Praise for *Rules for Being Dead*

"Kim Powers writes a glorious novel about a boy and his journey to feel whole after the mysterious death of his mother. Mr. Powers' prose is artful and searing as Clarke's story unfolds in a Texas town so vivid, the reader is there. Secrets are revealed, hope is lost and found, and redemption awaits in this beautifully rendered tale about love and loss, and the courage to face the truth with an open heart."

—Adriana Trigiani, *New York Times* bestselling author of *Tony's Wife*

"A tour de force in voice and structure, this uniquely heartbreaking novel—literary fiction meets boy detective—is somehow adorable and sinister at the same time. The brilliantly talented Kim Powers has created a poignant and remarkable story."

—Hank Phillippi Ryan, award-winning author of *The Murder List*

"We all know a few rules about being alive but who knew that the after-life could command equal attention. Kim Powers' *Rules for Being Dead* caught me by surprise with its intrigue, wit, and nostalgia. His incredibly moving novel takes you back home—no matter where, or when, you grew up. It reminds us that mothers and fathers can never be as perfect as we want them to be, and that childhood secrets can still haunt into adulthood. Get ready to be captivated by a lonely boy who's lost in the world of '60s movies and true crime and employs both of them to try to solve the ultimate mystery: what caused his mother's mysterious death? And one more thing? Despite its title, this book is about learning how to *live*, with every breath you take."

—Deborah Roberts, ABC News Correspondent

"*Rules for Being Dead* is a rich and compelling novel about a mother and her sons that is filled with nostalgia, heartbreak, and a love that will never die. Kim Powers has created an unforgettable story about discovering the world through movies, engaging with the tougher realities of life, and learning to forgive the people around us and ourselves."

—Will Schwalbe, *New York Times* bestselling author of *The End of Your Life Book Club* and *Books for Living*

"It's time well spent with the Perkins family, though the father should be locked up, one son should be disarmed, and the mother who might fix everything can't—because unfortunately she's a ghost. Unorthodox, quirky, funny, and heartbreaking, Powers' love letter to difficult families (and 1960s film classics!) is a blast."

—Wilton Barnhardt, bestselling author of *Lookaway, Lookaway*

"Tenderhearted and touching, *Rules for Being Dead* is imbued with the imagination and emotion of such beloved books as *The Lovely Bones* and *Ellen Foster*. The narrative is laced with nostalgic references (from Elvis movies to mentions of Don Knotts and TV shows like *Family Affair*) that bring to life a forgotten time. All these elements come together to create a vibrant backdrop to the story of one family's unexpected loss and journey toward healing."

—John Searles, bestselling author of *Help for the Haunted* and *Strange But True*

Narrated from multiple points of view but dominated by the two protagonists, a dead mother and her ten-year-old son, Kim Powers' *Rules for Being Dead* is intoxicatingly hilarious, smart, and deadly serious. Creola's problem is that she isn't sufficiently dead. She's hovering close enough to life to see everything and affect almost nothing. For anyone who has wondered what limbo is like, here's a startling answer, for Creola can't fully ascend until she remembers how she died. And not even the living know the answer to that. Ultimately, *Rules for Being Dead* offers a startlingly original perspective on misapprehension, forgiveness, and love and delivers its vision with a punch. I picked up the book and could not put it down.

—Elaine Neil Orr, author of *Swimming Between Worlds*

RULES FOR BEING DEAD

RULES FOR BEING DEAD

KIM POWERS

— BLAIR —

Printed in the United States of America
Cover design by Hannah Lee
Interior design by April Leidig

Blair is an imprint of Carolina Wren Press.

*The mission of Blair/Carolina Wren Press is to seek out, nurture, and
promote literary work by new and underrepresented writers.*

We gratefully acknowledge the ongoing support of general operations
by the Durham Arts Council's United Arts Fund.

ISBN: 978-1-949467-35-2

Library of Congress Control Number: 2020930164

In memory of my two mothers,
Creola Perkins Powers and Rita Cobb Powers

Memory is a complicated thing,
a relative to truth, but not its twin.
—Barbara Kingsolver

If you cannot get rid of the family skeleton,
you may as well make it dance.
—George Bernard Shaw

Lucy, you got some 'splainin' to do.
—Ricky Ricardo

RULES FOR BEING DEAD

— CLARKE —

The Ugly Dachshund is playing at the Ritz today, but my little brother Corey and I didn't get to see it because yesterday was the day our mother died. It was April Fools', so at first I thought it was a joke, but it wasn't. Daddy and Aunt Altha both said it wouldn't be right to see a movie because we're in mourning, which is the kind like when you're sad, not the kind like when you wake up.

At the funeral home tonight, Aunt Altha said they didn't do a very good job getting the red ink from grading papers off Creola's hands. Creola is her name for Momma because she's her sister, or was until she died. Then she started crying, and her eyes got as red as the ink on Momma's hands, which I didn't see because I was too afraid to look in the coffin. Aunt Altha is a teacher like Momma so she knows what red ink looks like. She held up her own hand and traced a line on her palm like she was pointing to the ink, except nobody could see it but her. She sees a lot of stuff that nobody else can see.

Red is the color of the ink in Momma's pen that she used to give grades with. So now I'm going to keep using it until it runs out, just like she did. The ink will be gone soon, but if I write down enough of what I remember about her, maybe she won't be.

———

P.S. I'm in the fourth grade at school and we're learning how to write letters to people. "P.S." is sort of like "pssst"—where you have an extra thought at the end, and you want to get somebody's attention after you've already said goodbye to them.

So this is my extra thought: I'm going to cut out *The Ugly Dachs-hund* ad from the *Courier-Gazette* and start a scrapbook with it, even if we didn't get to see it. Starting a scrapbook and writing in it every week will be a good way to keep my mind off things, which Daddy says we'll all need to do, until people stop talking.

— CREOLA —

This doesn't seem like heaven; not the one I've heard about all my life.

It doesn't seem like anywhere, actually.

It's foggy—but the fog is dark, not light—and I'm having a hard time staying up in the air. I thought that when I was dead I'd finally have a chance to rest, but this is hard work, staying suspended. It's like treading air and clouds instead of water. I don't have wings, but *something* is back there. It hurts, like something barbed is pushing its way through my skin, trying to grow out of me. A little notion goes off in my head, or what used to be my head; my shoulder blades twitch, my whole body shivers—a dog, shaking off from a bath: Cutie, Vincent, Penny, the parade of dogs we had for the boys that they promised to take care of, but you-know-who ended up doing all the work—and somehow, something happens. *Thought* happens, and I keep from falling back down to earth. I guess that's a version of flying. But after a while, my back aches so much from the effort, I think, *If this is heaven, then just let me die.*

Oh, wait. I already did. (*Haha*, Clarke, my oldest, will write on something called Facebook years from now. Wait. Where did that come from? Too much is happening all at once.)

The air is cooler up here, and considering the alternatives, I'm grateful for that. At least I'm not in hell. But there's that damn ache in my back and my ankle's throbbing from where I smacked it against Mrs. Bearden's chimney—the boys used to call it her "chimley," no matter how many times I corrected them—and my head hurts, left over from . . .

3

That's the part I can't remember.

Maybe *that's* what heaven is; not knowing how the end came.

Maybe that's why I'm stuck here, flying around, looking for clues. Maybe I can't go home—my *real* home, my heavenly home—until I know for sure. Until I remember.

I teach fifth grade—whoops, first rule for being dead: get your tenses right. I *taught* fifth grade, so I'm good at organizing and sticking to a lesson plan. It's a quick descent into chaos, being unprepared in front of a room full of eleven-year-olds who are hopping up and down they have to go to the bathroom so badly, so that's how I've decided to approach this . . . down time. This sabbatical. This *death*, I might as well call it; I've never liked mincing words, and now is no time to start. I'm dead, I know that for a cold, hard, backaching and ankle-throbbing fact, but as for the how and the why . . . I can't remember.

Did I say that before? Sorry, I'm still a little woozy.

What I *can* remember, what I sort of see when I close my eyes: my sleeping body in bed, my right hand, with veins that stick out too much from where I've lost so much weight with worry lately. My hand curled around something. I'm floating over my body; I seem to be a speck in that giant bed as I drift further and further away. A few early strands of gray are shot through my black hair, two weeks away from my hair appointment at Jean Ray's Beauty Salon. I'm only forty-four—I *was* only forty-four—but somehow, I look old.

I twitch, I shudder, I somehow *think* my way out of that room. My death room. Neither the ceiling nor the roof of the house gets in the way as I waft across the street to a tall tree in the Willises' front yard. It's spring, the very first day of April, so everything's green. I hide inside the leaves, up in the highest branches, and peek out to see everything that's going on across the street. (Later I will discover that I don't need to hide; no one can see me, no matter how hard I try to make them.) An ambulance without its siren on pulls into our driveway at 815 Woodleigh Drive. Two men get out of it and go inside the house; they come back out a few minutes later with my body on a gurney.

I *guess* it's my body. It's in a zipped-up plastic bag, so I can't tell for sure.

I fly from the Willises' tree to the TV antenna over Mrs. Bearden's house, trying to get a better glimpse, but the show is over. (Since I suddenly feel the urge to tell everything, I'll tell you this: Mrs. Bearden is old. And fat. And childless. And if you really want to know, not that friendly. So why didn't God just take *her* instead? Nobody needs her like my boys need me.)

No one sees me as I fly over Highway 24 and Louisiana Street to the roof of the school where I teach—there I go again, where I *taught*—to wait for my husband L.E. to be driven here by his buddy Forrest Goodman from White's Furniture and Appliance Store, where they both work.

So there Forrest is, behind the wheel of his station wagon, waiting with L.E., who is waiting for our sons to come out of school when the last bell of the day rings, to tell them that I am gone. Forever.

Oh, God, I think I'm dying all over again, seeing that.

Ten-year-old Clarke. Seven-year-old Corey. My two miracle babies, after so many years of trying with no luck to have children. My two heartbeats, except my heart isn't beating anymore.

That's the first time I cry that day, perched on the gabled roof of J. L. Greer Elementary School, where I'd done my best to prepare so many young minds for the future. For a second, I wonder if they'll rename the school after me, but that flies out of my mind the minute I see my sons walk out the school door and into a car they've never ridden in before. I swoop down to the roof of the car to try to hear what's being said inside, and I stay there all the way back to Woodleigh Drive.

L.E. takes the boys into the backyard and tells them that I am gone.

"*Gone?*" I want to scream. "I'm not *gone*. I'm up on the roof. Just look!" But I can't make any noise come out. I can't make them see me.

That's the second time I cry that day—April 1, 1966—the day I died.

Some joke, hunh?

— CLARKE —

SUNDAY, APRIL 10, 1966

The Ghost and Mr. Chicken with Don Knotts is at the Ritz today, and Corey and I really want to see it. Daddy hasn't let us go anywhere all week, not to school or even to Momma's funeral because he said it would upset us too much, and the neighbors keep looking at us strange when they come by and leave food. At least in the dark at the Ritz nobody could see us, but I don't know if a movie about a ghost is a good idea right now. All Corey's done since Daddy told us last week is cry, and I have to keep drying him out.

Daddy said, "Your Mumma is gone." He's from Vermont, and he says some words weird like that, because Vermont is closer to England than Texas, where we live.

"Gone where, Daddy?" Corey asked.

Daddy didn't say "dead" at first because he thought we'd understand what he meant. I understood before Corey did because I'm older, but I didn't say anything, so Daddy had to keep talking. "Well, she died, Corey. She went to heaven. Clarkie, you're going to have to help out with your little brother now, since your Mumma's not here anymore."

I told him I didn't want to be here anymore either; I wanted to be at the Ritz in the dark, so nobody could look at me while I was crying.

Daddy said we'd have to make do with *Dark Shadows* on TV for the time being.

7

P.S. My real name is Clarke, but sometimes Daddy calls me Clarkie, which has an "i-e" at the end of it. You add an "i-e" or "e-y" to the end of something when you want it to sound sweet, like "honey." Corey's name already has a built-in "e-y," so Daddy doesn't have to add anything extra to be sweet to him. They gave us names with r's and e's and c's in them so they'd be like our mother's name, which is Creola. I like thinking about sounds and letters and words like that, almost as much as I like thinking about movies. That's good for school but bad for me because Daddy says I'm "distracting myself."

———

P.S. P.S. I think I saw Momma's ghost the other night, but I'm not sure. It was something white, and it looked like it had arms, but it could have just been my white shirt. Daddy made us lay out our good clothes to wear to the funeral home, and my white shirt was hanging off the back of a chair, so maybe that's what I saw. I hope so. I don't want to be haunted.

———

P.S. P.S. P.S. That's not true. I'd give anything to see her again, even if it was just her ghost.

— CLARKE —

We finally got to go back to the movies today, except it was tonight. And it was at the drive-in instead of the Ritz, but it was still a movie up on a screen, and that's what counts. And it counts even more that it was the drive-in because that's where we saw our last movie ever with Momma, the night before she died. Jeanne Dixon, who's famous because she tells the future and sees ghosts on TV, says that it takes time for a spirit to depart. I hope so, because maybe that means Momma's still hanging around there. Just in case, I made our cousin Beverly park her car exactly where Momma had parked that last night. But even in the right spot, we didn't see Momma's ghost, we just saw Elvis Presley and Donna Douglas in *Frankie and Johnny*.

Elvis plays a gambler on an old-timey showboat, and he wears a floweredy vest, which is what they wore back then but also what "mod people" wear now because sometimes fashions come back like that. Momma got me a floweredy vest this Christmas to go with my Beatles belt and Beatles boots and paisley shirt, so I get to be Paul in our Beatles club at school. Also because my bangs hang down. When Daddy let us go back to school this week, the other Beatles gave me a sympathy card, but I think their mothers picked it out for them and made them sign it. Everybody says they have "sympathy" for us, but it's easier just to give us a card. It's like Beverly and her boyfriend Randy taking us to the drive-in. That's their way of saying they have sympathy without having to say anything at all. We can just look up at the screen and let the people there do all the talking.

But Beverly and Randy did start talking when they thought we weren't listening because they were in the back seat making out. Beverly's a senior in high school, and they get to do stuff like that. Corey and I were in the front. When Beverly came up for air, I heard her say something funny happened in our house. Not funny like when you laugh, but funny like when you whisper a secret.

"Pooch tried to find this bottle of blue pills that Aunt Creola used to take, but she couldn't find 'em. They're missing."

Beverly calls her mother Pooch, like a dog. She calls her sister Carolyn Cabbage because she likes to eat stuffed cabbage and cole slaw, which is made from cabbage. They all call Beverly Wheezer because she has asthma and has to use an atomizer to breathe.

"Pooch wanted to cut Aunt Creola open to see what was inside her, but L.E. wouldn't let her."

L.E. is our father's name, for Lloyd Edwin, which doesn't fit him at all.

"Pooch said, 'We could get a court order and have Aunt Creola's body exhumed.'"

"Your mom needs to have her *head* exhumed." That's the only thing Randy said. I could tell he wanted to go back to kissing, not talking.

"Exhumed" is like "examined" but with dug up added in.

In the rearview mirror, I saw Beverly hold up her thumb and finger about four inches apart, like she was holding an invisible pill bottle between them. It's the same as when Aunt Altha held up her hand at the funeral home to show how red ink was still on Momma's hand, even though she was just looking at thin air. Daddy says "seeing things that aren't there" runs in our mother's side of the family.

I closed my eyes to make the inside of my head see something that wasn't there—Momma's pills—and then I blinked extra hard to make myself remember to look for them when I got back home. That's a trick Mrs. Frye taught us this year, for how to remember things. You think of something like Elvis from the movie, then you think of what you want to remember, then you put an equal sign between them. Then you close your eyes and blink extra hard like you're clicking a camera to take a picture, and the thing shows up behind your eyelids like this: "Elvis = pills." So when I glue the ad for *Frankie and Johnny* in my scrapbook tonight and see "It's Elvis" at the top, I'll think of the missing pills and remember to look for them.

It's neat when something you have to learn in school can be used in real life.

— CREOLA —

Besides my boys, I think that I'm going to miss Elvis movies most of all. He was my personal tour guide for all of the places L.E. never took me. *Blue Hawaii, Fun in Acapulco, Viva Las Vegas.* I got to see the world with Elvis who, believe me, is a lot more fun than L.E. turned out to be. I'd come back from one of his movies, having dragged the boys with me, and then I'd assign a bulletin board based on it to my class, just to keep my pretend vacation going a little bit longer. The students never knew my secret: they thought I was actually teaching them something, but I was just thinking about Elvis and his pelvis, which is not something grade-school teachers are supposed to be thinking about. My kiddos would be struggling away, chewing their plump little lips at the corners, their chubby fingers cutting out the imports and exports of Hawaii from old *Look* magazines I'd bring in from home, while I was daydreaming about surfboards and ukuleles and Elvis in his bathing suit.

I watched the boys in that car with Beverly and Randy tonight while I was balancing up on top of the drive-in movie screen, forty feet up in the air. That's becoming one of my favorite new places to be, maybe because I spent so much time there when I was still alive. Day or night, it doesn't matter, I sit on top of that screen and look out around me, and I'm happy, for just a little while. I don't stray too far from home yet, from what I know, still too afraid to venture out much. I float back and forth between the Cottage Hill Cemetery and Woodleigh Drive. It doesn't feel like two weeks have gone by since I died, more like twenty minutes. Time is different . . .

here. Wherever here is. Wherever I am. Fast and slow, at the same time. And not just that, but it's stretching way into the future. Like *waaaayyyy*, which is something Clarke will write in the . . . well, future.

So there's that. (Which is another thing Clarke will write.) Yes, in addition to flying, I seem to have developed an ability to see what will happen years, even decades from now.

There will be something called Facebook. And Twitter. And Instagram. And emojis. And abbreviations. Lots of abbreviations. LOL. ROTFL. RIMCL. Rolling in my coffin laughing.

I wish I could be there to see it.

I wish I could have seen *my* future, so I could have stopped it. Whatever it is that stopped *me*. I'm getting better at being dead, I guess, but I'm not getting any better about missing the boys and all the things we did together.

I tried to make them both feel my presence tonight at the drive-in, to let them know I *was* still there for them. I rattled the speaker in the rolled-down window of Beverly's car and kept turning the volume up and down, but they just kept hitting the metal box to make it work right. The speaker kept going out the last time I was here with the boys, the night before I died, so I thought that would remind them. But it didn't. It only reminded me.

Tammy and the Bachelor. The drive-in. The night before I died.

It was almost April, and it didn't get dark until late, so the movies didn't start till late—so the boys slept through most of it. I usually didn't take them on a school night, but that night was different. (Well, it was different because it was the night before I died, but it was different for some other reason too. Only I can't remember.)

I'd seen the movie years before, on the third or fourth leave their father had spent in town. It wasn't until his ninth leave that L.E. had proposed to me, already an old maid at just twenty-seven, on a three-penny postcard. He was too bashful to ask in person and too cheap for a proper envelope. A marriage proposal on the back of a postcard, in the tiniest print imaginable:

Creola—

I'm not good with words, so I'm not going to make this long. I've known a lot of women, the ones who can get past the scar on my leg. I was flat on my back for so long, waiting for my leg to heal when I was little, so I know what waiting is like. I can't wait that long ever again, for you to say yes. I want us to be married, and I want us to have kids. I get out of the Army soon. I don't know what comes after that. Not Vermont, I know that much. And I know it won't be in the kitchen. I'll cook for you once a week, but none of the recipes I've learned here on KP duty. I've had it with dishing out shit on a shingle for a bunch of hungry guys who can't manage to say "Thank you." Maybe I can do something with electronics. I like using my hands and making things work. Maybe a farm, with a pond and a house I'll build with my own two hands. If you'll just have me, I promise you carousels and Tilt-A-Whirls and tornadoes of love.

L.E.

He didn't realize how scary that sounded: "tornadoes of love." He'd thought he was writing a love poem that didn't rhyme. I thought so too.

My last night on earth, watching *Tammy* again at the drive-in, was completely different, with two little boys instead of a man who didn't love me anymore. I'd gotten scooted to the middle of the front seat: Corey had his head in my lap from one side, Clarke the other. They'd conked out at how old-fashioned it was; thank God they weren't awake to see their old mother crying herself silly at an old movie that reminded her of a time when she was happy. (Forty-four. And I already felt as ancient as the boys probably thought I was. They had two words for parents: "new" and "old." I wasn't the first one.) A teenager from the concession stand shined his flashlight at us because we were the only car left in the parking lot after the final credits. A big embarrassed grin came over his face when he saw that it was me and realized I had taught him, years before.

"Oh my gosh, Mrs. Perkins, I didn't know it was you."

"That's okay, I hardly know who I am anymore anyway." I tried to make a sound like a laugh, but I started crying even harder.

"You stay as long as you like. My mother cries at old movies too." Old. See? There it was, everywhere I went.

Monkey Boy. That was his name, at least the only one I could remember. I'd had to take him to the principal's office one Valentine's Day because he climbed up a tree at recess and threw mud at one of the girls. Later he'd confessed to me that it had been an act of love. He'd given her a box of Russell Stover chocolates, but she'd told him he looked like a monkey and gave the candy to somebody else. Monkey Boy started crying in front of me—like I'd just done in front of him—and from then on, he became one of my secret favorites. It's odd the things I remember about my students: the first time one of them fell in love with another; the first time one of them fell in love with me; the way they always acted so bashful and out-of-place when they saw me away from school, at the grocery store, or downtown on the square. On the Day of Judgment, I used to think, I'd fail if I couldn't repeat all of their names. It would mean I hadn't been a good enough teacher.

And here I am—dead, but still waiting for judgment.

I guess "Monkey Boy" will have to do for now.

That night we finally left the drive-in parking lot—Monkey Boy waving his flashlight into the night sky behind us—and I drove home, leaving the drive-in dust and gravel behind us.

There's not much to see out there on the edge of town where the drive-in is, but because of God's little postmortem party trick of turning me into the Amazing Kreskin, I can see what it *will* become. (It's like His joke: like He held out His two closed fists to me and said, "Creola, pick one. You can either see the past and what killed you, or you can see the future. But you can't see both. At least not yet." I must have picked the one that held the future; I knew that was the only way I was going to be able to keep up with what happens to the boys.) The Haggar Slacks factory will be built soon, sewing machines and steam presses going nonstop, jobs for so many women in town, the mothers of my students. The only job in this town for women besides being teachers. A sacred calling of a different sort. The roller rink tent will come into town on an empty plot of land out there every summer. The only time you won't hear rented skates on that make-shift wooden floor will be on Sunday nights when it's reserved for revival meetings. The boys will be there on Saturday *and* Sunday nights.

When Clarke is in fifth grade, next year, Rhonda Sue Lewis will draw him a diagram of how to skate while they're supposed to be reading *The Witch of Blackbird Pond* during quiet time, and they'll both get in trouble shuffling their sheet of lined notebook paper back and forth. Clarke will get sad in a way that Rhonda Sue can't understand. Sad at me—and mad too—for being gone. He'll think that *I* should have been the one to teach him how to skate. He'll get mad a lot. He'll lie to Mrs. Laird, the music teacher who comes in once a week, that he knows how to play *Für Elise* on the piano for the school talent show, and then when he can't play it, he'll blow up. He'll overhear her say he has a "short fuse."

He will have a short fuse for the rest of his life.

I'll get mad too—at God—every time something bad happens to Clarke or Corey and I'm not there to comfort them. I'll get mad that I took them to *Tammy and the Bachelor* my last night on earth instead of staying up with them and telling them everything I knew, everything I wanted *them* to know to protect themselves, that I could squeeze into my last few hours.

Which I can't remember.

— CLARKE —

Every Saturday at noon, Daddy comes home from work to make us lunch and to eat his lunch too. He's tired from selling furniture and appliances all morning, so he takes a nap in the lounge chair while Corey and I play outside. Sometimes when he's sleeping I sneak back in and look at him and wonder how we got such an old father, forty-five, when all the other fathers we know are young. He almost looks like Brian Keith from *Family Affair*, but the worn-out version that would never be on a TV show. The week after Momma died, I saw him looking at his face in the bathroom mirror. He pulled back his droopy skin and put a dark brown washrag on top of his light brown hair, which he wears sticking straight up like Frankie Avalon's. Then he pulled himself up and turned around so he could see sideways in the mirror. He sucked in his stomach and puffed out his chest and pulled back a handful of tee shirt to hold it all in, but then he got normal again because it was too hard to not breathe. He let go of his tee shirt. He took the washrag off his head and put it in the dirty-clothes hamper. He looked at himself some more, then reached back in the hamper. I thought he was going to put the washrag back on his head, but he pulled out a whiskey bottle hidden under the dirty clothes and started drinking instead. That's his favorite hiding place, but he's got a lot of them.

One of them is up in the cabinet above the washing machine in the kitchen, where I was making Corey dessert while Daddy was taking his nap. I got out vanilla wafers and strawberry jelly and mini marshmallows and told Corey we could play like we were having "canapés," like rich people do in movies. To get the fancy silver tray Momma used to use, I stood on top of the washing machine and reached up into the cabinet over it. Something knocked over, something rattly. I knew it wasn't Daddy's bottle because that would sound liquidy. I reached inside and pulled it out, and it was Momma's little pill bottle, not Daddy's big drinking bottle.

My eyes blinked, and then I remembered. Elvis = pills, and now so does Momma.

There's something weird about the pills being all the way up in the cabinet in the kitchen, where she couldn't get to them fast enough if she needed them. Beverly says funny, I say weird, but I think we mean the same thing. Funnyweird. I gave Corey his canapés to keep him quiet, then took the pills to the medicine cabinet in the bathroom where medicine is supposed to go. I put the pill bottle on the shelf, but I kept the pills for myself so I could show Aunt Altha they weren't missing anymore. That way, she'd know nothing funny or weird happened in our house. I don't like people thinking we're funny.

I closed the medicine cabinet door and saw myself in the mirror on the front of it. For just a second, I thought it was finally Momma's ghost, because I look so much like her. That's what everybody says. She was short and had dark hair and eyes that could change from gray to green. So do I. When she smiled, she didn't open her mouth because she always had lipstick smeared on her teeth. I don't open my mouth when I smile, but that's because my teeth have big gaps in them.

I walked backwards out of the bathroom so I could keep looking at the mirror and play like I was looking at her. The further away I got, the littler her face got. One more step back and she'd be so little she'd completely disappear, but then a giant stomped in and scared her away.

It was Daddy, and he was big and screaming and dragging Corey with him. Corey's face was covered with blood, only it was strawberry jelly. Daddy's face was as red as Corey's, only it was the blood inside him. He pulled me into the kitchen where everything was smeared with strawberry jelly blood from the mess Corey had made. I snapped my eyes shut to keep from seeing it, and there it was again.

Elvis = pills, and so does Momma.

"Where are the missing pills?" I remembered and yelled, to keep Daddy from screaming at me the way he does when he's drunk and I'm afraid there will be real blood.

"*What*?"

"Beverly said Aunt Altha said you wouldn't let them cut her open to find them."

"Jesus Christ on a goddamn crutch, Clarke . . ."

"Didn't her pills help?"

"*What* pills?"

"The ones Aunt Altha was looking for." I almost said that I just found, but I didn't.

He almost turned into the Daddy he wants to be, all puffed up and big and young and strong, but he took a breath and just stayed the Daddy he is. "Let's get this mess cleaned up and get you boys to your movie. We'll deal with pills and your Aunt Altha tomorrow. I'd like to give *her* some pills." He whispered that last part, but I heard it anyway.

———

P.S. There was another ghost at the Ritz today, but I wasn't afraid to see this one. It was *The Ghost in the Invisible Bikini*, and Daddy said that a movie with "ghost" and "invisible bikini" both in the title is not meant to be scary. But I think he's just trying to be nice to us now to make up from when he got so mad. He picked us up at the Ritz after work, then we came home, then we had dinner, then we went to bed. That's where I'm writing this now, in bed. When Daddy goes in the bathroom, I hear him open the medicine cabinet because the door makes a rusty metal sound, but then I don't hear anything. Maybe he's just standing there, wondering where Momma's pill bottle came from that wasn't there before, and where the

four pills are, that *were* there but aren't there *now*, because they're
with me.

———————

P.S. P.S. I've never written so much at one time before, so now I
have a blister on my writing finger. I should hold it under cold water to make the pain go away, but I can't because Daddy's still in the
bathroom, not making any sound at all. Maybe he's seeing Momma's face in the mirror, just like I did.

— CREOLA —

My sister Altha had taken Polaroids of my funeral at Cottage Hill Cemetery, snapping away through her tears and counting the number of flower arrangements that had been sent to honor me. Sixty-one full-scale flower arrangements in planters and A-shaped stand-ups and grave blankets. They'd put a special blanket of yellow roses from Corey and Clarke over the top of the coffin where my head would be, even though L.E. hadn't let them come to the funeral. He thought it would scare them too much.

No, all those upright tombstones and grave markers would have scared them, spread over a plot as large as a football field. Not that they hung out at football fields that much. But in Texas, they were inescapable, plunked down on the landscape as much as these old country cemeteries in the middle of nowhere. Football field, cow pasture, cemetery, repeat. Goalposts and grassy parking lots and barbed wire fences forming the perimeters around them all, holding back high school boys in shoulder pads, cattle and ghosts in equal measure. The scary part for the boys was that they didn't yet know that there was already so much death out in the world, that each one of those carved pieces of stone connected to a body six feet underneath. They hadn't lost anybody before me; your mother shouldn't be your first, not when you're just seven or ten.

You could have carpeted the entire cemetery with all of those flowers—enough left over for all the old dead people who never got any—that's how much I was loved. It mattered to Altha, and I guess it matters to me. I'm learning to hang on to things like that since I don't get a lot of fresh information here. When it was over,

Altha asked the funeral home people if they'd ever seen that many arrangements. They thought she was just making conversation. She wasn't. Altha never just "made conversation." She wanted exact numbers. Emblazoned across the front of the photos, which she planned to give the boys one day when they were old enough, she'd written down the number 61—with an exclamation mark!—so she'd never forget, as if she ever could. She wouldn't forget anything about that day, the saddest day of her life.

Well, mine too.

You'd think a woman who had survived the Dust Bowl; who, as the wife of a farmer, had had to stick a knife in a cow's stomach to relieve it of bloat out on the farm, then keep it alive until the vet could get there; who'd endured class after class of unruly fourth graders, could move on with her life, but not my sister. She was stuck, same as me. She was grieving, same as me; I heard it all when I flew to her house in Plano, thirty miles away.

"You try being scooched up next to your own flesh and blood with a windstorm howling outside and sand seeping in every nook and cranny of your body, then coming out of that Dust Bowl alive, only to have your sister taken from you no more than thirty years later."

Thirty years, thirty minutes, time made no difference; Altha was still scrubbing out that sand as I heard her talk to her husband, Quentin. One indignity was as bad as the next; Altha's life was a string of indignities, and what had happened to me was just the latest.

"Hey, eyes up here! *I'm* the dead one," I wanted to scream, but I've never been able to get in a word edgewise with my sister. Neither could her husband, Quentin, always sunburned from working out in the fields. Or maybe it was just his blood pressure rising from having to listen to her.

"Altha, you're running off half-cocked . . ."

"Don't you tell me about half-cocked. I *know* about half-cocked, Mr. Man." (They'd had some problems in the bedroom.) "I know what I think, and I don't mind saying it. How else do you explain why Perkins wouldn't let them do an autopsy? Because he knows what they'd find! How else do you explain how a perfectly healthy woman in the prime of her life . . ."

"Creola was never that strong, and you know it . . ."

"Well, would *you* be if you were still picking sand out of your crack, day in and day out? That wears a person down. Just look at me."

It was the wrong thing to say, because Altha Robinson could slay Goliath with one hand tied behind her back. A hand that was still scratching the sand out.

"All I know is that a week before she died, she came here—a *week*, just seven days!"

"Altha, I know how long a week is . . ."

". . . came here to look for a nice new apartment to move those boys into. And Perkins was *not* going to be along for the ride! And if you don't think *that* takes strength, you would be sorely mistaken. Leaving that husband of hers who's always tight as Dick's hatband. She was going to move those boys here to start a new life, away from that man"—here she glared at Quentin, cursing him for his sex, or lack thereof—"and that apartment was pretty as you please, except for the landlady walking around with a can of beer in her hand. A can of beer. Honestly. Trying to conduct business, and drinking . . ." She glared at Quentin again; he had a drinking problem too.

"Don't they all?" I wanted to put in my two cents, but I didn't want to miss anything Altha was saying. This was news to me: I'd gone to Plano looking for a new apartment? How could I not have remembered that? A little flash of something came back to me: a decoration thing on the dresser in the main bedroom, purple glass balls that were supposed to be grapes, see-through grapes, on a ceramic branch that was painted brown, with twining green leaves. Something fragile the boys would break the first night we moved in. If we did. Which we didn't. But how could I have forgotten that?

But Altha was rambling on. "I wish the Good Lord had just taken

me instead. Sixty-one arrangements. Will *I* get sixty-one arrangements when the Good Lord sees fit to take me? Hunh?" She chal-
lenged him—Quentin or the Good Lord, it was hard to tell.

"Altha, nobody's taking you anytime soon, believe me. Nobody
has the strength."

"Those poor boys, stuck in that house with that man . . ."

"Perkins is a good provider. He keeps food on the table and a roof
over their heads . . ."

"And his wife's corpse in a coffin! And he put it there!" She took
a breath, the deepest breath she'd ever taken in her life. "The nerve
of that man, keeping those boys from their Momma's funeral. If
only she'd had time to move them all here, so I could watch over
them . . ."

Just a week before I died. Why had I wanted to do that? I was so
preoccupied thinking about it and everything I'd heard at Altha's
that I barely made the trip back home from her house to the cemetery at Cottage Hill. My little wing-nubs weren't decked out enough
for such a long trip, not yet.

Home. Heaven. Limbo. Wherever I am.

For the first time, I think I might be in hell.

— CLARKE —

Today is May 1, and Momma has been dead for exactly one month. So this doesn't have anything to do with seeing a movie; it's just to remember her by, which I do all the time anyway. But to make it official, I've decided to start calling her "Mother" instead of "Momma," because that's something a little kid would say. But it's weird to call her anything at all since she's not here to hear me. "Here" and "hear" are homonyms, which means they sound the same but mean different things, like "Momma" means something different than "Mother." And "Father" means something different from "Daddy," who's never told us how Mother died, which is something a father is supposed to do.

— CREOLA —

Something new is happening, and it's scaring me. I can't fly as high as I want to. Something keeps pulling me back down. I can get over the telephone poles, push myself all the way up to the top of the drive-in screen, but if I try to get any higher it feels like somebody's pulling at my legs, trying to pull me back down to earth. I can't actually see hands grabbing me—I can't see my legs, for that matter—but I know somebody's there, keeping me tethered. Little hands, big hands, they feel like they're clawing at me. They'll let me go so far, but then . . .

Stop lying to yourself, Creola. I said I wasn't going to lie anymore, but I just did. Those hands grabbing at me? I *can* see them. I know who they belong to. The boys. Those golden tans they get in the summer, the little peach fuzz hair on their arms turned white-gold, almost like gossamer. Spider webs. They've trapped me. How many times did I read *Charlotte's Web* to how many classrooms, and now I'm trapped in the same web that Charlotte spun for Wilbur the pig.

I'm still thinking like a human, unable to let go of the old fears. I'm still afraid I'll fall to the ground, that it will hurt. That it will break my body, maybe even kill me. *That's* a laugh. I'm afraid I'll get comfortable and fall asleep up in a tree somewhere, or on the ledge at the top of the drive-in movie screen. All those teenagers parked in the dark out front will see a body hurtling down past the screen. A split second, and then it would be gone. They'd think it was just a scratch in the print or a hair that got caught in the projector. Or I'll be outside the Ritz, hunched up on the marquee that juts out—just me and the gray-green pigeon doo—after I've watched

26

them change the big, red plastic letters to the next feature late at night, and I'll tip over and plunge to my death, headfirst.

In my heart of hearts, I know that I'm not alive, that it *won't* hurt. That I'm just . . . air? Thought? But what is it then that hurts so much—physically hurts, like a stabbing pain, or a heart attack—whenever I look down at the boys? It doesn't feel like the death I was promised. I'm alive *and* dead, one foot in each camp. Halfway to heaven. Stuck in between. It's like what they call "magic time" in the movies, dusk or dawn, those magical thirty minutes or so when night turns to day or day turns to night and everything is perfect for just a little while. When nature can trick you, but you don't mind because it's so still and beautiful and right. It's like every minute of my life now—my death—is "magic time." It's not day or night; I'm not dead or alive. I'm just . . . stuck. Wondering where it all went wrong and why I still feel so much pain.

To try and find out, I spend a lot of my time in the tree in the Willises' yard, across from my old house. The Willises' son Mike has his tree house up here—some boards he hammered together, an old bedspread hanging in the middle to divide it into "rooms." It's not much, but I like to call it home these days, when I'm not at the cemetery. It's the perfect place for spying on the house I *used* to have. It's an okay block, but the houses on it aren't as nice as the street name makes it sound. I could lose myself on a Woodleigh Drive; couldn't you? But it isn't like that. It's on the outskirts of town, a new development, or it had been when we first moved in. Empty lots dotted with leafless saplings and piles of earth that had been flattened by a tractor, their zippered tractor treads still visible. Now the trees have grown; all the lots are occupied. But the houses are small. Ranch-style with big picture windows, with carports and porches with supports that jut out like fins. I think they're supposed to look like the future. Jet set, or at least the Jetsons. The McKinney version of mid-century modern. Every fifth house on the block has the same interior design, although you wouldn't know that unless you visited them. (I remember my shock the first time I visited the Bruntons' house at the end of the block, and their layout was exactly the same as ours.) A few brick houses, although we don't—well, the boys and L.E. don't—live in one of them. L.E. will put aluminum siding on our house within the next year, when he and that woman . . .

Well, I don't want to get too far ahead of myself.

You'll find out soon enough, just like I did.

The street has nice lawns, for the most part. Corey and Clarke will certainly make their fair share of pocket money years from now mowing them in the summer, when they're not catching crawdads or poison ivy. (If I'd invested in calamine lotion early on, I'd have become a rich woman from all that pink gunk I had to slather onto their precious little arms and legs.) I just wish we could have done a little better for them. It was a starter house for a starter family, only we never escaped it. Nothing sadder than that, a starter house you're forced to finish in. Me on my small-town schoolteacher salary and L.E. nothing more than a salesman, working on commission. When the boys get a little bit older, they'll see that their neighborhood is more *lower* middle-class than *middle* middle-class. That "lower" will make all the difference, especially to Clarke, my oldest. He's not a snob—well, he will be for a while, but he'll grow out of it.

———

Anyway. Whatever. Whatevs. It is what it is. That's what they'll say in the future, meaning "let's move on."

I mostly stay here to see if the boys are doing okay, if L.E. is getting them to school on time, if their clothes are still decent. I keep hoping they'll get over their fear of heights and come play with Mike Willis in the tree house so they'll be closer to me, but they seem more scared than ever. They don't even look up at the sky, but down, at the sidewalk. Their little necks must be aching something awful. Corey hides in the hedges all the time with a sheet over him, thinking that makes him invisible. That big blob of white sheet, through the waxy green of the leaves. It doesn't matter if the ground's muddy or not, he just plops down in those bushes. Clarke gets out of his school clothes as soon as he gets home in the afternoon and puts on his bathrobe. Maroon corduroy with gold braid trim; that was my silly touch, to let him know he was a prince. He's started thinking his clothes are covered with germs—which he's just learned about in school—after he's worn them for only a few hours. He thinks that's how I died, from some kind of germ, because no one has bothered to tell him. Just like no one up here has bothered to tell *me*.

I thought they were supposed to greet me, all my dead loved ones. Weren't all of my friends and family supposed to be at the end of some tunnel of light or something, waiting for me? But they're nowhere to be found. Believe me, I've looked. I'm lonelier than I ever was in life, where I had no one but a roomful of children, a sister, and the occasional angry parent to talk to. Even in the cemetery, buried right next to my parents, Frank and Beulah. Nobody's home. I'd grown up near McKinney and I'd never been away, not even in death. I'd never really thought my life would end as it had begun, in the same small town. Flying above it at night is as close as I've ever gotten to being on an airplane and leaving it all behind.

I've done my best to remember the prayers of the living and ask them to come to me; I've begged them, I've screamed to God, but nothing works.

Once or twice at the cemetery, I've seen figures in the fog, but when I tried to chase them down, they disappear. Maybe they're afraid of me. I'd always read in the Bible that in hell, people constantly cast their faces down, as if they were ashamed at being there. But the few people I've seen floating around in this in-between look that way too: down at the ground, as if they're ashamed to be *stuck*. Not that they did something bad, but that they didn't do enough good to go straight to heaven. Looking at the ground, trying to figure out why they were still *here* and not *there*. It's the same look Clarke and Corey have now: bent over like little old men, looking down at the ground, like they're ashamed. Ashamed of having a dead mother.

If my heart weren't already broken, that would break it for sure.

One time, not that long before I died, I'd gotten them out of their separate classes at school. Their regular teachers were used to my strange ways when it came to my own children. I was taking my fifth graders to get ice cream at the Sabine Valley Ice Cream Parlor a few blocks away. (Sabine? Like the women who were abducted and raped in Roman mythology? What kind of name is that for an ICE CREAM PARLOR, I ask you? Why am I only now feeling this outrage when there's nothing I can do about it? Yet one more outrageous and unfair rule for being dead.) By the time we started walking away from the schoolyard, it was dark and cloudy and lightning outside. I said that wasn't going to stop us: "Just focus on the cloud formations and you'll see carousels and Tilt-A-Whirls and tornadoes of love."

I tried to teach them to be poets.

I tried to teach them, every chance I got, to see things that weren't visible to the naked eye.

I tried to teach them to use their God-given imaginations, which could get them out of many a jam.

Leaves were blowing off the trees and the sky was turning purple and green like a bruise; still, I made my twenty-five students—and my own two children—keep walking. A gestapo in a belted shirtwaist school dress, luring them with the promise of ice cream. Any flavor they wanted. I stood at the back of the line so nobody could run away, and I held Clarke's hand on one side and Corey's on the other. I held their little hands so tightly they started complaining I was hurting them.

Leaves were blowing and getting tangled in my hair. By the time we got to the ice cream parlor, it was pouring and we were soaked. Some of the girls said it was too cold for ice cream, but I made them get it anyway. I wanted to prepare them for future discomfort, more important that mathematics. That was my job as a woman and a teacher. Cherry vanilla or black walnut or honeydew melon; the store made their own special flavors you couldn't find anywhere else, and it was my treat. How many other teachers did that?

Finally inside, I licked my ice cream cone and looked out the big front glass window, even though Clarke pulled me back and said it looked like a tornado was coming.

"Yes! Your father's tornado of love! Just look at it!"

"You're gonna get hurt. Please. You're gonna get all cut up if the glass breaks and comes in!" Clarke was pleading with me. Pulling at me. But I couldn't turn away from the growing storm outside.

"Let it," I said.

I actually *said* that to my child. I said even more: that I wanted to see the roof blow off the Safeway across the street. I wanted to see the tornado blow us all to the Land of Oz.

What kind of horrible mother says that to a child?

That's why I'm not in heaven. Yet.

I went to see Dr. Hill the very next day, and he gave me pills for the first time.

At night now, I go back there, to that giant yellow-tile obelisk that stretches up above the front entrance to Safeway, across from the ice cream parlor. It's the tallest point in town, taller than the drive-in, taller even than the courthouse in the middle of the town square. Hundreds and hundreds of yellow tiles, building a stairway to heaven. I stand on top of the Safeway Tower and think of the tornado that almost came. I look across the street to the Sabine Valley Ice Cream Parlor, where I made crying children, *my very own children*, step over blown-down tree branches and walk through lightning, just to get an ice cream, and I think . . .

It's coming back.

I'm beginning to remember.

— CLARKE —

Mother's pill bottle is gone. When I went to the bathroom and looked in the medicine cabinet, it wasn't there. Corey's medicine is there, but not Mother's. It's a good thing I put her four last pills in my pocket, or they'd be gone too.

Before our movie started today, I took them to the drugstore to show Mr. Wilson. He squinted at the pill, then squinted at me and Corey, from under his glasses. He knows us from when we come in and get Corey's medicine, and he's always squinting at us.

"Where did you get these?"

I said, "I can't find the bottle anymore, but they're for our mother."

"You mean they *were*. I'm so sorry about what happened. I know it's been hard." Mr. Wilson wrapped his fingers around the pill and wouldn't give it back. "But you shouldn't be running around with this, even for a joke. This is strong medicine. This is Stelazine. For hallucinations, depression, anxiety, obsessive thinking, paranoia." He ticked off all the words; one problem for every finger he raised, each one closing together to make a fist. "This stuff could kill you if you take too much."

In my pocket, I made a fist too, around the three pills I still had left.

After that, we saw *Rasputin, the Mad Monk* at the Ritz, but I couldn't really keep my mind on it. It's about a long time ago in Russia when the royal family tries to kill this creepy guy who has a long beard and scary eyes that he uses to hypnotize people with. In his case, "mad" means crazy, not angry, even though he gets angry too and cuts off somebody's hand. You see it flopping around by it-self after it's cut off. The fingers on the lonely hand shoot out like they're trying to scream, then curl back in, one at a time, just like Mr. Wilson's hand did after he listed all of Mother's problems.

That's when I closed my eyes and blinked five times, to remem-ber every grown-up word he said, and that I guess Mother had.

> Blink = Hallucinations.
> Blink = Anxiety.
> Blink = Depression.
> Blink = Obsessive thinking.
> Blink = Paranoia.

I was glad I could remember them all, even if I didn't understand what they meant.

The Russians try all these different ways to kill Rasputin, like stabbing him and shooting him and even putting poison into his candy. But they should have just given him Stelazine.

— CLARKE —

"Corey is an angel with epilepsy."

That's what Mother used to say when she gave him his pills, which aren't Stelazine but phenobarbital. They're pink, not blue, and they make him sleepy on purpose. Otherwise he'd be shaking and jerking and biting his tongue all the time. She'd say, "Big jerks are called 'grand' but little ones are called 'petite,' just like you." Then she'd kiss him on the head when he cried that he didn't want to be an angel with epilepsy anymore.

Mother had Corey too early, when she was too old, so that's why he just weighed three pounds when he came out. That's why he's stayed more "petite" than the other kids in his class. He's never caught up with them like he's supposed to. The teachers are used to Corey and his pills, even though it used to be Mother who gave them to him. She'd put one on his tongue and make him swallow, then say, "You're going to get better and not have to take them for the rest of your life. But for now, just swallow this. It'll put an extra feather on your wings." I feel weird saying it, so I don't. But I still have to give him his pills anyway, to make sure he takes them.

"Is Momma an angel too, like in the movie?" Corey asked me tonight, after we'd seen *The Trouble with Angels* today. They aren't really angels in the movie, just high school girls who have to wear matching uniforms and get in trouble for smoking. Rosalind Russell is one of the nuns, but she was Auntie Mame first. It's supposed to be funny when the nuns call the girls "angels" because they're really more like devils. I asked my teacher, Mrs. Frye, about it, and she says it's called "being ironic."

"Of course Mother's an angel now, a real one," I said to Corey, trying to get him to go back to sleep. I feel weird saying that too, because it makes me have to think about Mother being dead, which I do all the time anyway. I can't forget it. I don't think Corey can either. He has nightmares now, where his eyelids jerk but don't open and his mouth screams but no sound comes out. It's like this book I got about the Ice Age. It had pictures of people yelling and screaming, but nobody could hear them because they were trapped inside mountains of ice that look like giant snow cones, without the food coloring. That's what Corey looks like when he sleeps, like the frozen Ice Age people.

"Will I get to be an angel, even if I've done bad things?" Corey asked me tonight.

"Sure. But not for a long, long time. So many years you can't even count that far. And you could never do anything that bad anyway."

The song from the movie today goes, "Where angels go, trouble follows, trouble follows." It's an example of a song that's "catchy," because it catches in your head and won't let go. I should know because it's been holding onto me all day. A little while ago I started singing it to Corey, to help him fall back asleep. But then I thought, "Trouble follows" won't give you good dreams, so I quit singing it.

———————

P.S. I hope what I'm telling him is true. I hope Mother's an angel in heaven now. She could be in the other place because she tried to kill Daddy with a frying pan. She yelled that the Great Apostle Paul was telling her to do it, so she was just following orders. She swung and screamed, "I know my Heavenly Redeemer liveth!" She used both hands to swing it, and Daddy used both hands to cover his face, and I used both of my hands to cover Corey. She finally got worn out because the frying pan weighed so much and she weighed so little. Her eyes started fluttering like Corey's do before he has a spell, then she fell asleep on the couch. Daddy wiped the spit off her mouth, then wrapped her in a blanket to keep warm, even though she'd just tried to kill him.

"Oh, Creola," he said, and all the air went out of his body. He told us not to tell anybody about the Great Apostle Paul or the Heavenly Redeemer, and Mother told us not to tell anybody about the apartment in Plano she wants to take us to, so everybody is telling us not to tell anybody anything, and nobody is telling us anything either about how Mother died.

— CREOLA —

I've come back here to the school, like I did on so many days when I was alive. It's a hard habit to break after nearly twenty years of teaching. But it's another way to stay close to the boys, to keep from driving myself crazy with worry and missing them. You'd think they could see me as I fly between their two different classrooms: Mrs. Moore for Corey's first grade, down on the lower level, closest of all the grades to the cafeteria, so their short little legs could make it, and Clarke's fourth-grade class, up by the principal's office. Next door to where my classroom used to be, near the boys' bathroom that always smells like that cake of something soapy they put in the toilets to keep them smelling fresh. It does anything but.

I do everything I can think of to get the boys attention so they'll know I haven't really left them: flapping my wings that aren't really wings but just thought, stirring up enough air to make the window shades shake, rattle, and roll all the way back up to the ceiling. Crouching up on top of the flagpole in their rooms as they say the Pledge of Allegiance. Surely the boys can see me then: that tiny, worn-out woman whose hair needs a dye job, looking down so proudly on them as they put their little hands over their hearts? But Clarke won't say the Pledge anymore. He says he's protesting like he sees the hippies do on TV. Only he doesn't know what he's protesting. He's protesting everything. He's protesting that I'm gone. He's protesting that neither one of us knows how I went.

I can't tell what Corey's doing today. They've finished the Pledge in his classroom, and now he's up at Mrs. Moore's desk putting out a fishbowl and a photograph of me. (It's in color, and my lipstick is bloodred; I've smeared it on my teeth and way outside the line of my lips. I wish someone had thought enough to take me into the teacher's lounge to fix it the day the school photographer came, but no. That is how my children will remember me, looking like I had blood pouring out of my mouth.)

Corey is telling Mrs. Moore that for his show-and-tell, he wants to have a séance, using his fishbowl for a crystal ball, like they do in the movie *Houdini*. Tony Curtis and Janet Leigh. We'd seen it one weekend when I took the boys away, just by ourselves, to a motel in Aquarena Springs in San Marcos, to get away from their father. In the movie, Houdini's mother has died and he goes to psychics all over the world trying to find her. To bring her back from the dead.

I'd told the boys I wished Houdini could make us all disappear.

Corey looks up at LouEtta Moore—just seven years old and he's already the most serious little soul you've ever seen, with deep purple circles of worry under his eyes—and she doesn't know what to do. Neither do I. I want to fly down off that flagpole and swoop him up in my arms and snatch him away, but I can't. LouEtta is glad he's coming out of his shell and talking again, but she's more used to stuffed animals and stamp collections and vacation souvenirs for show-and-tell. A pair of wooden shoes that somebody's uncle sent them from Holland. Not trying to contact the dead.

That would be me.

But she lets Corey do it anyway. Maybe she's as tired of teaching as I was by the end, and she's willing to do anything to vary the routine. She lets him pull down the shades and turn off the lights and make the room as dark as it can get. All his little classmates gather around their teacher's big desk where Corey turns over his fishbowl like a crystal ball and puts the photo of me underneath. It makes me look like I'm floating under wavy glass.

Then a voice I've never heard comes out of him. A voice nobody's ever heard, saying things nobody should ever have to hear. Certainly not children.

"Oh great Mother from beyond, please come back to your son

Corey because he has something to tell you. Something you need to know. Something about how you died."

If I didn't know better, I would think he was already going through puberty, his voice sounds so deep. It's like one of the made-up voices Clarke does all the time from watching so many movies, but I didn't know Corey could do it too. Then the voice changes to something a little more normal, like he's finished the acting part and is just speaking from his heart. He closes his eyes so he can't see anybody else, like when he goes into the bushes and puts a sheet over his head and thinks he's disappeared.

"It's me. Corey. You have to come back. Right now. I have to tell you something that can't wait. Something that happened that night. If you love me, you'll come back. Come to this séance . . . come to me . . . come back . . ."

He starts whimpering like a dog does when it's asleep, swaying his body in sync with his own words, and the other children seem to move in sync with him, as if he's hypnotized them the same way he's mesmerized LouEtta.

"Momma, please . . . enter our circle. Give us a sign." Now he's crying, and if there's anything a first-grade teacher knows, it's the sound of a crying child.

"Okay, Corey, I think that's enough. Show-and-tell is over."

But it's not over. Corey's whole body starts twitching and his eyes snap open. He jerks around and knocks the fishbowl off the desk, onto the floor, and into a million pieces. LouEtta tries to push the children away from the broken glass, and that's when Corey's full-blown seizure starts.

His body snaps, contorts, spasms. He hits the floor, and one of his tennis shoes flies off from all the shaking. LouEtta grabs him, yelling, "Somebody go get his brother!"

"No, no, don't get him. He'll hate me. You'll all hate me," Corey wails.

I'm watching my baby flail around on that cold linoleum floor, banging his head like he's trying to stamp out the fire in it. I can't reach out and comfort him. I can't protect him. That's the toughest rule I've learned in the days since I died: that I can't blind the other children from watching him and making fun of him. That hurts as much as dying.

Finally, the seizure stops, and Corey just lies there. A pool of urine seeps out of his dungarees and onto the floor.

LouEtta takes him to the bathroom to clean up; I vaporize myself to go with them. But all she can do is have him go into one of the stalls to take off his wet underpants, then give him a bunch of paper towels to blot at the stain on the outside. While he's doing that, she dabs at a little trickle of blood at the corner of her mouth, from where Corey accidentally elbowed her. She tries to pile her towering, cockeyed nest of gray hair back into place; she moves the ruby-red barrette she always wears this way and that way to fix it, but her bun just won't stay straight. She tests it, shaking her head, and the hair shakes with her, along with that barrette that no one knows if it's real ruby or not. And then she shakes her head again at the memory of what she's just seen.

I'm shaking too, and I can't stop it.

Maybe Corey *could* feel me, and that's why he was trying to call me with his séance. Maybe it's better if I don't stay at the school, so they won't have me so nearby. But I can't leave. After spending half of my life in that place, and now so many days since my death, I'm practically haunting it.

For a centralized command post, when I'm not visiting one of the boys' classrooms, I like to crouch on top of the glass display case that's in the middle of the hall opposite the principal's office. From there I can look in both directions—toward the front door the kids enter from every morning, the same door they stampede toward to get away every afternoon at three, and toward the back door, which leads to the teachers' parking lot. There's a sort of landing outside the door with concrete steps leading down to the ground in both directions. That's where Gary Losch, the visiting music teacher, will take the students one by one after they've played flutophone in the sixth grade, to tell them if they have a future in music and whether or not they should try out for the orchestra in junior high. (There are two choices of flutophone colors: a creamy white one or a black one, like an oboe. Only the most daring students ever chose the black in 1960s Texas. I'm proud to say Clarke will be one of them, saying he's doing it in "solidarity with my black brothers." He's ten. He has no black brothers. He has no black anything in lily-white and sometimes redneck McKinney, and he will barely even have black classmates until junior high. In high school, he will give himself a home perm Afro and wear a dashiki. "IN SOLIDARITY," he will yell at his befuddled father, who won't have a clue what he's talking about.)

How many other dead teachers still walk these halls like me without being seen? Surely dozens. It's a hard calling to let go of, this profession that every good little girl wants to grow up to be. You leave a little bit of yourself behind in a grade school every day you show up. The red ink I used to write down grades with might as well have been blood for all I gave those kids. That's what teaching was like; that's what giving your life to little children who aren't yours is like. And then just try to save something of yourself for your own children at home. That's the part of teaching they never tell you about back when you're dreaming and planning for a family of your own.

When the boys were little, in that first bare-bones house we had on Virginia Street—oh my goodness, L.E. and I were so proud of that, and it was little more than a shanty—I was taking night courses and driving to Denton on the weekend to finish up my master's degree in teaching. I remember how Clarke would "help" me with my homework, coloring in my school books. How much he loved dressing up in my cap and gown when he was barely out of diapers himself. He braided the tassel that went on my mortarboard, and I wore it that way for my graduation, all the way across that stage. The only mother up there, with her tassel in a French twist that her firstborn had given her for good luck.

So many memories; so many teachers who came and went before me. There must be a lot of them floating around these waxed halls, almost bumping into one other, no clue where to go now that their jobs are over. The hallways are so cavernous with their high, arched ceilings that it's easy to hear sounds that aren't there. I used to scare myself silly when I'd stay after class to do a lesson plan for the next day and the whole school emptied out. My high heels echoed in that hallway—those wood floors the janitor, Mr. Ring, kept so shiny—and I thought, *Somebody must be following me*, although I couldn't see anyone.

"Is somebody there?" I'd stop and call out.

Now I know. They were the sounds of teachers who'd gone before, cursed to walk those halls forever in the high heels we couldn't wait to get out of the minute we got home. The heels we'd kick off under our desks so the students couldn't see our stockinged feet with the seams across our toes. (Surely there's a joke in that: where do old teachers go when there's nothing left to teach? When they're dead? I just can't think of the punch line, not yet.)

What had kept me from going to school, from doing my job, my last day on earth? It must have been powerful. I could get ready for school with my eyes closed; I didn't even have to look at my lesson plans anymore. I just showed up and taught. That's what I did. That's what I was. A teacher. That's all they saw me as; they didn't see all my problems with L.E. They didn't see me following him around at night. They didn't see me . . .

What? Dammit! I almost had it.

They didn't hear me cursing; that's something a teacher never did in front of a student.

Did I leave some clue behind in my old classroom? My desk?

I think it, and there I am. Not therefore, but *there*. Not so much flown as teleported. Behind that beat-up old wooden desk, carved with names and soaked with wax, looking out at a roomful of fifth graders, a wall of low cabinets painted institutional mint green at the back of the room, a row of high windows above them. Blackboards, chalk dust, felt erasers, that little cluster of sticky gold stars I'd put on their tests or give out whenever someone needed a little boost of confidence. (And someone *always* needed a little boost.) I hope I taught Miss McLarty that in the three days she was with me, before I died. She was my student teacher, twenty-two, still in college, trying to figure out how to translate what she was learning in her college classroom into *my* classroom, a real classroom with living, breathing, hot-wired students, and she needed more confidence than the kids. The first day she was there I put a little gold star on her hand at the end of the day, and you'd have thought I'd given her the Miss America crown. Just three days together when . . . whatever happened, happened. That was barely enough time to teach her how to do anything except collect lunch money and take attendance, which had nothing to do with teaching. She'd been a willing student, soaking up everything I had to pass on. But did I pass on anything to her about how *I* was about to pass on?

Now that I'm gone, Mr. Walker, the principal, has already asked her to take over my class and finish out this year, and even stay on next year. She's beaming. No teacher ever smiles like that over those stupid question boxes in the geography book—because no student can ever get all the right answers, and everybody, students and teacher alike, just ends up mad as a hornet—but Miss McLarty is smiling now. She knows she has something to come back to after the summer. She knows she has something to . . . live for? I'm happy for her.

Looking into the future, I can see the new dress she wears for the first day of school next year: a red and rust jumper kind of thing with one of those mod rib-knit poor boys under it. It matches her titian hair, and soon, it will match the autumn leaves falling all over the playground outside. She's no Twiggy or Lulu; a poor boy and pale lipstick are as far as she's willing to go to be part of the mod generation. She's just an ordinary country girl like me. I can see her getting married and changing her name to Mrs. Roper, and the students getting mixed up for a while about what to call her: McLarty or Roper, Miss or Mrs. I see my boys at her wedding, drinking lime sherbet and ginger ale punch for the very first time. I can see her reading *A Wrinkle in Time* to her class and Clarke being the only one to stay awake enough after lunch to hear it while the others put their heads down on their desks and fall asleep. I can hear her tell them the world will never again end by flood, but it *will* end by fire. (I'm not too thrilled about that—not the fact that it might happen, just the fact that she's telling fifth graders about it. Children shouldn't have to worry about their futures. They already worry enough, the smart ones. And my children are smart.) I can see her having children and grandchildren of her own, and I can see her teaching much longer than I ever had a chance to. That makes me sad; I still had a lot more to give.

I can see everyone's future but my own, but nowhere can I see the letter that I think I left behind in my old desk, a letter to L.E. that I had just started working on, explaining how I was going to leave this all behind.

— CLARKE —

SATURDAY, MAY 28, 1966

Every week since Mother died, I've gone back into her old class-room and asked Miss McLarty if I could clean out Mother's *Instructor* magazines in the cabinets at the back. I like touching them because they have plays in them and I want to be an actor when I grow up, but also because Mother's hands held them when she used to read them to find out how to be a better teacher. I try to guess which pages her fingerprints are on, or maybe if she got a paper cut and left blood on the page. I hold them up to the light from the back windows to look for brown splotches, from where the blood might have dried. When it's in your veins it looks blue and when it comes out it's red, but when it dries it's brown. Miss McLarty probably thinks I'm weird, but she's getting used to it. So far I've gone to her room seven times, once for every week Mother's been gone. I've moved the magazines around so many times, arranging them in their right order according to date, that their pages are falling off. I got them all in order the third week I went, but I pretend they're still messed up so I can keep coming back. Miss McLarty has probably figured that out.

Yesterday was the last day of school for the year, so I went to her room one more time to thank her for letting me come in so often. I asked her if there were any of Mother's old pens left in her desk, because the red one I've been using from her purse is running out of ink. She looked at me funny, and sad, which is funnysad, which I guess is better than funnyweird. Then she looked in the drawer.

I could smell my mother when she opened it; all the old smells she used to carry around, like the smells she left at the bottom of her purse. Perfume and powder smells.

I took an extra breath to get Mother in my head, and Miss McLarty looked at me funnysad again.

"Hmmm . . . I don't see any red pens," she said, moving around some papers. "Here, I can give you this one. It's all I've got left from when she was here. It's black ink, but I think she used that too."

"No, you should keep it." I decided it wasn't fair that I'm the only one who got to keep stuff from Mother since she knew so many different people. Then neither one of us said anything for a while. I didn't want to leave, so I asked her if I could come back during the summer to keep organizing.

"I wish you could, Clarke, I really do, but it's not up to me. The building will be all locked up. But . . . maybe it's good to take a break from the magazines for a while and just run around and play." She said she hoped she'd have me in her class next year because seeing me would remind her of my mother who taught her so much about how to be a good teacher, even if it was just for three days. She said I could look at the magazines all I wanted to then, but maybe I wouldn't need to anymore.

"Sometimes it's good to let things stay messy, like the magazines used to be. Sometimes it's good not to organize so much, just to . . . let things happen."

I knew it was my turn to talk then; that she wasn't really talking about magazines. But it was easier just to leave with the crumbling *Instructor* I hid under my shirt while she was digging in the desk.

She gave me a hug goodbye and I thought maybe she felt it sticking out of my waistband, and I got so scared I called her Momma by accident. I apologized, but she said it was okay and hugged me even tighter. (I'm going to whisper it to myself now: "Momma." It's a soft word, softer than Mother, even though I can't use it anymore.)

Now, every time I leave the house, I carry the magazine so I'll have a part of Momma with me. I had it with me when Daddy took us to lunch at Shaw's Café today, to celebrate school being out for the year. He said not to get used to it because we won't be eating lunch out every day this summer. He said he didn't know what we'll do yet.

When Daddy's food came, he tucked his tie into his shirt so it wouldn't drag in the ketchup. He has a whole rack of clip-on ties that Mother used to pick out for him to wear, but now I pick them out for him every morning before he goes into work. At first he said my colors were too loud because he didn't want to "scare away the customers." But lately he's been saying, "The more color the better." He seems happier while Corey and I just seem . . . hungrier? What's the word for when you don't understand everything and all you're thinking is, "Who's going to make us lunch this summer?"

Then this lady came in and Daddy quit eating. He pulled his tie back out from between the two buttons on his shirt so it would look normal. He said, "Uh, boys, this is, uh . . . I want you to meet . . ." Then he stopped and looked at the new lady like he didn't know what to say next, but he tried to anyway. "These are my boys. My sons. Corey," he said, putting his hand on Corey's head, "and Clarkie."

He was making honey words again. I hate it when he calls me "Clarkie."

Corey said, "Are you going to make us lunch this summer? Are you our new babysitter?"

"Not unless you need your baby shoes fixed, or covered with bronze." She laughed and spun Corey around on his stool at the counter.

"Mrs. Cobb fixes shoes. Next door. She fixed my shoes. Well, actually, she helped me get new shoes, since I'd worn my sole out."

"You can say that again," the new woman said and winked at Daddy. "You boys ever have a shoe emergency, I'm the woman to see." Then she winked at us too and ordered a coffee to go. She winked the way I blink, like she was making herself remember something.

"She really did save my shoes," Daddy said after she left, after he

watched her walk out the door. "I'd be walking around barefoot if…"
Then he stopped again.

"We can go barefoot now that it's summer," Corey said, still
spinning.

"You boys. What am I gonna do with you? Corey, stop, you're
gonna make yourself sick," Daddy said, but not in a mean way. He
unclipped his tie and rolled it up in a ball and stuck it in his pants
pocket, like it had done its job and he didn't need it anymore.

Then we went to see *What's New, Pussycat?*, and Corey started
making drapey things on my face with his fingers and calling me
"Cobweb," like Mrs. Cobb's name, and which the Ritz probably has
a lot of because they never clean. I called him "Pussycat" and made
purring noises. When we got home, he helped me glue the movie ad
in my scrapbook. He likes letting glue dry on his fingers, then plays
like it's old man's skin and pulls it off and eats it. "Look, I'm eating
old man's skin," he says, then sticks out his tongue so I can see it.
Tonight, he stuck out his tongue and said, "Cobweb, cobweb, I'm
eating cobwebs, like that lady. Mrs. Cobb."

"Pussycat, pussycat," I sang back to him, like Tom Jones does in
the movie, "I love you." I went up high on "love," then did the rest,
"Yes—I—do, whoa-oh-oh-oh."

When Corey went up to the living room to show Daddy his gluey
tongue, I took the tie I had stolen out of his pants pocket and covered it with glue and hid it under my bed so Daddy couldn't ever
wear it again.

— CLARKE —

SATURDAY, JUNE 4, 1966

I'm sick of being nice to everybody when they're not nice to me, even though they don't know they're not being nice. That's why I loved *Village of the Giants* so much today, because it shows what it will be like when I'm a teenager who turns mean, who eats goo and becomes a thirty-foot giant. That's what I want to be right now, bigger than everybody else, so big they'll have to do what I say or else I'll step on them and crush them like the Ice Age is going to crush all of us when it comes back.

I told Daddy we have to buy extra sweaters for it, but he just laughed. He'll see how funny it is when he's freezing to death and running down the street trying to warm up and escape a giant iceberg. Then he can laugh all he wants, but I won't hear any of it because he'll have ice stuck in his throat and no sound will come out.

The drugstore man who said Mother had all those things wrong with her will see what it's like when I take one giant step on his store and crush him under my foot. All the Stelazine in the world won't fix him then.

That new lady at Shaw's Café who winked at us will find out what it's like when she keeps spinning Corey around and he throws up on her.

But mostly this strange kid I met where Daddy works will see what it's like when I hold him up in my giant fingers by his ugly red hair and drop him onto Daddy's crummy furniture and appliances. He'll crash, and I won't pick him up. I'll wait and see if Daddy does, so I can figure out who he is, because Daddy won't tell us. Just like he won't tell us how Mother died.

He was playing with Daddy at the store, calling him "Freddy" when his name is "L.E." "Freddy" doesn't fit him at all, even more than L.E. doesn't fit him.

"Hey, Freddy, let me ride on your back."

"Hey, Freddy, can I play with the TVs?"

"Hey, Freddy, you should buy this lawnmower for Grandma."

He was missing half his ear; not like somebody tore it off, but like he was born without it, like he drank the chemicals from *Village of the Giants* and now he's a mutant who's calling my father the wrong name.

Daddy was letting him play on the riding lawnmowers that run down the middle of the store. He never lets us play on them. They're set up on platforms that are covered with fake grass so you'll think it's real, but only a mutant with half an ear and red hair and freckles would think that.

"That grass isn't real. It's fake. You can't cut it," I said.

"You can so cut it," the kid with the weird ear said. "It just won't grow back."

"Like your ear?" I said, but he didn't hear me.

I went to the back of the store with Corey, where we play with the typewriters and tape recorders after our movies. I always leave my secrets and questions on them, and now I have a big one. I told Corey to go get Daddy while I turned on one of the tape recorders. The wheels started turning, moving the thin brown tape from one reel to the other.

"One two three, one two three," I whispered into the microphone.

I pushed RECORD as soon as I saw Corey coming back, and I put Corey in front of me so Daddy wouldn't see that the tape recorder was on.

"Who's that kid?" I asked.

"He hangs out here. His parents buy a lot, so I have to be nice."

Even Corey was bugged. "But he got your name wrong."

"Don't you think I look like a Freddy?" Daddy made a goofy face so Corey would forget that he hadn't answered him.

The tape was getting it all, except for the goofy face.

"He said you should buy a lawnmower for 'Grandma.' Who's Grandma? And anybody can tell that grass is fake."

"Number one, Clarkie, don't make fun of people, it's not nice, especially about something they can't control. Number two, you fool people into buying things by making them look like what they aren't. That's your first lesson in business. Follow that and you'll be a rich man."

Take things without paying for them and you'll be richer, I wanted to say, but I didn't. I just did it. I took the tape recorder home. It's not stealing; it's investigating. I've got a lot of questions now, and I can't leave them behind on a tape recorder at Daddy's store for complete strangers and an even stranger kid to listen to, who couldn't hear them anyway because he just has one and a half ears.

That's why I want to crush everybody today, because my father's name is L.E., not Freddy. And I'm Clarke, not *Clarkie*. That's a kid's name in a store where something funnyweird is going on, but nobody's laughing except that mutant kid.

— CREOLA —

Oh, Clarkie, I wanted to say—he never minded when *I* called him Clarkie—don't you get it? What's going on? Why I wanted to take us away? Because there's not room for two women in your father's life, and there was barely room enough for me? For us? Can't you read the signs? I taught you to read *before* you went to school. I took you to the movies. You're smarter than most kids. You *know* things. Grown-up things. Just *think*.

But then—do what? What did I want my son to do about it? Finish what I couldn't—which was what? What had I *tried* to do? That's what I can't remember, and I'm not getting to heaven until I do.

I know I saw her, before I died. I remember that much. I followed L.E. back to work one Saturday, after he came home for lunch, to see where he was going. Trip after trip to Cobb's Shoe Store. No man needed that many pairs of shoelaces. I stayed out on the sidewalk and pretended to be window-shopping.

She wasn't bad looking; she looked like a young Bette Davis, and that made me feel bad because I loved Bette Davis. She wore more make-up than I ever wore; her eyebrows dark brown and arched, definitely with a pencil. A touch of turquoise eye shadow. Her hair was thinner than mine, whipped up like a cloud of cotton candy on top of her head. Dark brown, like her brows, a lot of hairspray holding it in place and giving it a perpetual lacquered sheen. About my height, with a little extra weight. But it looked good on her, natural. My thinness didn't look like the result of being in shape; it looked like someone being eaten away from the inside. Not from cancer—at least I don't *think* I died from cancer—but from, well, life. Hollow and drawn. And that was *before* I was dead. Mrs. Cobb looked like a woman who knew she wasn't getting any younger, and that made me feel worst of all. We were the same in that department. She looked like a woman who did what she had to do to survive.

I could tell all that just from looking at her from outside on the sidewalk. I was too afraid to actually go in the store. At first. I did, later. I sort of remember that. But then—what did I do? That's what I can't remember.

Had I always known I was going to die young, at just forty-four? I think so. I used to hear all the other teachers, especially the young ones who were so thrilled to be hired, talk about the future and make plans. They made nothing but plans—lesson plans, wedding plans, children plans. I'd given up on that a long time ago, but was it because all my dreams had already "come true" or because I knew I wasn't going to last that much longer? Was that something I was born with? I worry my own boys have it, that I've passed it on to them.

They already seem old, both of them. They spend all their time sitting in the dark, watching movies up on a screen, living the lives of those characters instead of their own lives. That's what old people do. That's what *I* did. I cursed them with that, and I had thought it was a blessing. I was the one who taught them to pay their thirty-five cents in exchange for a ticket; the same amount they paid for their lunches at school. Food or a movie? Some choice. I'd always pick the movie, it was sustenance enough. I took them and stayed with them in dark auditoriums at night, watching *Bambi* and *That Darn Cat* and *Mary Poppins*, thinking I was keeping them safe from L.E. That was the one place he wouldn't step foot. There was no drinking there except for those watered-down Coca-Colas the boys love so much. Watching the movies in the dark, the boys couldn't see me cry.

We used to see Mr. Ring, the pint-sized janitor from school, there at night, just like us. He must have been hiding away from somebody too. After I'd run into him a few times and waved from afar, he finally said, "Call me Maurice. That's my name. Maurice, like more-RICE, except it's REESE. My mother likes to pretend we're French. We're about as French as French dressing. As French as Paris, Texas."

"Call me Creola. I like to pretend I'm . . . oh, I don't know what. Just anything good. Anything better than what I am."

"What a beautiful name. Sounds like an Indian princess."

"I'm a princess alright, watching the movies by myself, except for my court jesters here." I looked down at the boys, who were usually asleep by then.

"I guess we both like the movies."

"That, or getting out of the house. I'll just show up no matter what's playing. I don't even look at the paper before I come. I just show up."

"Me too." He might as well have said he was as lonely as I was. We both knew that's what we were talking about. It was the longest conversation I'd had with another adult who wasn't a teacher in I don't know how long.

"You ever want some coffee after the movie—or the boys want some pie à la mode—I can get it for free at the Townhouse. My employee discount."

When he wasn't watching movies or working as the school janitor, Mr. Ring worked at the Townhouse restaurant, which was attached to Woods Motel. He was the only waiter there who wore black tuxedo pants, a crisp white shirt rolled up past his elbows, and a bow tie that he tied himself. No clip-ons for Maurice Ring, no sir. Even carting around giant platters of chicken-fried steak or bussing tables, he looked so elegant; when he was sweating, his gleaming black hair always kept its perfect Pomade part.

"I'm trying to save up for a place of my own, got my sights set on one of those contraptions over by the high school. Apartments for young singles, they call 'em. That's me!" He took a cigarette out of a pack he kept in his rolled-up sleeve, and I saw his tattoo on a sinewy, bulging bicep. MOM, it said, surrounded by doves and a heart. Pale white skin, blue veins, no hair, and a red heart. He seemed a little embarrassed. "That's why I work so many jobs. Right now I live with my mother. That's how I'm getting out of Vietnam, because I've got to take care of her. And because I've got flat feet. And because I'm farsighted. And because . . . well, let's just say I'm a big ol' hot mess and leave it at that! Thank God. I wouldn't wanna fight. I can barely swat a fly, which is not good when you're a janitor."

(In the future, no one will ever know that my friend, Maurice Ring, the first homosexual I ever knew, was the first person to ever use the phrase "hot mess.")

I'd heard about men like him, but he didn't scare me. In fact, he secretly became my new best friend. He cried louder than anybody else at my funeral. He went up to my coffin and slipped in one of the programs they hand out at the Ritz every week that had the schedule on them. (He'd keep going to the Ritz after I died and always sit where we used to sit together, smack dab in the middle. "Not too close, not too far," he used to say. He'd see *West Side Story* and *Camelot* and *Finian's Rainbow*—he'd even see *Paint Your Wagon* and *nobody* saw *Paint Your Wagon*—and I wish I was there to see them with him. He'd make up his own dance numbers late at night in his apartment, which he'd finally get, until the neighbors downstairs complained he made too much noise and wrote something nasty on his door. He almost went with us to see *Tammy and the Bachelor* at the drive-in the night I died. If he had, maybe everything would have worked out differently.)

I try to make him see me now when he's the only one in the school, buffing the floors. Even with school out for the summer, he goes in once a week to make sure everything is just so. All alone, he wheels the record player cart out of one of the classrooms and plays the movie soundtracks he buys at Woolworth's at full volume and dances to them while he cleans, since he can't do it at his apartment anymore.

His apartment . . .

I tried to get an apartment.

I told L.E. I was leaving and taking the boys with me.

I went to Plano where Altha lives to look for an apartment; she'd said she could get me a teaching job there. They always needed teachers. They always needed women who didn't have anything better to do, or who were on the run from their husbands, or who were . . .

I wasn't worried about a job, I was worried . . .

I was worried about . . .

I was worried about staying alive.

Now I remember. Oh my sweet precious Lord.

There'd been a gun. L.E. had a gun. He kept it in his underwear drawer, next to his *True Detective* magazines.

I remember . . .

Was my husband trying to kill me so he could be with Rita Cobb? Is *that* how I died?

— CLARKE —

Daddy was going with us to the movies. Daddy never went with us to the movies. But tonight he came home from work and put Old Spice on his face and Vitalis on his hair and a fresh undershirt that tightened him up. I told him he could stay home if he wanted to, since he'd been on his feet all day. He could just drop us off like he always did.

"Nope, this is our Boys Night Out."

The boys—which was me and Corey and now Daddy—were going to see *My Fair Lady* on a Saturday night. Since Mother died, we never saw movies at night anymore, just on Saturday afternoon, but this was different. Yesterday, Daddy had cut out the ad for it from the *Courier-Gazette* with the same pinking shears Mother used to cut up our Chef Boyardee frozen pizza with every Friday night. She would make us pizza, then make him a steak in the same frying pan she tried to hit him with. He still made us pizza every Friday, even if he was drinking and the crust got burned.

Yesterday, he said he had a surprise for us, and I found the ad for the movie under my pizza slices. I had to wipe away tomato sauce and a gob of melted cheese to see Rex Harrison and Audrey Hepburn looking up at me from my plate. The ad said the tickets cost more because it was a musical "special engagement," and Daddy said, "That's an important lesson in business. You can charge more if you stick the word special on something. That one little word could make you rich."

He's never talked this much before. He's never taken us to the movies before. He's never cut out anything from the newspaper before, except for the printed obituary about our mother. He cut it out, but I never saw what he did with it.

Now I know why he wants to go to the movie with us. Mrs. Cobb, the lady with the shoe emergencies, was there, even though he pretended she was just an accident.

When we got to the Ritz, Corey and I stopped at the concession stand to get Cokes and popcorn while he went inside to save us seats. When we came back in, I saw Mr. Ring sitting with his mother. You know it was a special engagement because she never came with him, just like Daddy never came with us.

I started to find Daddy to ask him if we could sit with Mr. Ring, but then I saw Daddy talking to Mrs. Cobb. She was sitting by herself. Daddy motioned us over and told us he'd asked Mrs. Cobb to join us because it was such a nice surprise to see her, and he was "being polite, which is the most important business lesson of all." Corey started making those cobwebby things on my face so Daddy thumped us both on the backs of our heads. It hurt because he used the finger he still wore his wedding ring on, and the metal band punched into my head.

I felt sick at my stomach, like I did when he told us Mother was gone. Like when I smell too much Old Spice and Vitalis mixed together. I'd never smelled the smells of the Ritz before, but I did then—like when your drink spills on the floor and you step in it and the rubber on the bottom of your shoe mixes with all that sticky stuff, or the popcorn has too much butter and gets all shiny, or you smell the bathroom from the balcony upstairs. You even think you can smell the rust on the springs inside the cushions or the dust in the seats, because you can see it when the projector light comes up. You can smell things that aren't there, but you know they are. I smelled all those things, and I thought I was gonna upchuck, like when I get scared I have too many germs on my clothes and think they're going to kill me if I don't change outfits.

But then the movie started and I thought I could smell flowers because that's what Eliza Doolittle sells for a living, which isn't a very good one. She's dirty and talks funny—in a Cockney accent, like the Beatles—and she meets this fancy man who's from a different part of town. He teaches her how to talk better and walk better and sing at parties. He teaches her about the horse races and nice clothes to wear to balls, and finally he falls in love with her even though she never really turns fancy like him; she just looks like it on the outside.

I could smell the flowers because I can disappear into the movies. I can leave all the bad smells behind and go up inside the screen like I'm really walking around with the actors or riding around in their cars and hanging out on the set, being popular. That's what Mother taught me to do, to concentrate and pretend, and pretty soon you're not having to pretend anymore, you're just there. Inside the movie. And things are better. She said it was her favorite place to be, other than with me and Corey.

At the end of *My Fair Lady*, we all sat there like we didn't want to leave. We didn't want to break the spell. Even Daddy. He said, but kind of in a whisper, "Let's walk around the square and look at the stars. I haven't seen the stars in such a long time." He never talks like that. He never holds our hands either, but tonight he did. In the night air outside the Ritz, you couldn't smell anything bad on him anymore, like Old Spice or Vitalis or the whiskey he hides in the bathroom and drank before he brought us here in the car.

But then he called Mrs. Cobb "my fair lady," and all the bad smells came back.

When we walked past Woolworth's, she said, "Wait here. I've got an idea." It was just closing, but she asked them, "Please, please, let me in, just for a minute." She went inside then came back out with a package.

"This is a present for you boys, for letting me sit with you when I would have been so lonely sitting by myself." Inside was the soundtrack of *My Fair Lady* with a drawing on the cover of Professor Higgins holding puppet strings and Eliza Doolittle, the puppet, looking up at him like, "Now what?"

Daddy said, "What do you say, boys?" and Corey yelled out, "Move ya' bloomin' arse," like they do in the movie. Everybody laughed, and Daddy said he wouldn't even make him put a quarter in the cuss box when we got home.

In the car, Corey and Daddy sang, "I'm getting married in the morning, so get me to the church on time," which the Cockney people sing in the movie. It was the first time I've ever heard Daddy sing. He looked at me in the rearview mirror and said, "Clarkie, why don't you sing with us? It's what your Mumma would want."

I sang just to make Daddy happy, which I guess nothing else does any more except for Mrs. Cobweb.

— CLARKE —

SUNDAY, JUNE 12, 1966

Now nobody is singing because there's red on our hands, but it isn't ink from Mother's pen; it's blood from Corey's head. When Daddy let us sleep late on Sunday morning instead of getting us to the church on time, Corey put on our new soundtrack to *My Fair Lady*. He put on Daddy's bathrobe so he could be Henry Higgins, and I put on one of Mother's old nightgowns so I could be Eliza Doolittle. And then we sang "I Could Have Danced All Night" and danced along with the record.

When it came to the part where Eliza says, "I could have spread my wings and done a thousand things," Corey spread his wings too, running down the hall and letting Daddy's bathrobe flare out behind him. I chased him so Mother's floaty nightgown would do the same thing. Then we waltzed around the living room like we were at the Black and White Ascot Ball, only it became the Yellow and Red Ball when Corey's blond head went slicing into a sharp wooden corner of the couch that had lost its padding and red blood went everywhere.

I screamed, then pulled off Mother's nightgown in the time it took Daddy to wake up. I didn't want him seeing me in it, or waking up and thinking he was looking at Mother's ghost.

He wrapped up Corey's head in a towel, one he got from the dirty clothes hamper, and I heard his liquor bottle fall to the bottom of it when he moved things around. Then he took us to the hospital where Corey had an operation on his head, just like John F. Kennedy did in Dallas, which is forty-five minutes away from us. They shaved his head—Corey's, not Kennedy's—and then sewed it back together with black thread. But you can't see it now because his head is wrapped up in a cloth like the ones the fancy ladies wore in the movie.

"It's called a turban," Mrs. Cobb had said last night, not knowing Corey would be wearing one today.

I was so happy Corey wasn't dead, just missing some hair and blood and skin, that I thought we should all start singing again when we got home. But Daddy started screaming, not singing.

"GodDAMNIT nothing good ever happens in this shitass family!" He put a quarter in the cuss box and kept screaming. "Goddamnit to hell," he said, then threw all the change he had from the pants he'd pulled on over his pajamas at the wall. "There. THERE. Take all the shitass money I make. What ELSE do you kids wanna take from me?"

He put one arm against the wall to support himself like he does when he's drunk and has to prop himself up to keep from falling over.

"Why weren't you looking out for him? We go out and have a nice night and Mrs. Cobb buys you a present and I let you skip Sunday school. Then I wake up and there's blood all over the fucking house! Your brother's sick enough without you goddamn KILLING HIM!!!"

"Then YOU should have been looking after him instead of dreaming about THAT WOMAN..." I started saying, louder than I'd ever been to him.

"Don't you EVER..."

He started shaking and his face turned as red as the blood that had just come out of Corey's head.

"Go to your room right now and pray, PRAY that I don't come in and rip out your vocal cords for what you just said." Then he took our new *My Fair Lady* album and broke it into a bunch of little pieces instead of breaking me into pieces.

When Daddy left the house and the coast was clear, I took them and put them with the growing collection under my bed—Mother's

Instructor magazine, Daddy's clip-on tie that I covered with glue, the tape recorder I stole from his store, and, now, the shards of the record.

"Is Daddy gonna forget Momma now because of Mrs. Cobb?" Corey asked me a few hours later when his operation medicine finally wore off and he could talk again.

"He might, but we never will." I blinked my eyes, hard, to add that to the list of things I would never forget.

"Did Momma's head blow up and start bleeding like mine?" Corey's eyes were open, but he was looking up at the ceiling instead of me.

"We don't know how Momma died. Nobody does. That's what I'm trying to find out."

"I do. I caused it. This is God's revenge," he said, touching his turban. "He's making my head hurt as much as hers did because it was all my fault."

"I don't know what you're talking about. You're still all doped up. It's *my* fault, because I wasn't looking out for you. Daddy was right."

"I tried to find Momma at the hospital. I kept floating around to find her so I could tell her my secret."

"What *secret*? What are you talking about? Go back to sleep."

"I'm afraid to. I have nightmares where her head's bleeding and it just keeps getting bigger and bigger because there's nowhere for the blood to go except for out of her ears and nose."

He hadn't said anything in so long, and now he couldn't stop talking, like they were all the words he'd been saving up for months. "I'm afraid the same thing is gonna happen to me, from my angel disease. I have nightmares that I'm gonna die all the time now, just like her. Will you pray for me that I don't die like they said I would?"

"*Corey* . . . you're a kid. Kids don't die. So shut up about it and don't talk again until your medicine wears off because you're not making sense."

And then I made a turban for myself out of an old pillowcase and put red food coloring on it for blood so he'd know he wasn't alone.

— CREOLA —

Corey did die, at least for a few seconds. That's when I got to talk to him, or at least hear him; to see inside his head—through the gaping tear in it, blood smearing his beautiful blond angel hair—when he was floating along in the hospital, next to me.

Dying while the doctors tried to save him.

We only had fifteen or twenty seconds together, but it felt like a lifetime.

He floated up above his lifeless body on the operating table, covered with a sheet except for the opening where they worked on his head, pulling thick black thread through his scalp to close the wound.

When he died for those few seconds, they had to throw off the sheet and put electrical paddles on his chest. They should have put them on me, to keep me from dying all over again when I had to witness that. My second born, dying. Going once, going twice . . .

From his new position up in the air, I saw him look down on himself and smile, like he was finally at peace, not feeling any of the jolts pulsating through him and making his body jump like he was having a seizure.

It wasn't him down there anymore, just another little boy he could smile at.

I saw Corey waver out of the room and look at his father crying and smoking while a nurse tried to put out his cigarette, and I saw him also look at Clarke, barricaded in a pay phone booth, his feet pushed against the door so nobody could get in.

Corey just placidly observed it all—maybe there was a lesson for me there: just look but don't get so riled up—as he floated toward the snack room where he magically got a hot chocolate from the vending machine without having to pay for it. He just looked at the machine and grinned—my baby happy again!—and a little paper cup plonked out and filled with powder, then hot steaming water, then mini marshmallows.

He took the cup, but he didn't drink from it; he looked around for someone else to give it to.

That's when he saw me smiling at him.

That's what he had brought to me, my last night alive. I remember it now: a glass of chocolate milk, holding it out to me so carefully with both hands so not a drop would spill. He was just as mindful now, floating through the clouds with the hot chocolate calling to me. "Momma, momma, where are you? I have something to tell you. I'm here."

Now the look on his face changed. He didn't look happy anymore; he looked worried. He looked scared now that he could see me smiling at him, welcoming him. Company, finally! A child to talk to and read to and teach, like I was meant to do.

"Corey, it's me! I'm right here! Just keep following my voice!"

"No, I can't. I'm hurting too much. The hot chocolate is burning. My head is burning."

I knew he couldn't stay here with me. I knew it wasn't fair. As much as I wanted to see my son, to hear what he had to tell me, I told him he had to go back. That he wasn't finished. That it wasn't any fun to die too young. And seven was too young. Just like forty-four.

The second I thought it, he plummeted back down into his body and couldn't hear anything else, certainly not me. He could just feel things: a surgeon's scalpel slicing into his scalp. Those thick needles going into his skin.

And then I'm alone. Again. Naturally.

Maybe seeing me is what scared him into becoming the boy who fell to earth. I don't really know what I look like anymore; they don't have any mirrors here, so maybe it's not pretty, not that I was ever "pretty" in real life. I wouldn't want to look at me either, having to send my littlest angel back to earth. I felt like Judas Iscariot sending Corey back to earth. Like I've betrayed him somehow.

— CLARKE —

Usually we just see one movie at a time at the Ritz, not two, but Daddy says the Ritz is a good babysitter for us on the weekends. So today we saw *Fireball 500* with Annette Funicello and Frankie Avalon, where "they treat their dames and their cars the same . . . Rough!" That's what it says on the poster. We also saw *A Patch of Blue*, about this girl who is blind, and Sidney Poitier, who falls in love with her. She falls in love with him too, but she can't see that his skin is a different color than hers.

Tonight I wished that I was blind and deaf when Daddy started saying that Mrs. Cobb might be our new babysitter, only now we should call her "Rita." He took us to dinner at her house and made us get dressed up and wear shoes and socks even though it's summer and we usually go barefoot. Her house was leaning and her lawn needed mowing, and Daddy says it would be "a nice gesture" if we mowed it for her.

Rita made pot roast with potatoes and carrots and onions. She said it looked like it took a lot more trouble than it actually did because you really just "throw everything in a pot and turn it off two hours later." I could tell she was trying to be funny, but she was too nervous for the joke to work. She was nervous the whole night and kept bumping into things, like the blind girl in the movie.

She let me and Corey have our strawberry shortcake on TV trays in front of the TV, because she said that's what she'd be doing if we weren't there. Just watching TV in her housecoat. She said that she wanted us to feel free to do that anytime we came over, which she hoped was going to be a lot more from now on. I saw Daddy shake his head *No* at her, like he was trying to get her to notice him but not let us notice him.

We watched *Daktari* on her TV while she and Daddy sat at the table by themselves. I watched them out of the corner of my eye. She whispered, "It's going good, isn't it?" to him, and he nodded back, but now he seemed as nervous as she did and switched to drinking beer instead of iced tea.

The TV picture got fuzzy, so I got up to jiggle the rabbit ears that had little aluminum foil flags on them for better reception. Rita had a lot of pictures in frames on top of her TV—of a man in ice skates, of another man not as old, and of a kid with red hair. That was the big picture in the middle, which meant it was the most important one to her.

It was a photograph of that kid who had been playing at Daddy's store, calling him Freddy. He was easy to remember because of his red hair and freckles and the missing part of his ear. He was easy to remember because he shouldn't have been on top of Rita's TV.

"It's that kid," I said, without realizing I was talking out loud.

"Oh. That's my son, Gibson, and that's my grandson Ricky," Rita said. "You'd like him. Another little boy to play with. You should meet him."

We already have, I wanted to say, but didn't. And we *wouldn't* like him, but I didn't say that either.

A little bit later, we were saying goodbye and Rita was signing her name on top of Corey's turban—it was filled with so many names now from where his friends had signed it that it looked like his hair had grown back in black, not blond.

That's when I stole the picture of her grandson. I was shaking so much I thought the glass inside the frame would rattle and give me away, like it had just given Daddy and Rita away.

———

P.S. We're home now, and everybody's asleep except for me. I'm too afraid to sleep because I think I'm going to get in trouble if Rita finds out her picture is gone. But I'm not going to give it back. It's evidence, and I'm keeping it under my bed with Mother's magazine and Daddy's tie and the broken pieces of *My Fair Lady*. But now I've found something else that I never realized was evidence before.

It's the register from Mother's funeral, which in this case is a noun and not a verb, like when you "register" for school. This register is something that *is*, not something you *do*. It's the book you had to sign your name in if you wanted to see Mother at the funeral home. The outside of it is covered with padded white silk, and there's a watercolor drawing of a weeping willow on top of it. Sometimes when I look at it, which I do a lot, I end up holding my breath without even knowing it, and I have to make myself remember to breathe again. But I've never looked at it all the way through, until tonight.

It has pages telling you about what kind of flowers she had at her funeral and who brought them, and what kind of music was played, and what the preacher said. It's good to have a memory of stuff like that on paper because I don't have it in my head. Daddy wouldn't let us go to her funeral, even though he made us go to the funeral home the night before for the last chance we'd ever have to see her.

At the funeral home, they had colored spotlights pointed at her body to make it prettier, but they reminded me of those lights they point at roasting chickens at Piggly Wiggly's. The lights are red-orange to keep the chickens hot, and that's what the ones on Mother looked like; like they were there to keep her hot instead of let her get cold.

You buy the chickens when you're too tired or too drunk or too dead to cook, so we've had a lot of them this year. You cut them up when you get home, and that's how they're different from Mother, because Daddy wouldn't let them cut her up, even though Aunt Altha wanted to, to see why she died.

When I first saw Mother in her coffin, I stopped moving, but Daddy kept pushing me forward from behind. Daddy's shoes kicked my ankles—maybe he just bumped into me, but it felt like he kicked me—and it felt like little knives popped out of the tips of his shoes, like the ones Lotte Lenya wears in *To Russia with Love*.

When we got to Mother's coffin, if you didn't like the way she looked in it, you could see how she looked in real life because Daddy had them put a painting of her up on a stand behind the coffin. He'd had it painted for her years ago as a present. Her mouth is open just a little bit, like she's trying to say something.

Tonight, under my covers with a flashlight, reading her register, I think I finally figured out what she was trying to say. To me. I went through every page and saw all the names of people who came to see her at the end; teachers from school and people from church and our neighborhood. But there was one name at the bottom of the very last page that wasn't from any of those places. The last name, the last person to get to see her before they closed the coffin lid and put her in the ground.

It was from Shaw's Café.

It was from *My Fair Lady*.

It was from Rita Cobb.

— CLARKE —

I know what happened.

    I'd thought it, but I didn't want to believe it.

    Now I've thought it some more, overnight, and I know for sure.

    It happens in movies all the time.

    That's how I know.

— CREOLA —

Now I remember. I'd actually talked to her before I died.

Rita Cobb. The shoe lady. L.E.'s lady.

I did more than just watch her from outside her window; I went in and *talked* to her. With my red shoes. The ones L.E. had me buy to go with my Mexican "señorita" outfit, which I'd bought when L.E. won Salesman of the Year at his store and got a free trip to Mexico. There's a picture of us coming out of the plane, walking down the steps of that pulled-up stairway down onto the tarmac. You can see the heat radiating off it, even in black and white. L.E. is wearing that stupid ten-gallon cowboy hat he always wore when he was drunk, ridiculous since he was a Yankee from Vermont, and I was wearing the red suit he'd given me extra money to buy. Puffy, thick red cotton, *bouclé* they called it, with black piping around all the edges and seams.

He said it made me look like a señorita.

I said it made me look like a piñata, *after* someone had swung a stick at it. Bruised and puffed up.

We brought back a piñata for the boys, and serapes, and sombreros, and balsa wood bull fighting sabers they almost poked each other's eyes out with. Their hands would get sweaty playing with them, and the dye on the feathered crepe paper that was wrapped around the sticks would run off on their skin. They'd rub it on their little faces and . . .

Stop it.

Don't go there.

Every memory but the right one.

Every memory but the one I'm looking for.

Every memory that almost makes me wish I'd never become a mother in the first place, because it's too painful remembering everything about them being alive and me being . . .

Just stop. Focus.

The shoes.

The red shoes.

My red shoes. L.E. had insisted I wear them to the bullfights in Mexico. I'd stepped in a bull patty, and they were never the same since. Try as I might to clean them, I could never completely get rid of the shit.

Now, let Rita take a whack at it.

I didn't know if she'd know who I was—had L.E. shown her my picture, even told her about me? Had he shown her a picture of the boys to get her sympathy, tell her he was a widower, before he actually was?

That's what I would do, to trap her: I'd work in Corey's and Clarke's school pictures, the little ones I carried around in my pocketbook. Clarke in his Carnaby Street paisley shirt I couldn't get him out of, Corey in his red tee shirt and red-and-black sweater. I'd say I had to get the shoes cleaned up to wear to Clarke's baptism. Bring God into it. That would get her going. Or shut her up. Or get her to leave my husband alone. Or get her to . . . I don't know what. Just *something*. That's what I was casting about for—just something.

I walked into Cobb's Shoe Shop, a narrow storefront on Kentucky Street off the town square, two curved-glass display cases on either side of the door, the outside paneled with big dark maroon tiles. Almost cordovan, the shoe color, like an inside joke. But the once-white grouting was now dirty moss green, and there was a crack in one of the front windows, patched up with duct tape. I had my own shitty red shoes in a brown paper sack—the same kind L.E. carries his liquor bottles home in—and I thought, that's what her shop smelled like. Alcohol. Rubs. Dyes. Chemicals. It would be hard to work there day in and day out and come out with your lungs intact. That made me feel sorry for her for about five seconds before I remembered why I was there.

"I've got this problem, and I don't know if you can help me."

"If it goes on your foot, I can fix it."

"I don't know what ever possessed me to buy a pair of red silk shoes in the first place, and then wear them to a bullfight..."

"A bullfight? Not around here I hope."

"No, Mexico. With my husband. He won a prize."

I looked at her, to see if there was any kind of recognition in her eyes. Nothing. Not yet. I could be any of the ladies in this sweet little middle-class town with a husband and a pair of red silk shoes.

"I stepped in this stuff—the boys call it dukie—I don't know, maybe I should just throw them away ... the shoes I mean, not the boys..."

I tried to laugh, but my energy was flagging, like it did so often in those days just before the end. I'd show up someplace and not remember why I was there. I'd just want to sit down. I'd just want to go to sleep.

"Honey, are you okay? It's just a pair of shoes. Here, take a load off." Rita shoved aside some old *Courier-Gazettes* and *PennySavers* on the worn leather chairs and gently helped me sit down. I looked around to get my bearings, and I saw, of all things, a pair of ice skates hanging over the door. Black, the laces fraying and splintered, just barely hanging on, but the blades still shiny and sharp. Rita saw me looking up at them.

"Oh, those were my husband Harold's. One of the two things he loved most in the world. Ice skating."

"What was the other one?"

"Drinking. And when he drank *and* skated at the same time ..."

At least we had that one thing in common. Well, I guess we had my husband in common too.

"You should move those. What if they fall down and hurt somebody when they come in the door?

"That's what I keep hoping for, honey, every morning. The one thing that could give me a day off. Is *this* gonna be my lucky day?" She was as sad as I was.

I sipped at the water Rita gave me from a water cooler. "That's better." I was trying to catch her—trying to do *something*—and there I was hearing her life story, which wasn't so much different from mine, and falling apart on her. I didn't even have the energy to open the bag of shoes; I just held it out to her.

Rita opened it. "Let's see what we have here. Pretty shoes, although I don't know if I can save that red. They might turn out more . . . purple after I'm done with 'em."

I started saying more than I meant to, confessing myself instead of getting her to confess. "I never wanted those shoes in the first place. They were my husband's idea. Believe me, I'm not the kind of woman who wears red silk shoes. I'm a schoolteacher. Now you, I could see you in a pair of red shoes . . ."

There was a flicker, for just a moment—both of us, eye to eye. "I mean, you've got some style, you keep your hair so nice, your makeup . . ."

"Nothing wrong with a pair of red shoes to lift your spirits."

"They're fairy-tale shoes. That's all I mean. You know that story—Hans Christian Andersen? 'The Red Shoes'? They changed it for the movie, but it's really about this girl who dances so much she has to cut off her feet to stop, and all that's left is a bloody stump. Stumps. The kids want me to read it to them after lunch. It's all they want to hear. Bloody stumps."

I started crying, in the shop of the woman who was sleeping with my husband.

"I hate them." I'd never said that before, never even dared to think it.

Rita sat down next to me, on top of all those newspapers. She was going to get newsprint all over her dress. "Hate what?"

"Fairy tales, shoes, schoolkids . . . do you want them?"

"What? The shoes—or your schoolkids?" Rita laughed because she didn't know what else to do. She'd probably never had a customer break down on her like this before.

"You know what? I should just go."

"Wait. Whatta you want me to do with your shoes?"

"Why don't you keep them? Go dancing in them."

She watched me go. I could feel her eyes on my back. I could feel how pathetic she thought I was.

I opened my purse to get out a handkerchief to rub my eyes with, and that's when I saw what else I had put in there to take with me to her shoe shop: L.E.'s gun.

– L.E. –

Creola still came to him at night in his dreams. She'd say she wanted to go for a drive or wanted to show him something, and he'd go with her. Literally. He'd get out of his bed—the bed they had shared for years; the bed he had lovingly made for her by hand, along with a chest of drawers, from hard Vermont maple—and follow her outside the house and into the Plymouth that was parked in the carport. Sometimes he'd wake up there the next morning and not know how he got there, his face nestled into the upholstery and pebbled with its woven pattern. One time he woke up with the keys in the ignition and the car running; another time he woke up to find the boys standing outside the car in their pajamas, their faces pressed up to the driver's side window as if they were looking in a store at candy they wanted. He'd locked the door and they couldn't get in. For a minute, he thought he should just turn on the car, pull them in, and take them all away. They'd keep driving until they ran out of gas, then start a new life in a town where nobody knew their business. But there wasn't enough gas or money in the world to keep them going that far, even at thirty-five cents a gallon.

He didn't like the way the teachers looked at him now when he came to parent-teacher night at North Ward, where Creola had taught. L.E. would walk past them—the very same ones who had brought covered casseroles and cupcakes to the house when Creola died—and feel them staring at him. Judging him somehow. The same ones who hugged him then, when he had walked around in a daze with a stained tee shirt on, now had turned their backs on him. He'd never outrun Creola's ghost, not in that school.

When he met Rita, he thought maybe he could get away without anybody having to get behind the wheel. One of the first presents he'd given her was a box of maple sugar candy, shaped like oak leaves. They were fat little suckers, glistening on top with sugar crystals, and his brothers and sister in Vermont sent him a box every Christmas. He could never bring himself to tell his siblings how much he hated that candy; it was supposed to remind him of home, a place he hadn't been back to in years, a place he'd hated when he was there. (The only present he'd ever liked from them was a giant picture of John F. Kennedy shellacked onto a slab of maple with rough bark still around the edges. That had stayed up in the living room—L.E., the only Democrat in a town full of southern Republicans— until the president got killed, then it somehow seemed disrespectful.) Even the boys turned on the candy after a while, and they never said no to anything sweet. Rita didn't even try to pretend she liked it. She took one look and said, "That's a mouthful of cavities just waiting to happen." That's why he liked her so much. She could tell jokes. She had fun. Creola didn't have fun anymore.

He'd tried to be good, he really had. All the other women had been different—he'd never fallen in love before. Fucking didn't mean that much to him; he could do it, wipe his dick off, and go home at night or in the morning. Creola would stare at him— or sometimes throw things at him—and he'd sleep on the couch or in one of the spare rooms for a while until she let him back into their bed.

But then he came home one day—not even night, not early in the morning—with new brown shoes and an extra pair of shoelaces, and he knew that Creola knew he was back to his old ways. He never bought new shoes on his own. When he went to J. C. Penny's and bought three new ties (not clip-ons) she knew it was just a matter of time. She said, "I'm going to leave, and I'm taking the boys with me this time, and you'll be stuck with nothing but your cheap whore—whoever she is this time—and your bedroom suite. I hope you get some good use out of it."

L.E. had spent weeks making that furniture for Creola in their second or third year of marriage, trying to prove to her that he was worth something, that she hadn't made the worst mistake of her life. She thought he was having an affair the whole time he was working on it, he was out so late, coming home without any answers about where he'd been. He'd set up the bed and the bureau before she got home from school one day; he bought new sheets and covered them with fall leaves and lit candles. And they had been in love again, for just a while, until the newness of the furniture wore off and his drinking picked back up.

It was in his blood. L.E. had grown up in a family that drank, and it wasn't just the men. His mother too, and whatever man she happened to be with at the time. It was all four brothers; they said the alcohol kept them warm from the Vermont cold. They were drunk that Christmas when they'd chopped down every fir tree they could find and hauled them in a truck six hours away to just past the New York border to sell for Christmas. Little Lloyd Edwin—just six years old—was their shill, too little to tote the giant Green Mountain trees himself but pitiful-looking enough to get the city folk to buy them. They saw his poverty. They saw how cold he was in his threadbare coat. The New Yorkers melted at the sight of the little urchin, and he played it to the hilt until a semi-truck skidded off the side of the road and ran over him. He didn't hear it coming because of the flaps on his hat that covered his ears, so cold they were burning, so cold they couldn't hear.

He didn't hear it coming because his brothers were too drunk to look after him.

The doctors sewed his hurt leg back together and gave him the souvenir he'd carry for the rest of his life: the perfect imprint of a truck wheel tread on his left leg, in pink hairless scar tissue and the metal plate that replaced the bone inside. That was one of the boys' favorite things about him: they'd touch and prod the leg, trying to feel the outlines of the only kind of plate they knew, the kind they ate supper on. When L.E. was asleep—or pretending to be asleep,

to play along with them—they'd pull back the bed covers and show
it off to their friends, then giggle and run out of the room.

L.E. always said when he looked at it or touched it he automati-
cally smelled Christmas trees. And maple syrup. And blood. And
burning tires. And it hurt. That's why he stayed in Texas, after he'd
been stationed there for basic training. It was warm, downright hot
most of the year, and he convinced himself the heat made his leg
feel better, in contrast to the unbroken Vermont cold. He liked the
flatness of the place, that you could get around without straining
yourself, and didn't care if he never saw another mountain again.
He could be outside more instead of staying bundled up inside all
the time. It wouldn't matter if he didn't have the money for a nice
winter coat; he'd barely need one. And the people seemed friend-
lier. They could take their time in a conversation instead of rushing
home to where the heat was on. Their shoulders were more relaxed
because they weren't drawn up in protest against the weather all the
time. He thought you could tell a lot about a person from the way
their shoulders sat. The only thing that stayed the same, from Vermont to Texas, was the drinking.

He drank the week before he asked Creola to marry him, to give
him courage, and he drank the entire week after he asked her—
before she answered—because he was afraid she'd say no. He drank
the week his first son was born because he was so excited, and the
week his second son was born because he wanted to keep on having boys. He drank the week he got his job at Ellis Electronics, and
he drank the week he lost his job there because of his drinking. The
week Creola died, he drank some more. A lot more.

That's why he couldn't let them cut open his wife, to find out
what killed her; he knew what they'd find inside. Too many prom-
ises he'd made to her that hadn't come true. Too many times when
he'd said, "I promise, I'll quit, I won't take another drink." They'd
find all those drinks. They'd find all those nights he'd stayed away
from home, telling Creola he had to do inventory at the store.
They'd find all those bottles of Old Spice cologne he'd used, trying

to hide the perfume from other women. They'd open Creola up and the stench would come steaming out, along with the blood and bile and everything else.

He couldn't let the secrets of their marriage out. He couldn't let her be sewn back together the same way his leg had been, with a scar that would never go away, even if no one would ever see it inside her coffin.

He would see it, for the rest of his life, and know that he had caused it.

— RITA —

When she met Perkins for the first time, she'd just had her hair done. A dark brown rinse with a hint of coppery red, a wiglet teased in to add dimension to her thin hair. When it wasn't on her head, it was in a big turquoise carrying case; the girls at the beauty shop used to tease her that they should charge double because she took up one seat and the case took up another.

That was her big adventure every week: having her hair done but not having any place to show it off.

She'd just come back from the beauty parlor—the chemicals that fried her hair into place as potent as the ones in her shoe shop— when Perkins came in to get his shoes fixed. Cheap brown lace-ups; the sole was gone, and the width was stretched all to hell and back. He said they didn't "breathe" anymore, and she'd said, "Yeah, cardboard has a hard time doing that after a few years." He'd laughed, she'd laughed, the first laugh of the day for both of them.

"You want my honest opinion?" she'd added.

"If it's not gonna cost me extra."

"Let me start by saying a foot is a horrible thing to waste. They're all we have to keep us standing."

"I can already hear the meter running."

"I can call the priest if you want, or we can just do a private little ceremony right now, commend these shoes into God's green earth . . ."

"All God's chillun' got shoes."

"I think that's wings, but you've got the basic idea."

She didn't know what she was saying. Neither did he. Neither one had talked this way or this much in months.

She took him shoe shopping around the corner, pointed out some durable Thom McAns on the sale rack, and that was their first date. Back at her shop, she threw in an extra pair of shoelaces for free, and he put the slick little paper band they came wrapped in around her finger. He said it was for saving his life—"These dogs can *breathe*!"—and he left, his lunch break almost at an end.

The very next day he came back, asking if she had Dr. Scholl's cushions to put inside. But he pronounced it a strange way—"quishions"—and she had to ask what he was talking about.

"*Quishions*. You know, those paddy things."

"*Cushions*."

"That's what I said. I'm gonna take my ring back if you're already making fun of the way I talk."

"I've just never heard it pronounced like that."

"Then come to Vermont with me, where I'm from. That's the way we say it up there, in the cold. They need good solid shoes up there for tromping through the snow. You could do a good business, selling *quishions* to pad 'em with."

That was their second date, and they both knew it.

Third date, coffee next door at Shaw's Café, their elbows brushing up next to each other on a Formica countertop.

Fourth date, he bought her a tuna fish sandwich.

That's how their romance began. He said his wife called him L.E., so she called him Perkins, to give him a fresh start. She knew it was wrong. She knew he was married. She knew he had kids. She knew that her diet candy Ayds tasted like shit and wasn't working.

Perkins was the first man she'd gone out with since her husband Harold had died seven years earlier. He'd left her a grown son who had a life of his own now, a pile of empty liquor bottles, a pair of ice skates from his dream career that never came true, the shoe shop, and a cash register full of debt. She'd worked her way through paying it off with every shoe she repaired, every dye job she did for the fancy ladies in town who brought in their mother-of-the-bride dresses and wanted a pair of shoes dyed to match. DTM, as they said in the shoe trade. She punched holes in belts when the men who worked downtown got too fat and needed a little more room to buckle up, and she even shined their shoes, sometimes with the men still in them, sometimes when they stepped out.

It was all supposed to be so much better. She wasn't bad looking, but she wasn't the looker men left their wives for. She was short, and even shorter from standing on her feet all day. Her tits had fallen down as much as her arches, but she hid those with the right undergarments. She did her makeup every day—eyebrows plucked, some mascara, some lipstick. She always wore perfume; she put cold cream on her face at night and on her hands so her skin stayed smooth. But she had a mole that looked like a beauty mark that made her look cheap. Nothing she could do about it.

Maybe knowing Perkins it *would* be better. They'd keep it secret; it wouldn't hurt anybody. All those other men, sitting up on her shoe-shine stand, reading their papers, had flirted enough, but she just hadn't been ready. Now she was. She could laugh at Perkins's lame jokes and make better ones. She could feel okay closing up the shop for an hour and going next door to grab a sandwich with him. But she wouldn't go anywhere else with him, not yet. Not to his house, or a motel, or the back storage room of her store or his, just a block away over on Virginia Street.

A married man with kids.

Fixing shoes until she wanted to scream.

That's not how it was supposed to be.

Maybe it would be better if those ice skates just came slicing into her head and just-done hairdo when she opened the door to her shop, before anybody really got hurt.

— CREOLA —

I wish Clarke hadn't found out like that: Rita's name at the very bottom of my funeral register. I wish he hadn't found out *any* way. I wish I hadn't given birth to such a smart child. I wish . . . I wish a lot of things, far more than I ever wished on earth.

I wish he and Corey had never had to see me like that, in a coffin.

I didn't like how they made me look, but maybe I wouldn't have liked anything that ended up with me in a metal box. My lipstick was too red, and L.E. and Altha had put me in that stupid red señorita suit. A trip to Mexico, where nobody knows you, in a flashy red suit is one thing, but a trip to eternity in it is something else. The inside lining of the coffin was soft pink silk, but against that blood-red dress — didn't they have people who coordinated these things? Had Altha lost her mind? (In the portrait of me that L.E. had them prop up behind my coffin, I'm wearing one of my nice schoolteacher dresses, the dark blue one I liked so much. Why couldn't they have buried me in *that*?) Pink and red, two colors that were never going to go together in a million years, which was how long I was going to have to make my peace with them. Then they got panicky at the last minute because they couldn't find the red shoes I always wore with that suit, and they decided to let me just go barefoot in the coffin because nobody would know the difference with the bottom half of the coffin closed up like it was.

I'd be going to meet my Maker barefoot because Rita still had the red shoes I'd dropped off at her shop, the day I went there to . . . meet her?

Kill her?

I don't even know her.

Maurice Ring was there, at the funeral home. He knew about things like that, what colors went together. I thought maybe I could get his attention and get him to say something about how ugly I was put together, about how it wasn't the real me. Believe me, that's when you want to look your best, when you're about to meet your Maker. But Maurice was so busy crying that he probably couldn't even tell *what* color I was wearing; everything was blurry to him, and he was already blind as a bat anyway behind his Coke-bottle thick glasses. Wally Cox, that's who he looked like. Mr. Peepers. Miss McLarty, my student teacher, was there with him. They were huddled together on those brand-new gilt chairs Billy Wayne Turrentine was so proud of, that he had perfectly aligned on opposite sides of the room. They were all filled up; it was standing room only.

SRO, the kind of audience my Clarke, the aspiring actor, could only dream of.

That night, Billy Wayne just had a single building for his funeral home: an old Victorian a few blocks off the downtown square. Twenty-five years from now, Billy Wayne will move farther away and have his own perpetual care cemetery, acres and acres on the outskirts of town, complete with a sculpture garden and a mausoleum: one-stop shopping. And if you get hungry on the way there, you can stop at the nearby Stuckey's and buy an Indian-braided mosaic belt and some fudge to cheer yourself up.

I could have used the fudge back then; I needed cheering up. I wanted to stop the boys in their long march toward my coffin so they wouldn't have to see me like that, painted up with the wrong kind of makeup. They'd never seen a dead person before; I didn't want to be their first. No child, at seven or ten years old, should have to see his own . . .

No. Wait. They *had* seen a dead person before.

And I was the one who made them.

It just came back to me.

So much is starting to come back.

Mrs. Opitz was a widow who lived across the street and three houses down from us—the kind of woman I lived in dread of becoming, a sullen old biddy who wore the same ratty housecoat all day long and didn't have any visitors. The boys called her "Old Pits." I heard the news, a heart attack—news travels fast on a small street—and I began running down the sidewalk, screaming that she was dead.

And that I was going to die soon too.

(How did I just *know* that?)

It wasn't the kind of thing that women entrusted to take care of *other* people's children was supposed to do.

Clarke had just gone outside to pick up the *Courier-Gazette* from the front yard and there I was, for him and the whole street to see, crying and running down the block. He'd seen me cry before—and he'd seen me scream when I was telling his father about my visits from the Great Apostle Paul—but he'd never seen me sprint as if I were trying to outrun death itself.

It must have exhausted me because I remember being very quiet at supper that night. Maybe everyone else was just being quiet so they wouldn't set me off again. You could hear the silverware scrape. You could hear ice clink. (Me, giving schoolchildren sweet iced tea to drink for supper. No wonder they could never sleep.) You could hear the boys trying not to breathe. The only thing I said during the entire meal was that I had somewhere to go that night, and I wanted Clarke and Corey to go with me. I told them to go put on something nice and get in the car with me. They did, afraid that if they didn't, I'd start screaming again.

Of course, their father was nowhere to be found.

I put on something nice too, but I did it in a hurry. My bra strap was hanging out of my sleeve. I didn't notice, but Clarke did. He noticed things like that. He tucked it back under my blouse without saying a word, then looked straight ahead, out the front window of the car.

I drove to the funeral home—the very one I would be lying in several months later—and stopped the car. We sat.

"Why are we here?" Clarke asked.

"We're here to see Mrs. Opitz. To pay our respects."

"I don't want to."

"Neither do I," chimed in Corey.

"But *I* want you to. I want you to know that childhood ends. I want you to be prepared."

I marched all three of us into the viewing room. We saw a casket at the end of a long room with a light shining on it and heard organ music—coming from somewhere, but nowhere in the room because there wasn't an organ in sight.

I started walking toward the coffin and the body I knew was inside.

The boys didn't move a muscle.

I turned around to them. "Come on. She's waiting."

"NO. I didn't know you meant . . . I don't wanna see her," Clarke said.

"Me neither," Corey said.

"Either! And it doesn't matter because she wants to see *you*!" And with a ferocity I didn't know I had—my birdlike claws with ridged veins and chipped fingernail polish—I pulled both boys, *dragged* them, down the aisle to see their first dead person.

"There. Remember that. Look at her! That's going to be me one day. *Soon* if things don't change."

That's what death is, I know now, remembering every horrible thing you've ever said to your children. Terrifying them before they ever needed to be terrified.

I was remembering all that, floating above the crowd at my own visitation in the funeral home, when Rita came in the room. I was so busy trying to watch out for my boys that I didn't notice her at first. So many other people were there, hugging L.E. and the children, smothering them in middle-aged lady smells and soft bosoms. It's a wonder the boys didn't suffocate.

But then a room that was already quiet got even quieter.

Did everyone in the room already know that Rita was sleeping with L.E., the dead woman's husband?

The dead woman that was me.

— MAURICE —

"What a Friend We Have in Jesus" was playing in the background of the funeral home, but when Maurice Ring hummed along with it, to keep from making an utter fool of himself and wailing out loud, he changed the words to, "What a friend we had in Creola."

That's how much he had loved her, to change Jesus's name to hers.

He wasn't even sure he *believed* in Jesus, but he believed in Creola.

And he *still* made a fool of himself, crying so hard that his shoulders heaved up and down, and he accidentally tipped over in his fake Louis Quatorze chair and took out a row of flower arrangements with him. The very same arrangements that he had already shuffled around when he first got there, racing away early from his dinner shift at the Townhouse Restaurant. Somebody had just plopped the flowers down willy-nilly in the room with no sense of placement or order. Big flower pots mixed in with little ones; sprays of forsythia towering over orange day lilies that had been set up on leaning stands. So Mr. Ring had taken that job on, to keep himself from thinking about what was in that coffin. Shifting pots and planters and stands and frames around so that things started small and ended big, with the largest arrangements flanking the coffin. Pulling the eye in, to that final resting place.

The resting place he couldn't bring himself to go to.

Creola's gleaming white coffin: the top half of the lid open, the bottom half closed.

Hymn after hymn had played; person after person had gone up; Maurice had righted his chair and gotten his land legs back, but still, he couldn't do it.

So he just sat there, next to Suzanne McLarty—they'd gone in together on a flower arrangement—worrying at a grease spot on his black dress pants. When he'd ordered Creola's flowers from Crump's Garden, he hadn't been able to tell the woman on the phone what he wanted her to write out on the card. He stammered and then went silent as she kept saying, "Are you there? Are you still there, ma'am? Hello?"

On the phone, everyone always thought he was a ma'am until he told them otherwise. And sometimes he didn't even bother; it was just too much trouble.

Yes, he was still there, with no way to sum up what Creola had meant to him. So he just told the flower lady to write, "We'll always have the Ritz" and hung up. He decided to make his own goodbye card for her, to put in her coffin. He didn't know if it was against the rules or would be unhygienic or anything like that, he just knew that he had to do it.

And now he had to work up his courage and get it in there, on top of her body, into her hands, before they closed the coffin lid. So he made up a little story, using the titles of some of the movies that he and Creola had seen together at the Ritz. They gave out programs every time you went there, 8 ½-by-12-inch sheets folded over and printed on, front and back, advertising the current and upcoming movies from the Ritz and the drive-in, and Maurice had saved every one of them. He cut out the titles and put them all on a sheet of yellow construction paper so that the black and white of the lettering would pop. Yellow, the same color as the grave blanket of roses on the bottom half of Creola's coffin.

With all those cut-out titles, the final product ended up looking like the most bizarre ransom note ever delivered: "*Georgy Girl* says *Walk, Don't Run* if you want to learn how to do an *Arabesque*, but if you want to ask *Is Paris Burning?* then you'll have to *Follow Me, Boys!* all the way to *Khartoum*."

It didn't make any sense, but neither did Creola being dead.

He'd known she was planning to leave town, but it was just for

Plano, thirty miles away. Not heaven. What had happened in just a
few days' time—between her asking him to hide her suitcase in his
janitorial supply closet at school, to an ambulance taking her dead
body away? He didn't know what to do with her suitcase, no doubt
smelling of Pine Sol and ammonia now—whether he should give it to
Mr. Perkins or the boys. Whether he should open it himself. It might
put him over the edge, although it might have had something better to
wear than that red outfit they'd used to dress her for her coffin.

"C'mon. We're going. It's nearly over," Suzanne said to him,
yanking him out of his seat and his reverie. "You can do it."

Suzanne—who would never be the friend to him that Creola
had been, but who at least joined him for hurried cigarette breaks
out on the playground at North Ward—held his hand and pulled
him up, treating him as gingerly as she would one of her bashful
new students on the first day of school. He kept looking down at his
patent leather lace-ups and took slow steps, trying to match them
to the lugubrious church music that was playing; anything to think
about except what he was going to be looking at. Maybe this was a
bad idea. Maybe he just wanted to remember her like she had been.
He could say his goodbyes in his head. He had entire imaginary
conversations there, why not a final one with Creola?

"Just one step at a time. You can do this." Suzanne guided him
on, this still-in-college young woman who had only known Creola
for three days, now in charge. He knew she'd make a good teacher
just from that. "We're almost there."

And then they were. He'd kept his eyes squeezed tight, just like
he did when he made a birthday wish and blew out candles on a
cake, but he knew this wish would never come true: Creola would
never come back alive.

He looked at the painting of her propped up behind the coffin
and used that to steady himself before he looked at her face. She
was too pale, and her lipstick was too red—he could have fixed her
up if people weren't around—but she didn't look afraid. She didn't
look scared, like she had the last few days of her life.

— CLARKE —

When you say "Our Father" like God, you make the F a capital letter. When you say "our father" like Daddy, you keep the f a little letter. I will call Momma Mother, but I will not call Daddy Father. He doesn't deserve it anymore. I can't look him in the eye, and I can't look at Rita, because I know they were looking at each other over Mother's coffin.

I can't look at Aunt Altha anymore either because she is taking away Mother's dresses. She says she is "getting rid of them for your own good, just like your Daddy got rid of my sister so he could have a new life and a new girlfriend, never mind which one came first."

"Pooch, be quiet. Little pitchers," her daughter Beverly said, meaning us. She arched her eyebrows, then nodded her head in our direction.

Aunt Altha didn't see it because she was too busy yanking coat hangers out of Mother's closet and making piles of clothes on the bed. She came to Mother's pink party dress with swirly stuff on the bottom and sequins on the top.

"Why didn't we put Creola in this? Pink's the right color for a coffin, not red, like some whore would wear. Like *she* would wear."

"Pooch, shut your trap," her other daughter Carolyn said.

"You mean like L.E. shut Creola's?" She yanked more dresses out of the closet, the coat hangers almost poking her in the eye. "Carolyn, maybe you could wear this for your prom."

"I am not wearing a dead person's dress to my prom, no matter how much I loved Aunt Creola."

Aunt Altha kept on talking, not paying any attention. "Why

93

didn't I insist on an autopsy? She called me just a week before she died and said it was over. She was leaving. The last time I ever talked to her, and she said she had to hang up because L.E. just walked in. If only I'd kept her on the phone. If only they'd done an autopsy like I wanted, then we would . . ."

"Pooch, I'm gonna start calling you 'If Only,' if you don't be quiet. The boys." Now it was Carolyn warning her.

I was more focused on Mother's dresses than what Aunt Altha was saying. "You can't take that stuff. It's ours."

Aunt Altha said, "Funny, that's what I said to God when He took my sister, but it didn't get Him to change *His* mind."

"What does she mean?" Corey asked, to anyone who would answer.

"Oh, you know Pooch. She watches too many movies, just like you guys," Beverly said. "Come on, let's get this stuff out to the car."

That's when I got the most upset, when they put Mother's clothes into the trunk of Aunt Altha's car. "Now they're gonna smell like spare tires. I'll forget how Mother smells if you don't leave me something to remember her by," I said.

Aunt Altha grabbed one of Mother's schoolteacher suits off the top of the pile and shoved it at me. "Here. Remember this. Remember what a good teacher and mother she was." She held the suit up to me as if she were measuring me against Mother. But I could tell she didn't even see me anymore. She just saw her sister, because everybody says we looked so much alike. "She was so tiny when she died. He whittled her away. Just ask your father. And that woman. Ask *them* what's so funny about murder." Then she tightened up her mouth so much that all the wrinkles on her face bunched up all the way to her hair line. The color drained out of her face, and she pursed her lips tighter; more wrinkles shot out. She started hitting her palm like she did at the funeral home when she was showing where they couldn't get the red ink off Mother's hands. She was jabbing so hard Carolyn had to grab her wrists until she calmed down, but her hands kept shaking even though her arms stayed still. She was shaking so much Beverly had to drive their car when they left.

I was going to show Mother's pill bottle to Aunt Altha, but now I'm mad at her. And confused. She said "he killed her by whittling her away," but what does that mean? That he carved her up? Aunt Altha says he wouldn't *let* them carve her up, and that's part of her evidence.

I should ask Daddy, but I don't want to talk to him anymore after what he did. After what he's still doing.

He keeps trying to make us play little league baseball for the summer because he says we have to get out of the house and out of the Ritz, that we can't stay cooped up all summer long when the sun is shining. But when I look up at the sun, that's when the ball hits me in the head.

Then I saw the ad for the *Peter Pan* tryouts in the *Courier-Gazette*, and I thought maybe I could persuade Daddy that a spotlight is just as good as the sun. The Civic Chorus is doing it for the summer musical, and if Corey and I get in it, we won't have to play Little League. Or be around Daddy.

Last night was the tryout at the high school auditorium, which Daddy drove us to even though he was complaining the entire time. I sang "Edelweiss" from *The Sound of Music* for my audition. When I got to the part about "bless my homeland forever," I changed the words to "bless Mc-Kin-ney forever," so they'd think I was normal and liked where I came from and not just sad all the time because my mother is dead. "My homeland" and "McKinney" both have three syllables, so they time out the same.

Before we even left, they told us we got in, me and Corey. I'm Michael, the littlest brother in the Darling family, and Corey is one of the Lost Boys, which is how he looks when he has one of his seizures. I've wanted to be an actor for so long, I can't believe it's about to happen. That's why I go to the movies, to see the actors on-screen. That's why I love pretending, because that *is* what they do, like the girls who tried out for Peter Pan had to pretend they were boys, because Peter Pan is a boy.

The girls who tried out for Peter Pan had to play like they were crying. They had to do the scene where Peter sneaks in through the window of the Darling house. Wendy asks him, "Boy, why are you crying?" and Peter says it's because he's lost his shadow. Wendy helps him find it and sews it back on. Then she watches him fly out the window. But he comes back and takes all the children away, like play practice will take us away from Daddy. And Rita.

Sometimes I put on Mother's leftover makeup and pretend I'm her. When Daddy's at work, I sit on my knees in front of her old bedroom mirror and open the drawer she kept her makeup in. It's still there, and it smells like she's trapped inside. I take out the lipstick that she used to smear on her teeth, not the too-red kind they used at the funeral home, but the soft red she really wore, and the powder puff that isn't puffy anymore but flat and flesh-colored. Mother used to rub it against her cheeks and nose to keep them from shining, so I think it still has little flakes of her skin caught in it. I rub it on my face so some of Mother will rub off on me, even her germs.

Sometimes, when I do my acting lessons at the mirror and have a serious scene, I rub toothpaste under my eyes to make myself cry. Most of the time, though, I don't even have to use the toothpaste.

— CLARKE —

I'm not going to fly. That's what I found out tonight when we started play practice. Only Peter Pan is going to fly, when a man from Dallas comes in to teach her how. That's one of the main reasons I wanted to be in the play, so I could fly, but they told us we'll just have to jump off our beds at the exact second the lights go out and pretend.

The lady who plays our mother, Mrs. Darling, said she hopes we don't break our little necks, then she paused—actors call it "taking a beat"—and said, "Wait. I take that back. You know what they say about acting with children and animals. Don't!" She put her hands around my throat and squeezed while all the adults laughed.

We began working on our songs tonight at Dr. Hill's house, who's our doctor when he's not pretending to be our father, Mr. Darling. The first song we worked was "Tender Shepherd." We sing it with Mrs. Darling when she tucks us into bed, before we meet Peter Pan. The "Tender Shepherd" is really God, Dr. Hill said, but "the audience doesn't have to know that." So besides being a prayer, the song is also a round, which means everybody comes in at a different time and goes 'round and 'round. I put my hands over my ears so I could concentrate on just my part, and Mrs. Darling said, "Just remember not to do that when there's a packed house." The adults laughed again. They laugh a lot, and smoke too. After we learned our first song, they all went outside to light up.

When they began smoking, I began spying, because Rita's house is just down the block. It's the same street as Dr. Hill's, but his house is big and brick and two stories, maybe even three. Her's isn't.

It's little and wooden, on the other side of this creek that separates the good houses from the bad ones. Daddy said he was proud of us for getting into the play, but I think he really just wants to visit her when we're away at practice.

I told Corey to stay with the other Lost Boys while I snuck away. I learned what to do from my spy movies, like *In Like Flint* with James Coburn and the James Bond movies with Sean Connery. They're always sneaking away to some woman too. They put a glass to the wall to listen into the next room or put a hair on the door to see if it's moved while they're gone, but I didn't have to do any of that. I just had to look in Rita's window to see Daddy right there, drinking a beer and eating on one of her TV trays.

And then I saw them take off their clothes without even moving off the couch.

I went back to play practice at Dr. Hill's house. When we sang "I Won't Grow Up," I thought, *Too late, I just did.*

— CREOLA —

I smelled her on the sheets—White Shoulders, her signature scent—the week before I died.

Dead Shoulders; that would be my scent.

We fought that last week, L.E. and I. That's why I took the boys away on a vacation, lured by the promise of glass-bottom boats and mermaids who swam underneath them, to Aquarena Springs in San Marcos, five or six hours away. I told L.E. he wasn't invited; he was happy not to go. I told him he had to pay for the trip; he was happy to do that too, anything to be alone for the weekend with that woman who was trying to buy off my children with rubbery pot roast and stale strawberry shortcake. The boys didn't know L.E. was paying me off when he handed me a wad of bills through the rolled-down window of the car. I had taken up two parking places at an angle in front of his store, I'd driven in so fast, so angry.

I used to love being downtown on the square with the boys; now I couldn't wait to get away from it. (That damn square, the pride and joy of every old Texas town. A courthouse in the middle, where the high school chorale once sang selections from Gilbert and Sullivan's *HMS Pinafore*, and Clarke mistakenly thought it must be "MHS Pinafore," where "MHS" stands for McKinney High School. His only point of reference, the town's pride and joy, every storefront filled to the brim with "Go MHS Lions" signs and football schedules in the fall. Our entire little world on the square's four sides: Rita, L.E., the Ritz. No wonder they were all colliding in each others' lives. There was nowhere else to go. You were trapped. And every street there named after another state: Kentucky, Virginia,

Louisiana. Everything *but* anything Texan. Tell it like it is, and give me a Dead Armadillo Avenue. Cowboy Cul-de-Sac. Big Belt Buckle Boulevard. But no. It was all a lie.)

Before *her*, the boys and I could make an entire adventure out of visiting downtown. Going into White's, the furniture and appliance store where their father worked, and turning all the for-sale TVs on to a different channel. Woolworth's, where the boys would put their little faces up against the fish tanks, opening and closing their mouths like the goldfish. (How many goldfish did I end up making matchbox coffins for? Too many to count.) McKinney Dry Goods, where I'd let them look through the big glossy pattern books for their Halloween costumes while I tried on new dresses. Or the school supply store, where they'd get such a kick out of buying glitter and construction paper, rubber bands and paper clips. We'd go into the courthouse in the middle of the square and ride the elevator all the way up to the top—four whole stories!— because it was the only building in town that had an elevator. Or four stories.

Now I land on top of the courthouse and look down at what used to be mine, staring south, directly through the huge plate glass display windows into White's. In death, I have perspective—and a sense of history. It might as well have been called Whites Only, because it was, in 1966. Not that it discriminated, there just weren't any other kind of people in McKinney then, except for a smattering of Mexicans. L.E. used to tell the boys, "Study Spanish in high school. It will make you rich." This, to my children who each insisted on taking four years of Latin.

That's not all I can see, looking into the future. And into L.E.'s store. Three months from now, Forrest Goodman, the man who drove L.E. to the boys' school the day I died, will say he feels tired and plop down in one of the BarcaLoungers that's on sale, right up at the front of the store. He'll close his eyes and never open them again, and he'll stay that way for the next thirty minutes, taking a nap they all think, while that hateful woman Joann steals his customers. Practically grabbing at them the minute they walk through the door so no one else will get them first. (Not even L.E. can beat her, and he's fast. Or used to be.) Joann, who takes in foster children for extra money. Money she spends on herself, not on them. She will later say she heard Forrest snoring. She will be lying. She will get hers when they figure out her foster care scam.

––––––––

On our way out of the town square that last week, on our impromptu vacation to San Marcos, the boys and I were like bandits on the lam with L.E.'s blood money. I could turn even a desperate car trip into an escapade; teachers and mothers could make magic like that. We passed a fancy restaurant called Shangri-La, and I told them the story of the movie *Lost Horizon*. I said, "Let's pretend we're there, that we're on a plane that crashes, only it's our car that crashes into a snowbank. But nobody gets hurt. It's so freezing cold that the snow keeps our bodies numb and safe from hurting. And then a group of strange people dressed in wonderful warm clothes—fur hats and boots and thick, padded coats with wonderful colors—they come and save us. They pull us out of our wrecked car and take us to their wonderful village called Shangri-La, where nobody ever gets old, nobody ever hurts, nobody ever dies. It's the most wonderful place in the world, as good as heaven will be. And that's where we live for the rest of our days. Just us, without your father."

I told them all that because of a restaurant called Shangri-La that was shaped like an A-frame and had the most gigantic glasses of iced tea they'd ever seen in their lives. Iced tea with lots of sugar—that was *their* version of heaven. Giant metal spoons that had swirled handles. All the wonderful food we could eat. I bought the book for them when we got back, *Lost Horizon* by James Hilton, so I could read it to them for a bedtime story; I wanted them to know that wonderful movies come from wonderful books. I started the book, but we didn't get very far.

I left behind a bookmark fourteen pages into *Lost Horizon*.

I hope that's not all they think I left them.

Sunday night, when we got home from Aquarena Springs, just five days before I died, I came back into my house and smelled her. I knew she'd been there. She left her shoe shop smell, her perfume smell, her "we tried to cover it up" smell. Any wife knows that smell. It's the smell that says something is different, that says someone has been in your house while you were gone, someone you didn't invite. The boys were too excited to notice, telling their father about Shangri-La and the mermaids they saw floating under the glass-bottom boat. L.E. was in his lounger, watching *Bonanza*. He hugged the boys, but he didn't hug me. He barely even looked at me. Actually, I take that back. He looked at me guiltily, by looking down. Wives know that look too.

He was so busy not looking at me that he didn't see me go into the bedroom and sniff around some more, looking in the dirty clothes hamper to see if there was a dirty washcloth in there, from where he no doubt had her wash his back in the tub. I used to do it, and we'd talk about the future we had planned for our beautiful boys. Then he ruined that future, and I decided his back could go dirty. I wasn't going to touch it ever again.

He didn't see me go out to the covered garage, to the little shed where he kept his tools. He was still listening to the boys' recitation when I came back in with every weapon I could find—a saw, a hammer, a bucket of old semigloss white paint. I dumped the paint over all the furniture he had made in our bedroom. Our bed frame, which he had carved to look like a sleigh. He'd told me he'd never ridden one when he was a boy in Vermont—the rich kids did—but he swore he'd have one someday, even if he had to build it himself. The chest with three drawers on each side—three for me, three for him—that he'd never quite gotten the pulls right on, that always stuck no matter how much he oiled them. Even bunk beds that he'd made for the boys, which were in another room: I wanted to destroy *everything* he made.

Except them. Everything except the boys.

I was so quiet laying siege to his handiwork, except for the sound of the screwdriver plying up the lid of the paint can that had dried shut. It just made a little pop, a sucking sound. Silently pouring the paint—as slow and ponderous as his precious maple syrup onto the furniture. Even the first sawing sounds were quiet, when I took the handles off the chest of drawers. On his side. It was only when I began attacking the furniture with the claw of the hammer that I really made any noise at all. Vermont maple wood is hard and sturdy, so it took quite a few whacks to do any noticeable damage.

Even though I tried to stay quiet, I had to let loose a few screams —it helped as I swung the hammer over my head and landed blows on the headboard of the bed I swore I would never sleep in again, not after that woman had been in it. I could take a lot, but I couldn't take that.

Spoiler alert, as they'll come to say: that's why the boys don't sleep in their bunk beds anymore, because I destroyed them. It was the last thing I saw myself doing before I passed out. I grabbed the bottom rail bar L.E. had made to keep Corey from rolling out of his bunk during one of his seizures. He'd stained it so carefully, not a single imperfection; it all looked like it was carved out of the same piece of wood. No more. I grabbed it—the length and weight of a light oar—and I started banging it against the floor. About four good whacks and it split right at the middle, jagged stalagmites of dangerous splinters sticking out. It didn't break completely in two, so I snapped it over my knee. Now I had two weapons. L.E. ran into the room, and I attacked him with both of them.

I aimed one of those jagged edges at his face. Corey grabbed me before I reached my target. I thought about plunging the broken railing into my own heart, but I didn't want the boys to see that. The bedroom was destroyed, and so was I. That was enough for one night.

− L.E. −

He still slept in the same bed he found Creola in. The same bed they had spent their marriage in, made the boys in. If it hadn't been for Mrs. Angel, the new housekeeper he'd hired to take care of the boys now that school was out, he'd probably even be sleeping on the same *sheets* she died on, unwashed. Clarke told him that was a "funnyweird" name for her to have, "Mrs. Angel," because she doesn't look like one, but L.E. told him that angels come in all shapes and sizes.

And then Clarke told his father that their mother used to whisper that Corey was an "angel with epilepsy." L.E. had never heard that before. He got quiet when Clarke told him, then kissed the boys on their heads and said, "Lord help me. What am I gonna do?"

He didn't know how to use a washing machine; he didn't know how to use a dryer. He sold them for a living, but he didn't have a clue how to really use them, or what kind of detergent they needed, or how much. Creola had done all that. She'd made the breakfasts and dinners. She'd washed the clothes. She'd washed the dishes.

Those dishes. How could two little boys go through so many dishes, so many glasses, in just one day? Every time they wanted some iced tea, it was a new glass. Before Mrs. Angel, L.E. would come home at night and the sink would be filled to the brim with the jelly jars they drank out of. He'd stand over the sink and all he could see were plates and silverware and jelly jars, and then he'd start washing them. The steam from the faucet would make everything disappear and be replaced with his memories of the boys in the sink instead. That's where he and Creola used to give them their baths, when they were so little they could fit in each side, covered with bubbles, laughing and giggling and splashing. Creola would take one, he'd take the other, and that was the most fun they ever had together.

Now Corey and Clarke were growing up. They hadn't fit in the kitchen sink for years, and L.E. didn't know what to do. They needed uniforms for *Peter Pan*, and he didn't know what to do about those, either. They came home from play practice one night with a mimeographed list of the costumes they needed—the kids all had to provide their own—and how was L.E. going to do that without a woman in the house? They needed shorts and tops and flannel footie pajamas and nightgowns. They were playing lost little English boys and little English boys needed nightgowns. Mrs. Linstrum, the costume lady, sent them home with a pattern and told them to come back three weeks later with a nightgown. That's how they did it in the nice part of town, where Mrs. Linstrum lived.

L.E. didn't live in the nice part of town, but he told his boys he'd get them their uniforms. Somehow. He knew they laughed at him behind his back for calling them uniforms when they were really "costumes," but sorry, they hadn't had costumes in Lyndonville, Vermont. They didn't have plays. They didn't have Peter Pan to carry them away to Never Never Land. They barely had parents. They barely had clothes.

His boys didn't know how good they had it.

Maybe he could get Rita to help out. She had a sewing machine; he'd seen it in her house. An old Singer with a foot pedal that she never used, that magazines and big serving platters were piled on top of. But maybe it still worked. L.E. could give her some old sheets they had in the house to turn into the boys' nightgowns.

The sheets he'd found Creola on . . .

Maybe that's what they could use for their costumes?

He didn't see the sense in going out to buy fancy fabric at the

Dry Goods store when he had all the "dry goods" he needed right here in his house, washed and dried and neatly folded up after he'd found his wife's body on them.

L.E. couldn't just throw the sheets away, but maybe he could transform them into something useful. Creola would want that. But should he tell the boys that's what they were? There was an old white tablecloth too that they never used anymore, that Creola had insisted on, and maybe he could just get rid of everything at once—take the whole bundle to Rita and see if she could help him make his sons happy.

They could have their uniforms, their fancy English nightgowns, and they could wear their Mumma next to their skin. The sheets would be out of the house, and L.E. wouldn't have to remember what his wife looked like when he found her lying on them when he came home for lunch on that April Fools' Day. Or what she was holding in her hand.

— CLARKE —

Peter Pan is on in a week, and we had to rehearse this afternoon, so we didn't get to see *The Glass Bottom Boat* at the Ritz. I would have liked to, because we rode in one when we went to Aquarena Springs with Mother. I don't like getting behind with my movies—it's been weeks since we've seen one—so I'm going to paste the ad in my scrapbook anyway. I'm going to pretend like everything I see today is a movie up on a screen instead of my life down on the sidewalk.

I've been taking pictures with the Secret Sam Attaché spy kit Daddy gave me for my birthday, and when they're all developed, I'm going to flip them together at the same time so they make their own movie. My spy kit is a briefcase with guns and bullets you can shoot out the side and a camera with a little peephole that's hidden on one corner. You can aim it at people and take their pictures without them knowing it.

So far, I've taken pictures of Daddy at work and Rita at her shoe shop and them having coffee at Shaw's Café. I took a picture of the page from Mother's funeral register that has Rita's name on it and a picture of Mother's three Stelazine pills I still have left, and of the whiskey bottle that Daddy has left in the bottom of the dirty clothes hamper, and of the TV dinners we eat when we're not eating at Rita's, and a picture of the empty closet where Mother's clothes used to be until Aunt Altha took them all, and of the drawer where Mother's makeup still is, and one of the hall closet where Daddy put the painting of Mother facedown so he won't have to look at her anymore.

I've also taken secret pictures of Bobby Raines, who plays my

107

older brother John in *Peter Pan*. He came by our house today to take me to play practice in his go-cart. When he did that, I played like we were in *Fireball 500* with Annette Funicello and Frankie Avalon. There wasn't enough room in Bobby's go-cart for me and Corey both, so Daddy had to take him to rehearsal separately. I felt bad because I love Corey, but I also think I love Bobby. So I can pretend he's with me even when he's not, I had him record our scenes together on my tape recorder so I can "run my lines" when I'm alone. We did the part where Peter Pan tells us to "think lovely thoughts" so we can fly, and Bobby did all the parts but mine.

"Think lovelier thoughts, Michael!" Bobby says, pretending to be Peter.

"Picnics, summer, candy," I say, but none of them are lovely enough.

Bobby blows fairy dust on me and says, "Lovelier thoughts still, Michael!"

I scream out, "Christmas!" but I feel more like screaming out, "Bobby Raines!"

I almost got in trouble at rehearsal today when I broke one of the props. It's the poison cake the pirates use to lure the Lost Boys away with, which Tinker Bell eats instead. It's got wavy green icing made out of Dr. Hill's gauze bandages from his office, and I touched it, even though Dr. Hill told us not to. He looked at me funny, so I think he knows I did it. I think he also knows I used the special phone he brought with him to use backstage, because he's still a doctor even when he's an actor, and he's always "on call" in case people get sick. He said nobody should touch his phone, but I did worse than that. I called Daddy's store on it to see if he was there or at Rita's. I hung up before Daddy came to the phone but not before Dr. Hill saw me. He opened his mouth like he was about to start yelling, so I reached into my pocket and pulled out one of Mother's blue pills and yelled at Dr. Hill first. "Did you give these to my Mother the night you came to our house, when she couldn't talk backwards?"

"*What?*" Dr. Hill's face froze like it was in the Ice Age.

I had to keep talking before he melted.

"That night you came to our house. When she was all sleepy. You asked her who the president was and she didn't know, and what the days of the week were and she had to say them backwards but she couldn't do that either. Did you give her these pills, to help her remember backwards?"

And saying that made me remember backwards too, about that night just a few months before Mother died for real. She was moaning and her eyes were rolling around in her head even though the rest of her body was completely still.

But Daddy's mouth was moving. "Honey? Honey?"

Our mouths, mine and Corey's, were moving too. "Momma? Momma?"

Daddy called Dr. Hill, who came to our house and got down on his knees so he could talk to her where she was lying on the couch.

"Creola? Creola?"

Everybody called her whatever name they called her in two-by-twos, like Noah and the ark from Sunday school.

"Can you tell me who the president is?"

"Johnson." Her breath ran out near the end, and her chin slumped down on the "son."

"Can you count backwards from ten?"

Corey said, "I can," but Daddy shushed him.

"Ten. Nine . . ." Then her eyes rolled some more and she didn't say anything else.

Dr. Hill gave her a pill, putting it on her tongue like she used to put Corey's pills on his tongue. He propped up her head so she wouldn't choke when she swallowed it. Daddy gave her some water, but most of it dribbled down her chin.

Now that memory went away and I was back on stage at *Peter Pan* practice, holding one of the pills that Dr. Hill gave her that night.

"Where did you get that?"

"It was in our house. It was left over."

"That is *not* for children."

"Who's it for then?"

"People who get upset, like your Mother. Sometimes they need something to help them . . . calm down. To focus."

"Did Momma get upset? Is that why she had them?"

"Yes, but she took too many . . ." He froze a second time.

"*How* many? Didn't you tell her how many to take? You were supposed to help her *remember*, not forget . . ."

"I mean . . . just . . . ask your father. It's a family matter. And give me that pill before you hurt somebody with it."

He yanked it out of my hand and walked away. That's when I unplugged his special emergency phone so I could take away something of his since he took away something of mine.

— CREOLA —

The boys wander the house now, looking for a place to sleep at night. They don't really have bedrooms anymore; sleeping arrangements have been in free fall since I destroyed their bunk beds. (In their adult years, in therapy, Corey and Clarke will both look back on that time and not remember where they slept. Corey's shrink will ask him to draw a diagram of where the beds were in the house, and he'll be flummoxed and not know what to draw. They'll remember the *before*—the bunk beds that their father made for them, that we kept in our very own bedroom when they were little—and they'll remember the *after*—their new twin beds in their new bedroom that L.E. made out of the old den—but they won't remember the *in-between*. They'll be homeless in their own home, roaming from room to room, dragging pillows and sheets with them to spare rooms, a spare couch, anything soft they can find. And their father will usually be too drunk to even notice.)

It will be their time in the wilderness, just like this is mine.

The night I destroyed their bunk beds was the first night the boys slept in a different room. Their beds were a shambles, and the smell of paint I'd splashed around was everywhere. Nobody could sleep through that. I put all three of us in the big guest bedroom and put a chair against the door so L.E. couldn't get in. He hadn't ever hurt them, or me, but I never knew when he might start. I held Clarke and Corey in bed with me like I hadn't held them since the nights they were born.

I started to plan our departure the next day, when L.E. went to work. I packed a suitcase for each one of us, just enough to get us through a week or so of school until we could come back and take whatever we needed for good. My teacher dresses, the paisley shirt and flowered vest Clarke had begged me to get him for Christmas, his Beatles boots and Beatles belt, some extra dosages of Corey's medicine. I called Altha and told her I was coming, with or without a job. I'd get something; I just had to get away. I called the woman at the apartment we'd looked at and told her I was taking it. She asked if my husband would be coming with me, and I told her no, unfortunately, he'd just died. It wasn't far from the truth. He was dead to me.

I was on automatic pilot teaching that day, helping the kids put up their bulletin boards for World Geography week. One group used cotton batting for the fog around the top of the Matterhorn in Switzerland, and another group cut out yellow construction paper tulips for Amsterdam. I kept telling them to add more tulips, more fog, anything to keep them busy. I told them to add windmills and cuckoo clocks and chocolate candy.

During lunch, I stayed at my desk and wrote out a week's worth of lesson plans to leave behind for Miss McLarty. I got Patty Rollins, the other fifth-grade teacher, to cover my class for lunchroom duty in the cafeteria. I boxed up a few school supplies I'd need to get started: construction paper and safety scissors, little pots of glue with those pink rubber tops. (Is that all being a teacher was? Cutting out and gluing, turning cotton batting into fog?) I packed my framed diploma, and then I began writing a note telling L.E. I was leaving.

I can see myself getting out a piece of paper from my desk, and my red pen . . .

But what did I write on it? That's where my memory short-circuits. What came next?

— CLARKE —

Ivette Quattelbaum, who plays Peter Pan, is only in high school, but she already smokes and keeps her cigarettes in a gold lamé case tucked in her bra. When she has to go onstage, she says, "Here, hon, hold my cigs." I do, but I don't let Corey. He's too young to hold cigarettes, even though Daddy smokes all the time. Corey's also too young to know what I figured out tonight, when *Peter Pan* opened.

I figured out I was wearing Mother on one of my costumes, the sheets she died on, that Rita turned into a nightgown for me. It happened when we flew into Never Never Land, and Bobby Raines was holding my hand. We're wearing our nightgowns, and we jump in from the wings together like we've just flown in from London and are finally landing on solid ground. They've got a fan going to make our nightgowns look like they're blowing in the breeze. Our sister, Wendy, isn't with us so we look up in the sky to see what's taking her so long, and one of the Lost Boys sees her and thinks she's a bird and shoots her with a bow and arrow. Our eyes jerk down like we're watching her fall out of the sky, offstage, then we go to the wings—the curtain kind, not the angel kind—and carry her in like a giant dead pigeon. The Lost Boys call her "the Wendy bird" and lay her out onstage with an arrow stuck in her chest, only she's really holding it in her armpit.

I play like I'm sad because that's how Michael would feel if his sister was really dead, and being sad about Wendy makes me think about Mother, who really *is* dead. Actors call that a sense memory, except nothing about it makes sense. That makes me think about her the last night she was alive, when I said goodnight to her, and that's when I realize that I'm wearing her dead sheets. I remember her lying on them, and then I see me on them.

In them. Dressed in them. Onstage. That's when I start getting dizzy.

Peter Pan pulls the arrow out of Wendy's chest and she comes back to life, and the Lost Boys are so happy they start singing and dancing. The stage lights in my eyes make me think about the orange chicken lights on Mother in her coffin, and I start imagining that she's come back to life too, only she's sitting up in her coffin and I'm pulling blue pills out of her instead of an arrow.

In my head, I'm pulling out blue pills because that's what Dr. Hill said she took too many of, but onstage, I'm singing and dancing with the Lost Boys. They're building a lovely little house for Wendy, even though it's just Martha Hill's old playhouse painted green, and singing about how at last they have a mother.

They're all wrong, the words in the song, because they say "at last we have a mother," and actors have to believe what they're saying, and I don't believe any of this because Corey and I *don't* have a mother anymore. We just have Daddy and Rita and the dead sheets I'm wearing. We just have a song that's speeding up while everything else in my head is slowing down.

I look out in the audience and I see Daddy and Rita, sitting in the front row. He takes something out of his pocket. I think it's a bottle of little blue pills, but that can't be. It's just the sweat in my eyes making everything go blurry.

Bobby jerks my arm to make me pay attention, and everybody else, even Corey, tries to pull me around in time to the music. *"We have a mother, at last we have a mother . . ."*

I'm trying to find my place in the song and remember all my dance moves, but just then we move to the front of the stage and I see Daddy pop a pill in Rita's mouth. It's probably just a breath mint, but I don't know for sure and I screw up the song because I sing: *"We have a mother, at last we have a mother, Ri-ta's here to stay . . ."*

·

I sing Rita, not Wendy, and that's when I see it all come together in my mind: Daddy doing something with blue pills and Mother. Somehow, he made her take too many of them, and that's why there were so few left when I found the pill bottle, because Daddy had already used most of them to murder her with.

That's what Aunt Altha meant when she talked about getting the body "exhumed," because then they could cut it open and look for the pills inside her from where Daddy made her take them so he could be with Rita instead.

That's what Beverly meant when she said Pooch watches too many movies because that's what husbands do in movies: they kill their wives that they don't love anymore.

I started crying, but I kept on dancing and singing.

At intermission Dr. Hill put drops in my eyes to make the red and burning go away, but I kept blinking them anyway, so I'll never forget.

— CREOLA —

A few weeks before I died, I went to the elementary teachers' convention in Denton with Altha, who also taught fifth grade. One of the strange new things they showed us was how strong aluminum foil was, and how if you folded it up in a very specific way and put it under an elevator that was falling, it would stop the crash. And that led to a discussion about how if the elevator was plummeting, you should just start hopping up and down so you weren't actually standing on the floor when the elevator landed. You were up in the air, even if it was just an inch or two, even if it was just for a second or two. Altha turned to me and said, "That's all well and good if you work in a school that has an elevator, but how many schools actually do? Why aren't they teaching us something useful, like picking pencil lead out of a small child's nasal cavity? *That* I could actually use!" Her voice got louder, as Altha's voice always did when she had a bone to pick with someone. "Why the hell are they talking about aluminum foil at a grade-school convention? I'm going to write a letter to somebody to complain. WHERE THE HELL IS THE USEFUL INFORMATION?"

I thought the very same thing—WHERE THE HELL IS THE USEFUL INFORMATION?—when I saw my firstborn fall apart on stage. That's the only kind of plunging elevator I would ever experience, when I saw my little boy stagger around and start crying on the stage of McKinney High School.

I did the same thing, tumbling from the rails of the high school auditorium balcony where I was perched.

I understand gravity now, really understand it, for the first time. Ever.

You fall, you hit rock bottom, you go splat.

I wish I'd known that when I was alive so I could have explained it better to my kids at school instead of that stupid Sir Isaac Newton and the apple trick. I'd take my class out on the playground and have one of the boys climb up a tree and drop an apple from the highest branch he could get to. Ha! And I thought I was so clever, showing science in action, instead of just talking about it. That's what I felt like when I saw Clarke on that stage, only I wasn't *seeing* gravity, I *was* gravity. I was the apple, hitting the dirt of the playground.

If I had it all to do over again, I'd tell my fourth graders that gravity is what you feel when you see your oldest child fall apart in front of an audience of paying customers, his eyes as wide as saucers, but you can't be there to ask him what's wrong.

You can't be there to put a cool rag on his forehead, or even a kiss.

You can't see what made him so upset on this night when you know so many things have changed.

You can't be there to congratulate him after he takes his first bow on a stage.

You can't be there at the cast party after the play with all the other mothers—"the alive ones," as Clarke now calls them—ladling out lime sherbet punch, when you see Clarke try to talk to that Bobby Raines, who keeps flirting with the girl who played Wendy instead. (You *can* be there, as a ghost, to see Clarke's heart break and in that instant know that your son is like Mr. Ring. A mother knows these things, even when she's dead.)

You can't be there for him when he's ready to tell you the first time he falls in love.

You can't be there in person to tell him, "It's okay. I just want you to be happy."

You can't be there with him in that cavernous band room behind the stage where they have their cake and punch, the same room where they rehearsed their songs all during July smelling of summer sweat and nerves and leftover makeup, where giant wooden shelves hold tubas and trombones and drum sets that the children played with even though they weren't supposed to.

You can't be there when his father and Rita come into that room to pick him up and go to hug him, and he shouts something about blue pills and dead sheets and murder.

All you can do is keep falling.

— CLARKE —

It's very hard to kill someone; you have to really want them dead. That's what I learned from Alfred Hitchcock's *Torn Curtain* today at the Ritz. Paul Newman tried to kill this Russian creep who was a secret agent or something; he tried strangling him and stabbing him and finally holding his head in an oven with the gas on. He didn't want to die, like Rasputin didn't want to die, like Mother didn't want to die, but Paul Newman killed him anyway while Julie Andrews stayed in the background. She didn't sing like she does in most of her movies, but I thought that would have been good, to distract from all the death rattles going on in the oven.

During that part, I kept wondering if Mother tried to fight back while Daddy was killing her with the blue pills, and if she made a death rattle. Was she already so drugged up that she didn't know what was going on, or was she wide awake? Did he kill her because she hit him with the frying pan? Did he kill her because she found out he was boyfriends with Rita?

If I get enough evidence, I'll take it to the police and they'll arrest him. I've already taken a bunch of spy pictures with my Secret Sam Attaché spy kit. Last year at school we learned how to make lists to get organized, so this is my list I will take to the police.

Clue number one: Daddy knows Rita's grandson, who calls him Freddy, which is an alias, which is when you don't want someone to know your real name.

Clue number two: Mother found out about Rita, and that's why she wanted to leave Daddy and move to an apartment in Plano near

Aunt Altha. That's why she told us not to tell Daddy about going there, because she didn't want him to stop her before she did it.

Clue number three: Daddy found out she was going to leave him anyway, so he killed her with her blue pills. He knew she'd take us, and he didn't want to look like he'd lost us on top of everything else.

Clue number four: He wouldn't let them cut open her body, or they'd have found the rest of the pills inside her.

Clue number five: Rita came to see her at the funeral home and signed the register, the very last name to get in before they closed the coffin forever, which is proof that she already knew Daddy, before he killed Mother.

That's all I dream about now, people getting killed. I dream about this crazy man named Charles Whitman who stood up in a tower and shot people at the University of Texas in Austin, which is not that far from where I live. I dream about Lee Harvey Oswald who shot John F. Kennedy in Dallas, which is even closer. I dream about another crazy man named Richard Speck who killed all these nurses in Chicago, and I'm afraid he's going to kill me too, even though they caught him. It's in all the newspapers and magazines, and Mrs. Poston down the street told us about it, even though she didn't tell us the worst parts like how he took them to a bedroom one by one, except for the one who managed to roll under her bunk bed and hide. Corey and I used to sleep in bunk beds before Mother chopped them up, and that's what I have nightmares about: that I've rolled under our old bunk bed and I see something horrible happening to Mother from there. I see a man's feet walking to her, and then I see blood splattering on the floor. Aunt Altha said Daddy "whittled her down," so that's what I see in my dreams, Richard Speck whittling down Mother with his knife.

In my dream, I'm the nurse who escaped, but I can't do anything, just like she didn't, because I'm too afraid to yell. But I'm still afraid Richard Speck will hear me breathing and figure out where I am and come to kill me anyway, last of all, after he's finished everyone else.

— CREOLA —

My family's falling apart, and there's nothing I can do about it.

Clarke wears his blue flannel "Michael" footie pajamas from *Peter Pan* to bed all the time now—flannel, in a Texas summer, in a house that's not fully air-conditioned—because he thinks it will help him dream about Bobby Raines, but it doesn't. I don't know what he dreams about, but whatever it is, he just tosses and turns all night. At least L.E. had the good sense to make him cut the bottom feet out of the pajamas so he's not completely sweltering in them. (After Clarke sees the James Bond *Goldfinger* movie in a few weeks, he'll be afraid to ever have anything covering his feet at night. He'll somehow hear—mistakenly—that they killed the actress in it by completely covering her with gold paint, even the soles of her feet, and that you have to have the soles of your feet free to breathe or you'll die. For the rest of his life, Clarke will sleep with his uncovered feet sticking out from the covers, even on the coldest nights of the year. Just to stay alive.)

Clarke seems afraid of everything now. When he's talking to his father, which is rarely, he's bugging him to fix up the crawl space in the bottom of the linen closet in the main hall, the one that has a trap door that takes you all the way down to bare earth underneath the house. He wants to turn it into a bomb shelter, to use if the H bomb comes or a tornado. Thank you, *Wizard of Oz*. All he does is think about death, and prepare for it.

Corey too. He's become obsessed with getting baptized so he'll go to heaven when he dies. *Ha!* I want to tell him. Don't believe everything you hear. I believed the same thing, and just look at me.

He's made up a game he calls "Buried Alive," where he lies face up in an empty refrigerator box from his father's store. He turns off all the lights and only lets his eyes move around, nothing else; not his arms or legs or even his head. Just his eyes, moving side to side in their sockets, and crying.

Clarke tries to joke with him and asks him the same thing that Wendy asked Peter Pan. "Boy, why are you crying?"

"That's what it's going to be like when I'm dead," Corey answers back.

"Corey, I don't know what you're talking about. You're getting better. You've got your pills. You've got me to give them to you. And I promise to not give you too many at once."

What Corey *doesn't* have is his mother taking that box out to the trash and burning it instead of just watching him pretend to die.

I was there when he walked the aisle at North Baptist Church to get baptized. The minute the church choir started their first chorus of "Just as I am, without one plea, but that Thy blood was shed for me," Corey was on his feet, catapulting off the red velvet cushion in the pew he shared with his brother, looking at the shine coming off the new Plexiglas covers the church had installed over their ancient stained glass windows to keep them safe from storms.

Brother Joe Bob watched Corey walk down the aisle, then greeted him with open arms. Corey was the only one to accept the invitation that day, so Brother Joe Bob had an especially long time to whisper to him as Joanne Welles kept pumping out the hymn on her organ, trolling for more comers.

Brother Joe Bob asked Corey, "Do you really know what you are doing? Are you doing it all by yourself, without anyone else making you? Do you know how proud your mother would be, to see you do something so brave all by yourself?"

I *was* proud; I was there watching every moment, hearing every word as I hovered above. My little boy was growing up, and getting ready to die at the same time.

Corey answered "Yes!" to all three questions, then whispered, "If God doesn't cure my angel disease, I don't know what I'll do. It's more like a devil disease."

Brother Joe Bob had heard a lot during his years as the minister of North Baptist—he heard a lot of whispering about what put *me* in my coffin, the one he presided over—but he'd never heard that.

At the end of the service, the old people in the congregation waddled up to hug Corey and pinched his cheek, and the same message kept getting repeated: "Your Momma would be so proud. She's up in heaven now, beaming down on you!"

Actually, I was up in the balcony of the church, fluttering my wings to keep from pitching over, but close enough.

Clarke waited for all of them to have their say with his little brother; he patiently waited while Mrs. Kissinger removed her two big flower arrangements from the pulpit and two of the deacons started counting all the tithes that had been collected in the offering plate. It had been the day of the Lord's Supper, which they did once a month, and Clarke watched two women in the little kitchenette off the main auditorium pour out the grape juice that had stood in for Christ's blood and box up the leftover wafers so they could be reused for Christ's body.

Soon Corey and Clarke were the only two left in the church, Corey standing by himself, looking lost, in front of the baptistry. It had a painting of the Sea of Galilee on the back wall and a rounded glass partition in front that you could see through, like an aquarium. Now it was dry as a bone; they only turned on the water faucet when a baptism was about to take place.

Clarke shook Corey's hand, imitating what he'd seen the adults do. "Better make sure the water's hot or you'll catch pneumonia and die."

"Shut up."

Clarke was trying to make Corey laugh, as I'd seen him do dozens of times before. He knelt down and put his lips against the glass

wall and started moving them back and forth, like they used to do
with me at Woolworth's when they imitated the goldfish.

"Stop doing that. It's not funny," Corey said. "We're in church."

"I know. I'm just goofing off."

"Well, now I believe in the Holy Ghost, so you can't make me
laugh anymore. I had to, so when I get to heaven, Momma won't be
mad at me."

"I don't know why you keep saying that. Nobody's mad at you."

"They should be." And he wouldn't say anything else except, "I
believe in Momma's ghost, and now I believe in the Father, the Son,
and the Holy Ghost. Now I'm protected, three times over."

— CLARKE —

SATURDAY, SEPTEMBER 3, 1966

I think I'm going blind. I noticed it when we had to go back to school this week, and Miss McLarty, who I got for fifth grade, asked me to read from the blackboard. I couldn't. I lied and said I had allergies in my eyes from the chalk dust, but I can't keep using that excuse. I guess I could say I have tears in my eyes from being back in Mother's old classroom because it's weird sitting in there every day as a student and not just a visitor, and it *is* weird so it wouldn't be a complete lie, but people will make fun of me if I keep saying it. Miss McLarty writes a new vocabulary word on the board every day for me to learn because she knows I like new words. The other kids can learn them too if they want, but they never do. But now it's getting hard for me to read them unless I'm just two inches away.

I don't like looking at my spy pictures either because I keep thinking I'm supposed to see something I can't. I don't know if it's because nothing's there or I just can't see right anymore. The pictures aren't proof of anything, nothing I can take to the police at least. They just show an old man being happy with a new woman. They don't bring the old woman back to life. They don't show him killing her, like I see in my head.

The only things I like looking at anymore are movies at the Ritz because they take my mind off things. Today there was a double feature of *Dr. No* and *Goldfinger*, which the ticket lady let us see even though the ad says they're "Not Suitable for Young People." I didn't think anybody could make me forget Bobby Raines, but Sean Connery has. He takes off his clothes and puts on bathing suits and diving suits and bathrobes and towels and shows off his muscles and chest hair. He lies on a table and gets back rubs and makes pouty lips and kisses beautiful women and shoots a gun and drives a fancy car and wears tuxedos and cuff links. He drinks martinis that are "shaken, not stirred," like Daddy drinks whiskey that is "swallowed, not sipped." But when Sean Connery drinks, I don't mind.

If I do the same things as James Bond, maybe I can catch Daddy.

Spy Tip Number One: Get close to the villain so they'll think you're their friend, but you're really their enemy trying to get information out of them.

Spy Tip Number Two: Get the villain drunk so they'll let down their guard and tell you things, but not remember doing it in the morning.

Spy Tip Number Three: Hide a microphone in the villain's bedroom so you can hear what they say in secret, especially if they talk in their sleep.

As soon as the movies were over, I took Corey to Woolworth's to buy him two goldfish because he's been acting so weird since he became a Christian. Maybe having something he has to take care of will make him start acting normal again.

Then we went to Rita's shoe shop so I could start using my spy tips, like making her think I'm her friend when I'm really just getting information out of her. I could also get her fingerprints with the special powder that came in my spy kit. You brush it on over the greasy part, then lift them off with tape.

Fingerprints = evidence, but I'm not sure of what. Just that she works there? I already know that. Her name is on the front door. That Daddy visits her there? I already know that too.

She was wearing an apron over her dress and fixing shoes, gluing on new heels and tapping little nails into them, then holding the heels against a machine that set off sparks. That's what her store smelled like, sparks and burns and shoe polish and leather. She turned off her machine when Corey held up the plastic bag with his new goldfish in it. "Look. Oddjob and Pussy Galore. Guess which one is which."

"Uh, the big one's Oddjob and the little one is, uh . . . the other one?"

"You're right!" Corey said. "We saw James Bond today, and that's where I got their names."

"I'm gonna paste the movie ads in my scrapbook when I get home. I use glue too, but I don't think mine's as strong as yours." I said something friendly like Sean Connery would have said, to make Rita think we had something in common.

"Take that jar of glue behind you. It's super strong, and that way your ads won't fall out. I've got plenty. I buy it by the caseload."

Corey put his goldfish bag down on the counter and started picking through Rita's shoe dyes. "They sprayed that woman all gold, even her face. That's what killed her. They made her turn gold just like my goldfish. Except they're really orange. Why don't they call 'em orange fish?"

"No, see," Rita said, picking up the fish pouch and turning it around to catch the light, "you can sort of see the gold in their scales. See, how they're sort of shimmery there?"

"I'd hate to be killed by being painted gold," I interrupted, trying to get back to spying and killing and getting information. "Or by any of those ways James Bond uses, like when he throws that radio at the guy in the bathtub and he gets electrocuted? Or Oddjob throws his hat through the air and it's really all metal and it chops off that guy's head? Or when they put that giant tarantula on James Bond when he's in bed and he almost gets poisoned to death. The only thing they *didn't* do was force somebody to take an overdose of pills. I've heard that's the worst way to die of all."

I was looking at Rita when I said that to see what she'd do, but she just turned her shoe machine back on and didn't look at me.

"Clarke, you want to learn how to use this?" She put me in front of her and had me hold a shoe against the wheel and then put her hands over mine. Up close like that, I could see where the shoe dye had gone into the wrinkles on her fingers, and where her nail polish was chipped off and she had little scabs from where the shoe needles poked her skin. She used her foot to move a pedal on the floor, and the machine slowed down or speeded up, depending on how hard she pressed it. While the machine was on, she sort of whispered to me. "I don't know if Corey needs to hear all that, do you? I think it's nicer to talk about goldfish than ways of killing people."

"He saw the same movies I did. He knows what I'm talking about."

"But maybe he doesn't *understand* like you do." She guided the shoe in my hand along the sandpaper on the metal band, so the heel got evened out. I could see how good she was at her job. "He's having to grow up awfully fast this year. You both are. I did too, when I had to take over this shop."

"Isn't it yours? It's got your name on it."

"Well, my husband's name, but when he died I had to . . ."

"He died?"

"He drank too much. I guess we *both* know what that's like."

I didn't know she knew that part about Daddy. I didn't know what to say, so I said something else to make noise. "I think it'd be fun to have your own store."

"Oh, yeah, it's a *lotta* fun. Murray's Jewelry Store on the corner? Now *that'd* be a fun store to have. Wear pretty jewelry all the time? Something different every day? But Cobb's Shoe Shop? Doing *this* all day?" She took the shoe we'd been working on to a bench. "Corey, you want to have *fun* with me and Clarke and put these shoelaces in?"

At the shoe bench, there was another picture of her grandson in a frame. I picked it up. "Did your husband know him? Was he born before . . ."

"Ricky was born, but he was just two when Harold died."

"What happened to his ear?" I wasn't saying it to be mean. I really wanted to know.

"He was born without it. They're making him a new one now with skin grafts, that's why it looks like he just has half of one, but he won't ever be able to hear out of it. But at least kids won't make fun of him."

Was she looking at me when she said that? I couldn't tell because I was looking down at the floor. I had to make more noise because the silence was making me feel bad. "Kent Brailey? He's in my class at school? He's got a glass eye from when he got hit in the head with a baseball bat, and the only way you can tell him apart from his twin brother is when he takes his eye out to show you which one he is. But nobody makes fun of him for that. We all like his glass eye."

That's when I realized I was just talking to Rita, like a normal person, instead of spying on her or trying to get information like James Bond, so I told Corey we had to go.

Rita said wait, and she gave us both a pair of moccasins from her shoe store, even though it's not our birthdays or Christmas. She said, "This is for you being such good boys, and for being so good to your Daddy. He's hurting too, you know. He misses your Momma."

James Bond didn't have a scene like that, so we left.

When we got home, I took a spy camera picture of the moccasins to add to my evidence, of how she is trying to be nice to us. And then I said a prayer for Ricky's half ear and one for Kent's glass eye and another one for Rita's fingers with the shoe dye on them. Then I said a prayer that Sean Connery would love me the same way Daddy loves Rita. I put my elbows inside my pajama top so I'd look like a woman with big titties, then pretended Sean Connery was kissing me and telling me how beautiful and nice I was, even though I know I'm not.

— RITA —

She'd made up her mind to leave L.E., but that was before those little boys came into her store with their goldfish and stories of James Bond.

She didn't want to ruin his marriage; she didn't want to upset his sons. She'd been with them a few times already and could tell they were the upsettable type. It was better to just end it. Things like this didn't end well for her, ever. She didn't have any girlfriends in town, and now she'd have one less man friend. She even talked it over with her son, Gibson. He was grown and had his own wife and child. He knew what Rita was doing.

"Mother, do not get mixed up with that man. He's married."

And then he wasn't.

Creola hadn't been sick, not that Rita knew about. Rita didn't even know what she looked like until she saw her in her coffin and put it together that she was that same woman who'd brought in the red shoes. How was Rita supposed to know that was his wife? Perkins had never shown her a picture; he'd only ever shown her pictures of his sons.

From that first tuna fish sandwich she and Perkins had shared at Shaw's Café, the boys were all he talked about. Not the best way to seduce her, but certainly the best way to win her heart. How Clarke was so smart and always reading books and going to the library. How he wanted to be an astronaut one day and an actor the next. How he liked order in his life and picked both professions because they began with an A, then decided he wanted to be an archaeologist after he saw Victor Buono play King Tut on TV in *Batman*.

How he could do anything he set his mind to, as long as it began with the letter A.

How Corey wanted to be an artist and how good he already was, even at seven years old. How he made a cat picture out of dyed orange popcorn, with green for a collar, and didn't let a single kernel go outside the line, which was hard to do because of his epilepsy. It was the first time she ever saw Perkins cry, talking about his son who was sick. She fell in love with Corey then, when all she knew of him was from a first-grade picture with a cowlick and buck teeth.

Even when Rita slipped up, when Perkins got her to drink too much and sleep with him at his house while his wife was away that one weekend, all he could do was talk about his boys as he took her on a guided tour. The toy boxes he'd built into the walls of the den for them. The bookshelves he'd built into the wall above the toy boxes. The *Childcraft Encyclopedias* he bought for them, with a little bit from his paycheck every week. The play they'd put on for their mother in that room, covering the entire place with sheets of newspaper that Corey had tempera-painted to become a lake and grass and sky and sun.

They spent the night together, and the next morning for breakfast he made her okra gumbo and pancakes with some of the maple syrup his relatives sent down from Vermont. He said he didn't know what he was going to do when Creola came back; he didn't know what he was going to do if his life couldn't be like this all the time now.

Is that what Rita had wanted: him free and clear for her? She didn't know what she wanted anymore. She couldn't think after she found out Creola was dead. Perkins had called her the night it happened. So many people were pouring into his house, bringing food and smothering the boys with love, that he made up some excuse, got into his car, and drove to a phone in the office at White's and told her. He was crying, Rita knew that much. He was drinking, she knew that much too. And he was hurting.

She just lived a few blocks from the town's square where White's was, but he wouldn't come over. He wouldn't risk having her smell on him when he got back to his house and all the neighbors and teachers who'd come to pay their respects were there.

Rita decided to go to Creola's visitation on her own; she wanted to show her support to Perkins. She got there, and half the town stared at her. She couldn't even go over to Perkins and tell him she was sorry.

She didn't need any mystery in her life. She didn't need any tiptoeing around or people looking at her or boycotting her shoe shop, so she made up her mind to leave him. That night, at Creola's visitation. What they were doing wasn't right.

But then he brought the boys over to her house for their birthday, and she couldn't. She could leave *him*, but not *them*. They were starved, and not just for the birthday cake she bought at the bakery: chocolate cake with white icing, studded with jelly beans. She loved them already, even though she knew they didn't love her back. In fact, they probably hated her, but it didn't matter. She was going to win them over, no matter how many pairs of moccasins it took.

— CLARKE —

Pussy Galore is dead. That's how my day started, with one more dead thing in the house. Corey fed her too much, so now we'll have to see if Oddjob makes it through the next few days. "Go easy on the fish food," I tell Corey. "You've turned Oddjob into a widower, just like Daddy. If he makes it, I'll buy him a new wife." Oddjob I meant, not Daddy. Daddy doesn't need a new wife, he's got me and Corey. He doesn't need anybody else.

To make sure things stay that way, I've been working on a new plan all week. Since I didn't find out anything from spying on Rita, I'm going to have to do one of the other spy things James Bond does, which is get Daddy drunk and ask him questions, then put my tape recorder in his bedroom so I can hear what he says when he's asleep. The drunk part shouldn't be hard since Daddy gets drunk every night.

It was almost a great plan. The drunk part worked, and then Corey and I started to go to bed. We do that when Daddy gets all blurry and sad. But tonight he said we should all sleep up front in the living room, under the air conditioner, because it was too hot in the back of the house. But that's where I'd already set up the tape recorder, in his bedroom with the microphone hidden in the pillow. Daddy wraps it around his face and slobbers in it when he sleeps now, so the microphone would catch everything he said if it didn't get wet and electrocute him first. I couldn't get to it without him seeing me, so I'd have to become a human tape recorder and remember everything he said.

Lying on our mattress that we'd dragged up to the living room and put on the floor, I was still trying to decide what to do when I saw Daddy looking at me. At least I think he was looking at me. He had one eye open, but the other eye was scrunched under him on a throw pillow. And even the one good eye that was open looked like it wasn't seeing anything.

"Daddy?"

Nothing.

"Daddy?" I said, a little bit louder.

The good eye blinked. "Go 'sleep." His mouth was smushed against the pillow like his eye, but I could still smell something coming out of it, like whiskey and iced tea and bad breath and sleep all mixed together.

This was my chance to ask him my James Bond questions, when the alcohol would be like truth serum, only I hadn't figured out what my questions were. There was only one question, "Did you kill Mother?" but I couldn't ask that straight out. Truth serum didn't work like that. I had to warm him up first, so he wouldn't know I was tricking him.

"Do you ever dream about Mother?"

"Hummmm." Hummmm yes or hummmm no, or hummm he was falling asleep?

"How did she die?" I already knew the answer, but I thought I'd ask it anyway.

"What?" He unsmushed his mouth and turned it toward me.

"How did she *die*? You never told us."

"*Christ*, Clarkie."

"I have nightmares about it. I dream about Richard Speck killing her."

"Go back to sleep. It's . . . I'm too tired to talk about this."

"I can't sleep until I know." I hadn't found out what I needed to know yet. "Why did Rita come to the funeral home? Did she fix Momma's shoes? Did she *know* her?"

"Your Mumma's shoes?" He was falling asleep. The eyelid on the good eye was closing. "Altha has your Mumma's shoes. Altha took everything that wasn't nailed down."

I got closer to the couch so I could hear what he was saying and tape-record it in my head.

"I didn't want her to take Momma's stuff." This was my one chance, even if it wasn't a question. "And I don't want Rita to take Momma's place."

"It's . . . ummm . . . late." He was shifting around so he was facing the back of the couch, away from me. Did he say "so late" or "too late"?

"Daddy," I said, and pulled at his back on the couch. He didn't move, he just snored.

"*Daddy.*"

I stood up and peeped my head over his so I could look at his face. I wanted to see what he was dreaming, if I could tell by the way his eyelids moved if he was dreaming about killing Mother or loving Rita.

In the dark, I thought he looked like Sean Connery because they've both got pouty lips and sunk-in cheeks and five-o'clock shadow. They've both got extra girlfriends. They both drink, only Sean Connery smells like martinis and Daddy smells like beer and whiskey. I got close enough to Daddy's face to see if I could pretend he smelled like a martini, whatever that smells like, and that's when I heard him whisper.

"Creola."

It was sort of a whisper and sort of a breath and sort of a snore all rolled together. Maybe it wasn't even a word, just something I imagined. But then he said it again, like maybe he thought I was her, like maybe he forgot she was dead. Or maybe he thought she was haunting him, like she haunts me.

"Creola."

He snored really deep then, through his nose, and his body tensed up like it was deciding what to do next. He swung his feet off the couch and stood up like it was morning and he was going to work; he reached into the orange glass ashtray that's on the side table to grab his car keys. He didn't slow down. He didn't seem like he couldn't see. He didn't seem like he was asleep, even though his eyes were still sort of half-closed.

I didn't know if I should wake him up or not. They say you're not supposed to wake up somebody in the middle of a dream or they'll stay stuck there, and since I didn't know what he was dreaming, I didn't want that on my head.

He opened the front door and went out on the porch. He stood there, stretched his arms up, then stepped off the porch into the holly tree that was in the corner, about three feet below.

That's when he woke up, down on the ground with prickly leaves poking through his pajamas.

He saw me looking at him, even in the dark. Then he saw four eyes, two sets, because Corey was looking at him too.

"What the hell happened?"

"You got up from the couch. You got your car keys, like you were gonna drive away."

That's when he noticed the keys for the first time.

"You said Momma's name."

"I said your Mumma's name?"

"I thought you did."

"Jesus Christ." Then he said it again, but just the first part: "Jesus." He licked his lips to make the gluey spit go away. One string of it connected to both lips, like when Corey eats glue.

"I hurt my leg. Help me up. I'm caught in this shitass bush."

Corey and I went out and helped him get up. He didn't seem drunk anymore, or dreamy, or sleepy. But instead of going back in, he just sat down on the front step of the cold concrete porch. We plopped down too, and he put his arms around us like he was hugging us, but I think he was really just using us for support. He looked up at the sky.

"Your Mumma's up in heaven, you know that, right?"

We didn't say anything.

"You know there's only heaven, right, that there isn't hell? That's just what they say in church to scare people. God wouldn't make anybody go through that, being on fire all the time. If He wants to play with you, He does it right here, on God's green earth. Trust me on that."

Corey said, "That's not what Brother Joe Bob said."

"He can say whatever he wants. Doesn't mean you have to believe him. That'll be our secret. I don't want you boys scared of anything."

I said, "Richard Speck's going to hell for killing all those nurses."

"I don't want you saying that name, let alone thinking about that. Clarkie, you've gotta start thinking about happier things. You know, like Peter Pan. 'Think happy thoughts.'"

"Were you gonna get in the car?" I said, trying to change the subject. I didn't like thinking about Peter Pan anymore.

"I don't know. Let's just get you guys back to bed."

He looked up in the sky one last time—like he was looking for Mother, or daring God to prove there really was a hell—and said, "I need a cigarette." And then he said, "We need help."

This time, there was no mistaking what he said.

He went inside the house and brought his cigarettes out to the porch, and we sat there for the rest of the night. Corey and I laid our heads in his lap and fell asleep, but Daddy didn't. I could tell because when we woke up in the morning, there was a pile of cigarette butts next to us.

Normally that makes me feel bad, but tonight it made me feel good.

— CREOLA —

I watched them all night long from a branch of the giant tree across the street. At one point, some of the ash from L.E.'s cigarette fell on Corey, and I wanted to swoop down to keep it from burning him, but Corey just shrugged it off like a tickle. Once or twice I thought L.E. even saw me as he sucked on his cigarettes and the red tip of each one flamed up and then died. But if he did, he didn't care about getting me back, or more likely, I'm as invisible as Corey thinks he is when he hides under his ghost sheet.

They finally woke up and went inside just as the sun was beginning to peep up and the streetlamps were flickering off. I've always thought that was the best time to see Woodleigh Drive (so aptly named, on the edge of a forest on the edge of the town): against a sky-swept background of purple and Buena Vista blue, with just a hint of orange from the rising sun. I like seeing the sun come up from the tree house; that's as good a home as any for me now. Staying there beats the long trip back to the cemetery every night, and it has everything I'd need if I were alive: a kerosene oil lamp, some old candy, pillows and a blanket, even a Boy Scout handbook. Could I get a merit badge for Coming Back from the Dead? (Another thing I can see in the future: Clarke will be the only Boy Scout in the history of his troop to get a merit badge in theater. He'll make a model set of a Japanese pagoda and a hanging full moon for *The Teahouse of the August Moon* in an old shoebox turned sideways, and he'll use my makeup to turn himself into a Geisha girl. Herschel Witherspoon, the scout leader, will be horrified by the very idea of a Scout liking theater, let alone dressing up like a girl, but he'll still give Clarke a free sweet iced tea at the Dairy Queen franchise he owns a few days later to congratulate him, saying how proud I would have been of him. Why does everybody keep saying that, speaking for me? Why won't God give me a three-day pass to say it to them myself? It's not enough to just see them. I need to be able to *talk* to them too! *That's* hell.)

They say "write what you know," but for me, it's more like "stay dead *where* you know." So I do; I stay drawn to Woodleigh Drive, still looking for that final answer that has been denied me. I float over the Postons' house, where Clarke plays with their Ouija board, asking why I died; over the Morrises', where Garnett Morris killed a copperhead snake that had slithered onto their flowerbed on the 4th of July. Fireworks exploded in the night sky just as the hoe came down, cutting the snake in half. I float over the Watsons' house, where they always yelled at you if you stepped on their perfectly manicured front lawn. I float over the house of the three Holy Roller sisters, who will take the boys to sign language classes at their church.

Further back, past Inwood Drive, the houses are nicer: big brick ranches, a step up from the frame and aluminum-sided houses on Woodleigh. There's a rickety wooden bridge and a creek where I once saw a man catch on fire. He'd been working in a nearby house and lit a match near some paint thinner. Actually, I witnessed just the aftermath of it all, his body rolling down the beautiful green slope of grass into the creek, leaving behind the pattern of a man in agony and freefall etched into the lawn. When he finally hit the water, there was a sizzling sound like a hot skillet makes when a cold stream of water hits it.

Those skillets have been a big part of my life.

I used one to hit L.E. with, just before I tried to leave him.

I remember I had started writing a letter to say goodbye to him, one of my last days at school, but where did I leave it? Was it with Maurice? He'd become my confidante, my partner in crime, the only adult I could talk to. Did I ask him to keep the letter behind so the boys and I could get a good head start, then take it to L.E. at the store? Maurice was so devoted to me, he'd do anything I asked.

Maurice Ring, shining those floors outside my classroom.

He always kept them so shiny; there every day after the final bell rang, revving up that polisher with the giant circular bristles, before he had to switch clothes for his waiter shift at the Townhouse. I'd never met a man who worked harder than Maurice Ring, who went from hanging crepe paper scenery for the sixth-grade talent show, to fixing the audiovisual cart, to mopping up pools of vomit without ever complaining.

I went up to him after school—this was the Tuesday, before I died on Friday—and told him I had to talk to him about something. Something important. He told me the same thing. He said let's meet at the Ritz tonight, they're showing *The Sandpiper* with Elizabeth Taylor and Richard Burton. I got LouEtta Moore to babysit for me, then had her take the boys to her house to spend the night. I didn't want any of us running into L.E. again.

Maurice and I met in the balcony. I trudged up those narrow steps on that maroon-and-gold carpet one last time. Popcorn kernels were smashed down into it—did they ever vacuum the place?— and the smell of butter got stronger the further up you went. Old movie posters lined the pale-green walls, which were beginning to flake. You could see the layers of other colors underneath: pale blue and gray, the same timid colors every schoolroom I had ever been in had been painted. Did they all get their discount paint at the same place? Didn't anybody have any imagination and know that dull, bland colors like that made children nod off instead of stay alert? Didn't they want children to learn and imagine in Technicolor?

Maurice had changed out of his waiter clothes and into a nice sweater set. He gave me popcorn and some Mary Jane candies, and while "The Shadow of Your Smile" was playing on-screen, before I could tell him to look in my school desk for an envelope if I didn't show up for work one day soon, he whispered that he was in love with me.

He told me he'd never met a woman as wonderful and beautiful as I was, who liked movies as much as I did, and he wanted us to be together.

"But I thought you . . . I didn't think you . . . are you sure you like brunettes?" It was all I could think of to say.

"I like anything as nice as you."

Oh my Lord. This was a pickle.

And then we slept together.

I was about to meet my Maker, and here I was, sleeping with a homosexual grade-school janitor in room 214 of Woods Motel, where he got a staff discount because he worked at the adjoining Townhouse restaurant. It was a crazy thing to do, I know, but no more crazy than preparing to sneak away from McKinney like a thief in the dead of night with two little boys in tow. And I have to give Maurice credit, he did the best you could with a ratty old motel room. Rose petals, Shalimar—I think he'd taken that from his mother—and a stack of movie magazines he said we could look at "after."

That's what he said. "After."

I'd laugh too, if I wasn't fleeing for my life and watching the saddest thing I think I've ever seen: Maurice Ring trying to be something he wasn't. Me trying to be something *I* wasn't. I thought maybe I should sleep with him, just to get back at L.E. But L.E. would just laugh, and I'd feel bad, using poor Mr. Ring . . .

So there was no "after."

There was no "during."

There was really just a long, extended "before." We sat on the bed, each of us facing opposite directions—from the corner of my eye, I saw his fine manicured fingers play with the little chenille nubs on the bedspread—and I said, "You know this can't happen, Maurice."

"Yes, ma'am."

"And you know why."

"But I love you so much."

"And I love you. You've helped me survive the worst year of my life. You've been my best movie date ever. You shine those floors better than anyone I've ever seen and you can balance a tray of piping hot food like you were born holding it. But . . ."

"Please. Don't say anything mean. I need this to have a happy ending."

"Sometimes a happy ending is just knowing you did the right thing, and you didn't lie to yourself. We're both in situations we don't like, and we're both looking for a way out."

If only I could have been as clear in my own thinking—then and now—as I'd been with Maurice that night, looking at that cheap laminate furniture with yellow-brown cigarette burns on it. A big hollow depression in the middle of the bed where the mattress sagged. A blue-green water stain that no amount of Comet would ever rub off under the faucet in the bathtub. And a constant *plink plink plink* from a drip you couldn't stop no matter how hard you twisted the handle. I know. Mr. Ring had tried.

Plink plink plink, instead of violins.

"You're gonna find somebody so great someday, somebody who's just perfect for you . . ."

We couldn't use pronouns, not in McKinney, Texas—population 17,847, soon to be three people less—in March 1966.

"Can we at least be spoons?"

"We can certainly be spoons. And knives and forks too."

"Don't remind me. That's all I'm ever setting out. Knives and forks."

And Maurice Ring, the only homosexual I'd ever known—well, besides Clarke—laid down on that nubby turquoise bedspread with me in his arms, and I think I did forget about my troubles for the first time since I'd found out L.E. had been seeing Rita.

And for an hour at least, I slept like a baby, the last Tuesday night

I would spend alive on this earth. I woke up and pulled some motel stationery out of the nightstand and wrote some more of my good-bye letter to L.E. on it. I had so many thoughts pinging around, and I wanted to get them all down while I could.

When Maurice woke up, he called the restaurant to order room service while we lay on the chenille bedspread and laughed and cried and looked at gossipy movie magazines. We talked about movie stars and the teachers at school we liked and the ones we didn't, and he told me what he found in their wastepaper baskets and we talked about the best detergent to use on dishes, and we didn't talk about anything we couldn't laugh about.

Before we left, we opened the Gideon's Bible in the room there and prayed together, to find happiness. I remember I went to my favorite Bible verse, which was, "I look to the hills, from whence cometh my help." But nothing, or nobody, came.

It was three days until I died.

— MAURICE —

Maurice Ring was going to get a library card, and the first book he was going to check out was *Valley of the Dolls*, which he'd been reading about in his movie magazines. But first he had to settle the matter of his name with the librarian, Mrs. Jerry Lewis. It said so, right there on the plastic name tag she was wearing.

"Maurice? That's an unusual name for Texas," she said, rolling the little orange card into her typewriter so she could set up his account.

"I know. Blame my mother. I do. She says she thought everyone would know to pronounce it 'Morris'—like the English do—but it just came out 'Mau-REESE' instead. It's my cross to bear."

"Try living up to 'Mrs. Jerry Lewis.' My husband couldn't tell a joke if his life depended on it." She ratcheted Maurice's card out of her typewriter and looked it over through the bifocals on her cat-eye glasses, then handed it to him. "Guess the joke's on me, being married to him. There. You're all set."

"Well, let me start with the new Jaqueline Susann. *Valley of the Dolls.*"

It was a special request book, and they kept it behind the front desk, to be checked out only with the permission of Mrs. Lewis.

"It's our only copy, and it's in high demand, so don't keep it overdue. Otherwise I'll have to track you down and cut off your library privileges. Ha ha. That's just between us chickens." She made a gesture with her elbows like she was clucking.

He went off into the stacks in search of the other books on his list, *The Unexpected Mrs. Pollifax* and Stanley Green's *The World of Musical Comedy,* which he wanted because he had volunteered to choreograph First Baptist's production of *Good News,* the new Christian folk-rock musical, and he needed to get some good ideas for the dance numbers. He was skimming through the photos and wondering if he could get away with stealing "Dance at the Gym" from *West Side Story,* when he heard Mrs. Jerry Lewis again.

"Oh, those are way above your reading level, hon. Mine too," she said, and for a second, Maurice thought she was still talking to him. But then a little voice that he recognized—earnest and soulful, a boy soprano not yet affected by puberty—answered her back. "I've been tested and I read at the high school level."

"Well, that may be, hon, but I don't think your mother would want you reading smutty literature like this, now would she?"

"My mother *told* me to get these books for her!"

"I know who your mother is, little mister, so I don't think that's a Christian thing to say. Not Christian at all," Mrs. Lewis answered, her voice getting testy and shrill.

Mr. Ring peeped through the stacks of the dramatic literature section of the library to see Clarke going at it with Mrs. Lewis.

"If you want something scary, why don't you go find a good Lois Duncan or Phyllis A. Whitney?"

"No. I want *these.*"

"*In Cold Blood* by that fruitcake Truman Capote and *The Boston Strangler* are *not* appropriate for little children. And whatever my name tag may say, I am not joking. But I'll show you something your mother *would* want you to read."

She reached into a drawer for a ring of keys like the matron in a prison. "Come with me," she said, clinking and clucking, and Clarke trudged along behind her, leaving his books on the check-out desk.

Maurice hadn't seen Clarke or Corey since their father stopped bringing them in for breakfast at the Townhouse every morning. Clarke always got a sweet tea and a single biscuit; Corey got waffles. Mr. Perkins just got coffee. Black. And he didn't talk. The only time he said anything was when Maurice showed Clarke how to wear his sweater like a girl, by not putting his arms in the sleeves but draping it over his shoulder. Mr. Perkins told Maurice that Clarke was afraid of the Ice Age coming back and he needed to get as much coverage out of his sweater as possible, so he needed his sleeves. Like a boy. They quit coming in after that.

Mrs. Lewis marched Clarke past the big wooden card catalog to a smaller room, next to where the magazines and newspapers were displayed. The room's long windows were covered with curtains so you couldn't see inside. You'd almost miss it if you didn't know it was there. She unlocked the door and there was a whooshing sound, almost a sucking sound, as if she were having to do battle with something that had been hermetically sealed. She reached her hand over to a switch to turn on the lights, and fluorescents slowly flickered to life.

Maurice had followed them to the door; if they wanted to kick him out, they could. The first thing he thought when he looked inside was that it wouldn't be a very hard room to clean. There wasn't any dust in it. Just old books that nobody ever checked out—that nobody even knew about—inside glass-covered cabinets on rich, golden-hued wooden book shelves.

Mrs. Lewis spied him. "You might as well get a lookie-loo too, since it's nobody here but us chickens." She clucked again.

Maurice whispered, "Hey, Clarke," too struck by the solemnity of the room to raise his voice much louder or say anything more. Even Clarke seemed awed by the silence and mystery of the place and why he'd been brought there, this secret room he'd never even noticed before.

In the very center of it was an upright display case on four legs, about four and a half feet tall. Everything in the room drew your eye to it, as if that were the sole purpose for the room's existence. But Clarke hung back, afraid to see what was inside.

"We'll look together. It'll be okay." Maurice gently put his hand on Clarke's back and led him up to the display case, much as Su-zanne McLarty had led Maurice up to Creola's coffin.

Clarke was barely tall enough to look inside at a dark, red velvet cushion. And a single book resting on the middle of it.

"This is the book that the other teachers gave in honor of your mother, to show how much they loved her," Mrs. Lewis told them. "*Sonnets from the Portuguese* by Elizabeth Barrett Browning. None of that killing nonsense you've been looking for. *This* is what you should be reading."

She carefully unlocked the case, and a second whooshing sound filled the room as the glass top swung open on hinges. She pulled out the thin volume, a solid outer shell of blue binding that nestled the book itself. "Do you know what a sonnet is? It's another name for a poem. Do you like poetry?" she asked Clarke, or maybe she was talking to Maurice too. She was talking to both of them as if they were children, so it didn't really matter.

Clarke broke his silence: "They didn't love her very much if that's the best they could come up with. It's so little."

Maurice agreed. He would have pitched in money if they'd just asked him. And he knew Creola would have liked her own copy of *Valley of the Dolls* with a fancy engraved name plate in it a lot more than she would have liked this.

"It's not the quantity, it's the quality," Mrs. Lewis said, opening to a page and declaiming, "'How do I love thee? Let me count the ways.'"

She then balanced the book on the edge of the case so that Mau-rice and Clarke both could see the inscription that was inside the front cover.

Maurice read it aloud. "From the teachers of J. L. Greer Elemen-tary School, in memory of Creola Perkins. We do hereby adopt this resolution, that the Good Lord in His infinite wisdom has chosen to call His Loyal Servant Creola to her heavenly rest . . . ."

"But He hasn't," Clarke yelled out. "She wasn't ready. She got all the rest she needed at home! She didn't need to go somewhere else for it!"

And then he ran out of the room. A few seconds later, Maurice and Mrs. Jerry Lewis both saw him outside, racing past the front windows of the rare book room that looked out onto the parking lot.

"Aren't you going to go after him?" she asked Maurice.

"Do I look like a runner?" he said.

"Do I look like I'm laughing?" she said right back.

But the joke was on her when they got back to the checkout desk and saw that Clarke had snatched the copies of *In Cold Blood* and *The Boston Strangler* on his way out the door.

— CLARKE —

SATURDAY, SEPTEMBER 24, 1966

I have something new to add to the evidence collection under my bed: the true crime books that I took from the library, to prove that a real true crime took place in our house. I can't go back to the library now or they'll arrest me for stealing, but I don't care. I have the books as evidence I can give to the police when they get ready to arrest Daddy. I guess if they take him away, we'll have to go live with Aunt Altha, but living with somebody who scrunches up her face all the time will be better than living with a killer.

But I've got to trap him first. Since my "tape record while Daddy was sleeping" plan didn't work out, I needed something new, and Mr. Sardonicus gave it to me. He digs up a grave to see what's inside, so that's what I'm going to do: dig up Mother's grave to prove how she was killed. If I can't trap Daddy with my spy pictures or James Bond tricks or tape recordings or Mother's portrait, I'll go in the other way, through her body.

Mr. Sardonicus was the movie we saw at the Ritz today, about this man who's so ugly he has to wear a mask whenever he goes out in public. His mouth is frozen in this scary grin they call a "sardonic sneer" that shows his gums and teeth and cheekbones without any skin covering them. Early on in the movie you see how his face got that way, when he dug up a man's grave because he thought a lottery ticket worth a lot of money was buried with him. He sneaks into the cemetery late at night with a lantern and shovel, and when he pries open the coffin lid you see that the dead man's face is screaming and his eyeballs are popping out. That lets you know he was buried alive and screaming for help inside his coffin before he ran out of air and finally died. The face of the man who's digging him up freezes the same way and stays stuck like that. Forever.

When that part came on, Corey screamed like the man in the coffin and ran out and wouldn't come back in. He said that's what it's going to be like when he's dead, and he doesn't want to see a preview of it. But by then I'd seen enough too, enough to make my new plan, so I didn't have to see how the movie ended.

Somehow, I'll open up Mother's coffin and see if there are little blue pills stuck inside her body, which should be all skeleton by now since it's been there almost six months. I'll be able to look through her bones and see if the pills are still there, if they haven't turned to dust like her body's supposed to.

At supper tonight, I started asking Daddy questions to figure out how hard my plan will be. "How much dirt is on top of Mother's grave? Are there bugs in it? Snakes? I don't like snakes. Has all her flesh fallen off her by now?"

"*What* has gotten into you lately?"

"I just wanna make sure she's okay."

"Clarkie, remember how we discussed this? Corey, you too. I wanna make sure you both understand this. Your Mumma's in a big thick metal coffin that's closed tight, and nothing can get through it to hurt her. But remember what Brother Joe Bob said?"

"I thought you told us not to pay any attention to him," Corey said, still poking at his Salisbury steak from his frozen TV dinner tray.

"Well, most of the time not, but this time he was right. Corey, look at me."

Corey looked up, a kernel of corn, a green bean, and a slice of carrot speared on his fork, from his vegetable medley. "He said she's not really in there anyway, in her coffin. Her body may be, but that's just the space suit she left behind. What really made her your Mumma has flown the coop. Her soul. That's up in heaven now, flying around, and looking down on us to make sure *we're* okay. Believe me, your Mumma's doing just fine."

Soon, I'll know for my own. I just have to be careful that my face doesn't freeze like Mr. Sardonicus, whatever I see in her coffin.

— CLARKE —

I went to see another scary movie this afternoon, to make myself as strong as I could be for tonight. It was called *The Psychopath*, and Corey wouldn't go because he says he's still recovering from *Mr. Sardonicus*.

I'm still recovering from *The Psychopath*.

It's about this crazy man who kills people and leaves little dolls that look just like them next to their bodies. Right before he does it, you hear this little voice that goes, "Mother, may I go out to kill?"

And his mother says, "Yes," but only the crazy man can hear her.

When the movie was over, the ticket lady was outside taking down the poster from the glass case. It shows a man who looks like Barnabas Collins from *Dark Shadows* holding a knife up to this doll, but with all these other real people looking on. And then at the bottom, it says, "Don't Cross the Path of the Psychopath Unless You're Tired of It All!" Which I am.

I asked the ticket lady if I could have it since they don't need it anymore.

She said, "Yes," just like the mother in the movie.

To keep the poster from scaring Corey, I rolled it up and put it under my bed with all my other secret things.

After everybody was asleep tonight, I kissed Corey on the head. He wiggled like something was itching him or like he was having a bad dream, but he didn't wake up. I looked at Daddy asleep on the couch in the living room where he sleeps all the time now, but I didn't kiss him goodbye. He was shaking like he was having a bad dream too.

We all have bad dreams all the time now.

Then I set out on my bike with a collapsible shovel in my basket, wearing my black sweatshirt with the Batman decal, a yellow and black iron-on that was already flaking off. I thought it would help me blend in with the dark. But it wasn't too dark for me to see. The stars were out and the street lights were on. There was a breeze, and the dead leaves that had fallen off the trees made scary noises like finger bones had fallen off a skeleton and were scraping along on the sidewalk. I think it was a sign that I'd find those when I opened Mother's coffin: finger bones, and other bones too. I had to be ready for anything. Maybe a little flesh and some little blue pills stuck in her throat that she couldn't cough up.

I stopped the way I was supposed to, just before I turned onto the highway, right at the corner where the big light pole was. The same place where Patti Coffey had left her secret Valentines for me, but I figured out who my "secret admirer" was anyway. Then I turned right and pedaled past Derryberry's Animal Clinic, where they say they turn horse hooves into glue. I guess that's what I use, pasting my movie ads into my scrapbook.

There wasn't much traffic on the highway, and I started thinking about this one time when we were all in our car together, leaving our house early in the morning to start a vacation. Daddy made us get up at three or four to beat the traffic, but Mother let us stay in our pajamas for the car ride and Daddy gave us sips of coffee from his thermos, so we could pretend like we were adults. Corey and I played a game from the backseat where we'd look out the window for signs of civilization, like telephone poles or street signs. When we were on old country roads that didn't have them, we played like we were the first explorers ever to see that part of the world. Mother and Daddy played with us, to see who could find the first signs of civilization, with the sun just beginning to come up.

They loved each other then, but not like I love Mother now. Sometimes I think I love her more dead than alive because I miss her so much now, and I didn't miss her that much then. But that's because I didn't ever think she'd be gone. I'd wait after school with her, and she'd let me write words on her chalkboard while she put numbers in her grade book. She'd tell me how the teachers had a party and served little mints and nuts in paper cups or let me take care of the silk worms she finally brought home from school in a big box, even though we weren't in her class and hadn't studied how to keep them alive. She showed us how to keep them in a dark, warm space because that's what they liked, and it was like having a teacher and a mother at the same time.

When I got off the highway and was finally on the back road to the cemetery, I played like I was telling Corey all those happy things about her that he might not remember. If anybody passed me in their car, they'd think I was talking to myself or to somebody invisible because I was moving my face one way when I was me, then moving it a different way when I was Corey. If people in their cars played the same game we used to, they'd think I was a sign of civilization.

It was a long ride, but I'd been practicing on my bike longer and longer to build up my leg muscles. Daddy was glad because he thought I was beginning to like exercise and the outdoors. He wants us to live outdoors one day in a house like the Cartwrights have on *Bonanza*. He works on his cardboard model of it every Sunday before the TV show comes on, and he says he's going to build it for real one day, on a plot of land he has his eye on. He says he's got "a plan and a plot and a promise." When he's happy like that, I think maybe I've imagined everything. That maybe he didn't kill her. That maybe he and Rita are just friends. That he doesn't drink more than anybody else.

It took about an hour to get to Mother's cemetery, but finally I rode through to the front gate where there was a church to keep you safe. The walls had long stained-glass windows in them, and even though there was no light on inside, they seemed to glow in the dark. I was sweating from the ride, but I couldn't tell if I was hot or cold or wet or scared. I was feeling so many things at once, I almost couldn't feel anything.

It took a while to find Mother's grave because they all looked alike in the dark, but I knew I'd found it when I came to the one that had "Wife, Mother, Teacher" carved into the tombstone. None of the others had that; it was Daddy's idea and was another good thing that made me think maybe I was wrong. I moved my fingers over the letters and turned the printing into cursive, which made a prettier shape than printing, like Momma made a prettier sound than Mother.

The digging didn't make a pretty sound at all; it made a crunching sound, a metal sound. Daddy told me the coffin was deep so I knew it would be hard to get to, but it was almost impossible because there was so much dirt on top. I dug and dug and dug, but I didn't get anywhere. I was so sleepy from being up late and riding all the way that I didn't think I could do anymore, so I put the shovel down and leaned against the tombstone to take a break. I pulled my arms inside my sweatshirt to stay warm. I was still shivering even with my arms covered up, so I pulled my knees up to my chest and stretched the sweatshirt over them too, like a little blob of black. I put my head down on my knees, and I guess I fell asleep that way because I had this dream.

I think it was a dream, but I couldn't tell if it was a good one or a nightmare.

I was digging deep in the dirt and grass, down five or six feet, and my shovel hit something hard: Mother's coffin. I cleared off the dirt from on top and saw that the metal was still shiny and new looking even though it had been underground for more than five months. What does a dead person look like after that long? I've prepared myself for this moment, and now I pried off the lid to find out.

Only Mother wasn't there.

Something was, but not Mother. It was a jumble of bones tangled up in the threads of a red suit that used to belong to Mother. Some of her face was still there, but there wasn't any expression on it, no smile or scream or eyes popping out, just bones and . . . nothing. At least I knew that she hadn't been buried alive like Mr. Sardonicus. Or Mrs. Sardonicus.

I poked through her neck bones and the tatters of her suit. I didn't see any blue pills, but that didn't prove anything. I looked at the skeleton some more, wondering where else the pills could be, and something started happening.

Mother started reappearing.

First, her suit started coming back together. That made me feel better because she wasn't naked anymore. She wasn't just skin and bones; now she was covered up and warm, like me. Then all new flesh started covering over her cheekbones; her gums and teeth came back into place, and her lips plumped up, nice and rosy, healthier than they ever looked in real life. She smiled, and I could tell she was as happy to see me as I was to see her. She smiled bigger and better than she ever did in real life.

"My precious, precious baby, my oldest son. You've traveled so far to come to see me, so you must know what I want you to do," she said, smiling so broadly her cheekbones begin to crack.

"What?" I was so excited to hear her voice again that I'd do anything for her, anything to keep her smiling.

"You saw it in the movie today. I don't even have to tell you. That's how I've been talking to you since I died, through the movies you see every weekend."

I thought back to the movie and the Ritz and the poster I had in my room, hidden under my bed. "Mother, May I Go Out to Kill?" it said, in big, scary letters.

"That's right, my son," she said, hearing me even though I didn't open my mouth. "What he did unto me, you must do unto him."

Without her having to say anything else, I knew who she was talking about. What she was talking about.

"If you want to ever see me again . . ." she whispered, beginning to fade away.

"No, don't go, Momma! Stay . . ."

". . . then do what I say. An eye for an eye, a tooth for a tooth, a murder for a murder. How can you kill him? Let me count the ways."

Inside my dream, I blinked to make myself remember what Mother wanted me to do, although I don't think I could ever forget it.

She wanted me to kill Daddy.

— CREOLA —

Years from now, there will be this thing—well, there will be two things. There will be a thing where young people say "that's a thing," and there will be this other "thing" where they say, *Mother, May I Sleep with Danger?* It's a joke they'll make based on a TV movie with someone named Tori Spelling. Everyone will laugh, no matter how old and tired it gets. (That actually reminds me there will be a *third* thing: TV movies.)

Can you imagine a child growing up on so many scary movies that it puts things like that in his head—although maybe I was the one who originally put things like that there by introducing Corey and Clarke to the movies in the first place? By teaching them that reality in the dark, looking up on a movie screen, is sometimes preferable to the reality at 815 Woodleigh Drive?

The Psychopath. Mr. Sardonicus. Some other one I can't remember with this sort of nursery rhyme sung in a child's whispery, breathy voice. You couldn't tell if it was a little boy or a little girl: "*The worms crawl in, the worms crawl out, in your stomach and out your mouth.*" And then a giggle, in that same high, breathy voice. A *giggle.* I guess I'm not one to talk since the worms *are* crawling in and out of me—well, the body that's left there, that Clarke tried to get to in Cottage Hill cemetery, not the one I'm flying around with.

I tried to get Clarke to see me that night. Not in my coffin or grave; he fell asleep on top of it before he barely had four or five shovels full of dirt upturned. And that barely scratched the surface. The dirt that got displaced from where they buried me is still somewhat fresh; spring and summer rains over the last few months have tamped it down a bit, but it's still fresh. The grass hasn't reclaimed it yet and completely sealed me in, so you could still look at the mound of it and think, "New in town?" Altha's the only one who comes to bring fresh flowers, once a week like clockwork. She's stuffed so many arrangements of gold and orange mums wrapped in brilliant foil-covers into the ground on top of me that I look ripe for the picking. A field of high school girl corsages, just waiting to be snipped and festooned with ribbon for homecoming. Altha sits on the ground with her feet stretched out and her back against the grave marker that L.E. picked out and just wails—the deepest, most wracking sobs I've ever heard come out of a human being— and I can't stay mad at her. I can't reach out to tell her I'm okay. Well, sort of okay. Except for the being dead part and not knowing how it happened.

I couldn't reach out to Clarke that night either, but I could roost on a tall nearby statue and keep watch over him through the night, to make sure he stayed safe. Nothing more horrible than the dreams he had to disturb his sleep.

Clarke didn't go to school the next day; he said he was too tired, and for once, L.E. believed him. Anyone would have; he was lying atop his covers, covered with dirt, dressed in that sweaty black Batman sweatshirt instead of his flannel footy pajamas. He seemed to have a fever.

Wait. A *fever*. I had a fever too, right before I died. Hot. Sweating. Almost radiating with heat. I . . .

Damn it! I almost had it. My last day. Something about me being sick in bed with a fever, too tired to get up.

I'm getting closer. I can feel it. There's something I keep trying to see that's just up ahead of me, turning the corner just before I can catch up with it. But maybe I don't even want to see it all the way to the end. Because if I finish that, what will I have left to stick around for? Would that mean I didn't get to see my boys anymore? That would be a fate worse than death, which, I already know from firsthand experience, is very bad indeed. But I can't stop the memories.

They keep coming back, and they're starting to come faster and faster.

Now I'm up to the Wednesday morning before I died on Friday.

It was the day after I'd slept with Maurice—well, slept on *top* of the covers with him. I didn't want to go to school and face him, but I knew I had to. I knew I had to get there that day for Suzanne. We didn't get our pick of the student teachers; they were assigned to us. (Student teachers. Humph. We weren't "student teachers" when I started out; it was just *bam*, us against them, and good luck if you survived that first day. But I wouldn't hold that against her, how old I was, how young she was.) For a joke, I bought a bag of apples, gave one to each student, and made them walk up to the desk Miss McLarty now shared with me, tell her their name, and then give her an apple. The place smelled like an autumn garden by the time we were through, but it was fun. And then she gave them back to each student and recited their names perfectly as we took a break to eat them all the way down to their cores. I reminded myself that I needed to do more of that, to have fun. To do silly things.

I would, once I got to Plano.

Then Suzanne moved to the crafts table at the side and just watched as we got started on our day, her eyes as big as saucers, taking it all in. My eyes were as big as saucers too, from the pills Dr. Hill gave me, and I knew I would need more soon.

I took her to the cafeteria for lunch and introduced her around at the teachers' table. I introduced her to Mr. Walker, the principal, and I showed her where the mimeograph machine was and the fluid we used for it and the teachers' lounge and how to fill the coffee machine and make a donation for cookies, and I thought, *Is this what it's come to? Coffee and cookies and cleaning machines . . . doing everything but teaching children how to see the world?*

They'll see the world soon enough, I remember thinking.

I even took the high road and introduced her to Maurice, who sheepishly brought me a leftover flower arrangement from one of his tables at the Townhouse. He told Suzanne that if she became half the teacher I was, well, that was a goal to shoot for. He kept coming by my room to say something, but I wasn't up to talking. He lingered by the display case that was just outside my room, shining it and shining it until it was a streaky mess and asking me if I had any erasers that I needed him to beat on the front steps. He sat down at the upright piano that was left out in the hall for the music teacher to use once a week and banged around on the keys until I had to tell him to stop.

At the end of the day, I made a special point of telling Suzanne how well she had done and how nice she looked. A plaid jumper, little flat shoes. She beamed, and I could tell I had made her day. That's a nice thought to have, knowing that I was good to someone before I left.

I drove to the square to pick up more of Corey's medicine at North Side Drugs so he'd have enough to keep him going until we got settled in our new home. There was something else I had to do down on the square besides pick up the medicine, but I can't remember what. It was something important though.

I'm floating here *now*, trying to figure it out, and I remember I was *standing* there *then*, feeling the same way. Something had happened, something bad, or at least confusing, and it stopped me in my tracks for a minute.

It will come back to me if I don't try to push things.

What I *do* remember is walking past the Ritz and seeing the poster outside in its glass case for *The Pied Piper of Hamelin*. It was an old movie from the late '50s with Van Johnson and Claude Rains, and I thought it would be the right movie to see for our very last time there: someone playing a flute and leading children out of town, just like I would be doing soon with the boys. I went to buy our tickets, and the woman inside the glass booth looked at me and seemed to say, *You know there won't be anyone else here. You know there won't be a crowd. There never is. Why are you buying your tickets now?*

Wait. Did she actually say that, or did I just imagine it?

I'm having more and more trouble separating what's real and
what I've just imagined.

I looked at her and saw myself in the reflection off the thick glass,
and I thought *why indeed? Why buy tickets in advance? Why do anything?* That was the problem with the world: people didn't plan
enough. They just went off half-cocked and *did*. No one could ac-
cuse Creola Perkins of not making plans.

I slid my money—a whopping dollar and two dimes, thirty-
five cents each for the boys, fifty cents for me—through the little
scooped-out tray that was cut into the marble of the counter. "If
more people took an active interest in things, the world would be a
better place indeed," I said to her with a haughty sneer. I wouldn't
have to ever come back here anymore and face her again, so I felt
like leaving a strong final impression. We'd see the rest of our movies in Plano for the rest of our lives. Maybe I'd even take the boys
into Dallas once in a while.

We had plenty of options that didn't involve the Ritz.

I used to think it would be fun to work in the ticket booth there;
no responsibility other than making change. No children's minds
to mold. No more schooley-dooley. All the movies you could ever
want to watch, for free. Your own office, of sorts. Behind that three-
sided glass shield—surely thick enough to be bulletproof—you
were safe, but you still had a prime location for looking out over the
entire downtown square. A window on the world, like you were in
and out at the same time. No one could touch you behind that window unless you wanted them to. Say, if you touched their fingers by
accident when you were giving them change or just wanted to make
a little contact, as if to say, "We're more alike than you think. We're
part of a secret brotherhood, and this is our secret handshake."
How many times had my fingers rested there in that little money
slot when I was the one giving the money? Maurice would no doubt
be horrified by all the germs left behind (as would Clarke), but I felt
a strange sort of communion in all the fingerprints that must still
be there; a history of cinema, a history of the entire town and the

citizens like me who had found sanctuary inside. You could pass on your pearls of wisdom about the movies—thumbs up or thumbs down, as two men named Roger Ebert and Gene Siskel will do in the future, or you could tell certain customers to be on the lookout for coming attractions. I would never abuse my privilege of working there; I would never say anything sarcastic or unkind to a customer. People came to the movies to be cheered up, not to be dismissed or made to feel "lesser than." Oh, well. Another time, maybe. If I couldn't find a teaching job in Plano, maybe I'd become a ticket-taker, on the lam from life.

The possibilities for reinvention were endless.

Now, with tonight's tickets in hand, I walked to L.E.'s store and stared at him through the window. He was a good salesman, I give him that. He could charm the skin off a snake and leave them walking out with three more things than they had come in to buy. That's why I fell in love with him. He charmed me. Well, he could be charming by himself now. With *her*.

The Pied Piper. How fitting. That's what L.E. had been to me, once upon a time, taking me away from the spinsterhood I thought was going to be my future. Maybe once we got settled in Plano, I'd tell the boys stories of our courtship, or I'd write them down, so I wouldn't forget. Maybe I'd put them all in the goodbye letter I was writing to L.E. and be done with him once and for all. Maurice would come visit us in Plano and we'd laugh about what had happened between us and maybe we'd *both* find good men to love us.

Hope springs eternal, doesn't it?

— CLARKE —

"Clarke needs to have his eyes examined." That's what Miss McLarty's note to Daddy said. I brought home so many notes from her that he finally had to take me to the eye doctor, who put drops in my eyes that made them sting and feel all big and gluey, like there was something in them I couldn't get out. Then he made me get glasses. Now the kids will call me "Four Eyes" on top of everything else they call me.

Daddy says I'm acting weird and he's tired of it. He's afraid I'm going to scare Rita away. He doesn't say that part, but I know it's what he's thinking. Yesterday, he came to school to talk to Miss McLarty about what he should do. They made me go out of the room, but I listened at the crack of the door and heard what they were saying anyway, like James Bond would.

MISS MCLARTY: "He's showing classic signs of delayed grief. He'll grow out of it, when things settle down."

DADDY: "Things aren't *going* to settle down, not the way he wants them to. His Mumma's dead. He's got to face that."

MISS MCLARTY: "It hasn't been that long. Half a year. She was my friend too. I was her student teacher. She taught me how to teach. And she must have taught him a lot too because he's very smart..."

DADDY: "You've got that right. Too smart for his own good..."

MISS MCLARTY: "He's creative, he's got a vivid imagination..."

DADDY: "Have you *seen* some of the things he writes?"

That *proves* it. Daddy has been looking at my scrapbook that I keep under my bed with all my evidence.

DADDY: "He thinks he's covered with germs. It doesn't matter how often Mrs. Angel washes his clothes, he still thinks it. He says he can't wear anything that's touched his skin for more than seven hours or he'll die. When he gets home from school every day, he throws his clothes in the dirty clothes hamper, then takes a scalding hot shower. Like he's been contaminated. Try keeping up with that! No wonder he thinks he's got germs, sitting in that flea trap Ritz all the time! You tell me how to deal with that! And he says he sees the germs even better now that he's got glasses to wear!"

Miss McLarty didn't say anything then.

Maybe Daddy doesn't want me to see better with my new glasses because he doesn't want me to see what's going on with Rita, but I do. Daddy told me I'd better not say anything crazy to her tonight because "it's special." He's taking us all to the drive-in, me and Corey and Rita. It's "special" because he never used to go with us and Mother, and we never go to the movies on Sunday, and he never misses *Bonanza*.

It's also special because it's the last night the drive-in will be open this year because it's getting too cold to keep your car window down for the speakers. I like when the weather starts getting cold and scary, all dead leafy and dark early. I like standing outside without my coat on so I can feel my goose bumps and hold my arms across my stomach and pretend I'm holding in my nerves, like they'll fall out if I don't.

Tonight, Corey's with me, standing by our car outside, waiting for Daddy. Corey starts to say something, but I go, "Shhhh, just listen." I'm trying to teach him something, maybe just to listen to what's not there, because there's always something there, even if you can't see it or hear it. Maybe I want to see if he'll say something about Mother, let me know if he feels her around him as much as I feel her. Maybe I'm just trying to tell him I love him without using any words because my words are beginning to get me in trouble.

Corey stops talking and closes his eyes. Then I unwrap my arms from my stomach and wrap them around him. A tremor runs through me, like the kind Corey gets when he has a seizure, and I squeeze him even tighter, to protect him. I'm not sure from what.

Something's going to happen tonight. My whole body feels it. Something's going to die. Maybe just the leaves on the trees, maybe just the drive-in itself, for the winter. Maybe . . . maybe I just feel weird because my new glasses are messing everything up. I can't quit feeling them on my face and seeing their edges when I try to look around, and I keep tripping when I walk because I see steps where there's just flat ground.

We get to the drive-in early to get a good spot; Daddy gets a good spot in the front seat next to Rita. I've heard about *The African Queen* before, but I've never seen it, even though they play it a lot for old time's sake. Daddy says he loves it, and I've never heard him say he loves anything before except for me and Corey and our Mumma and now probably Rita, although he hasn't said that out loud yet.

In the movie, Katharine Hepburn plays a missionary who goes to Africa with her brother, but when he dies, she has to escape. She gets Humphrey Bogart to help her, even though he's dirty. He has a boat called *The African Queen* that they go down the river in, where they get attacked by alligators and blood-sucking leeches and natives and waterfalls. While all those bad things happen, Katharine Hepburn and Humphrey Bogart fall in love. I start crying then. Rita does too. She doesn't know I can see her, but I can; I'm looking at her with my new glasses in the rearview mirror from the back seat where we're sitting. By the time the movie's over, it's eleven o'clock and Corey's asleep in my lap, stretched out across the back seat.

When we drive home, the streets are so deserted it seems like everybody else in the world is asleep too, that we're the only people left awake or maybe even left alive. The drive-in's all by itself out by the old highway, so there's no other light around, just the streetlight we stop at. I play like it's the first sign of civilization we see, blinking yellow yellow yellow, not red or green, just yellow. That means you don't have to stop at it, you just have to slow down, but Daddy *does* stop, all the way, like he's making up a new game where we see how long we can stop, completely still, until somebody says something or another car comes along.

And that's when the weird feeling comes back. What I was afraid of all night long is about to happen. Daddy starts to talk, looking at me in the rearview mirror, but I don't hear him because I see Mother there instead. This is the exact spot where we stopped with her the night before she died, doing the exact same thing, stopping and waiting and not moving. Only she wasn't saying anything. But Daddy was.

"Clarkie, you listening to me?"

"What?"

"We need to get your ears fixed, like your eyes." Now Daddy's looking at me in the rearview mirror instead of Mother. "I was saying . . . listen, I want to say this right, but . . . I'd like Rita to be my new wife. We need help, and you boys need a new Mumma. Aren't you tired of me cooking? *Trying* to cook?" He tries to laugh, and he looks at Rita, and she tries to laugh too, but they both sort of cough instead and keep looking out the front window of the car.

The yellow light's rocking on its cable, blinking on and off.

I'm blinking on and off, remembering what Mother told me to do.

An eye for an eye, a tooth for a tooth, a murder for a murder.

"Of course nobody can replace your Mumma . . ."

"*Momma*. Her name is *Momma*. It's not even that anymore. It's *Mother*."

Daddy looks confused, like he doesn't know he sounds funny because he's from Vermont. He doesn't know he sounds mean, trying to make us forget her. He doesn't say anything for a minute, and he leans on the steering wheel with one hand, the same way he props himself up and leans against the wall with one hand when he's drunk to keep from falling over.

"Clarkie, I'm away at work all day, and your little brother needs looking after..."

"I can take care of Corey by myself. It's just giving him medicine."

"I know you can, Clarkie, and you do a great job of it, but it's more than just medicine. He needs a Mumma. You do too. So do I. We need somebody to help us, I can't *do this* by myself anymore..."

He almost starts crying. I see him blink his eyes like I do when I'm trying to make myself remember something, and then he grabs Rita's hand, like he wants her to take over talking.

"I love you boys, I do, I love you just like you were my own..." At least Rita turns around and looks at me, even if Daddy doesn't. "I think we're all too tired to talk right now, but... all I wanna say is... I love you boys. One day I hope you'll know I love you as much as I know your Mother did. And I love your Daddy, just like Katharine Hepburn came to love Humphrey Bogart." She says that because she knows I like movies. She's trying to trick me.

"If you had a new Mumma," Daddy says, "then she could cook for you and wash your clothes... so they don't get germs on them. I know I haven't kept them as clean as I should. Maybe we could even move and start over somewhere..."

"I don't wanna move. Our friends are here. Momma's here."

And she is. I see her skeleton face again looking back at me in the rearview mirror, hypnotizing me with her eyes and blinking to remind me of the promise I made to her. Only she doesn't have any eyelids or eyeballs or skin left on her face so I just sort of imagine she's blinking. I imagine she still has eyes.

"Son... Clarkie... we're stuck. All of us. We need help. I can't do this by myself. I can't take care of us." He sounds as tired as I felt when I woke up from on top of Mother's grave.

Another car comes up, so Daddy doesn't say anything else and drives us home. He carries Corey in, and I put him to bed. Then

I hear Rita in Daddy's room, next to ours. I put my pillow over my head and try to make my brain go as big and blank and white as the screen at the drive-in, but all I can see in my head is Mother's pillow that Rita's sleeping on now, next to Daddy.

I knew something was going to die tonight, and it is.

It's Mother, being killed all over again.

— CLARKE —

This morning Mrs. Cobweb wasn't here, but I know she wasn't a dream. I looked at the sheets on Daddy's bed, and there were two shapes in them. I won't call her Rita anymore because that sounds like a friend. Friends don't twist up the sheets and use our mother's pillows like Mrs. Cobb did.

When we came into the kitchen for breakfast, Daddy was mixing pancake batter. "How'd you boys like the movie last night? As good as one of your new ones at the Ritz?"

I didn't say anything. He poured batter in Mother's skillet, the one she tried to kill him with.

"Sometimes the old ones are even better than the new ones. It's a shame we didn't get to the drive-in more often last summer. I'd forgotten how much fun it was."

He stuck his finger in the batter and tasted it, then started peeling strips of bacon from a package.

"Corey, would you get down the maple syrup your Uncle Bill sent us from Vermont? And get down some of those jelly glasses for juice. Clarke, check the icebox and see if we have any . . ."

"The pancakes are burning," Corey said.

"Shitass." Smoke was coming out of Mother's frying pan. Daddy grabbed the handle. "Fuck!" He pulled his hand off, then used a dishrag to grab it and throw the whole thing in the sink. "Fuck. See! That's what I mean. I can't do this! I need some goddamn help!" He turned on the faucet and let cold water sizzle over the pan and the ruined pancakes, and then his burnt hand.

I went to the sink and started cleaning up the mess. I wouldn't talk to him.

"Let's start over here." He grabbed me from behind and turned me around, then lifted me up and put me on the ledge of the sink. He did the same thing to Corey. Now we were both eye level with him.

"I think we need to clear the air here, and not just from the burnt pancakes." He opened one of the kitchen windows so the house wouldn't smell like it was on fire. "I'm sorry I sprang that on you guys last night, but . . ." He seemed to forget what he was about to say and went to the icebox to get out a stick of butter to rub over his burn. He looked at his hand, but he wouldn't look at us. "Let's *really* start over here. I should have told you this a long time ago. . . . Your Mumma loved you, but . . ." He shook his head, trying to decide what to say. "Your Mumma got really sad. Remember when she'd get sleepy, then she'd get all excited? And you never knew which one she was going to be? Dr. Hill tried to help her, and he gave her pills for that, so when she finally hurt her head . . . you're too little to understand, but when you're bigger . . ."

"I'm big enough to understand you're fucking Rita. On Mother's pillow. You did it last night."

"Don't you talk that way in front of your brother."

"He *heard* it. We *all* heard it."

"Corey, go to your room and get your school clothes on. Right now. You too, Clarke."

"I know what happened. I know what you did to her."

"We're all upset, so go to your room . . ."

I pushed Corey behind me and walked backward down the hall, still facing Daddy. "You *killed* her. You killed Mother, so you could be with Rita. I've got evidence. I've got proof. Under my bed! I took pictures with my spy kit! I've got the tie you wore when you were with Rita. I've got Mother's *Instructor* magazine. I've got true crime books to tell me what to look for! I've got it all," I screamed at Daddy, grabbing my plastic cardboard spy kit and holding it in front of me like a shield, so he couldn't hit me.

But he did anyway. He slapped me across the face with his buttered-up hand, so hard an imprint of his five greasy fingers stayed there, as red as he was. And my brand-new glasses flew off my face. He grabbed the kit and tried to break it over his knee, then got even madder when it wouldn't break with a snap; it just crumpled up into a wad of plastic and cardboard. He told me he was going to do the same thing to me if I didn't shut up.

"Don't you EVER . . . go to your room right now." He turned on Corey. "And you too. If I find out you're in on this . . . this bullshit your brother says . . . I've got another hand. Go!"

I grabbed my glasses and Corey, and we did what Daddy said. We ran to our room, and I pushed Corey under my bed then crawled in with him, squeezed in with all my other secrets that I'd just told Daddy about. We were breathing so hard and big and scared that every time we breathed, our backs hit the wooden slats of the bed frame that kept the mattress from caving in on us. We kept listening for Daddy to come in after us, but after a while we heard the frying pan slam and then the front door slam and then the car pull out of the driveway.

"Is he gonna come back?" Corey asked.

"I don't know. I don't care."

"Is your face gonna be okay?"

"I don't know. I don't care about that either. I *want* everybody to see what he did. To me *and* to her."

"Do we get to skip school today?"

"No, we've gotta go. Mother would want us to. From now on, everything we do, we do it for her. Not for Daddy."

"How're we gonna get there?"

"We'll walk. We'll collect leaves on the way for evidence, so we'll never forget what happened today."

But there was no chance I'd ever forget with the same red burn on my face that Daddy had on his hand, and the red look in his eyes that told me he hit me because he knew *I* knew the truth.

"I won't let him scare you like that ever again," I said to Corey, and then I blinked to keep from crying in front of him. I blinked to remember what I had to do if I wanted us to stay alive.

— CREOLA —

L.E. had never hit them before. He'd done a lot of things to terrify them when he was drunk, but he'd never done that. He'd never really even hit me, except when he was fighting back against my forged-from-the-gods frying pan. I use all the power I can muster to try to touch Clarke's cheek, the way I would have if I were still alive and he got hurt, or burned. Because that's what it looked like—a burn, a tattoo of a hand in fleshy pink and red. I close my eyes and concentrate more fiercely than I ever have—even harder than I have trying to remember how I died—so I can become manifest for just one second, long enough to kiss Clarke and make the hurt go away. I feel my body vibrating with the effort to become 3-D, but nothing materializes. I'm still just air and feeling, nothing more. Vapor. If I could even cry, that would work: for just one tear to drop onto Clarke's cheek and cool it off, like in a fairy tale. But God has taken even that from me. He's taken everything.

No, not everything. I suddenly remember the one thing I have left: thought. I can still seep inside their thoughts, at least Clarke's. I can make him think to go to my makeup drawer and cover his bruise. At least L.E. hasn't emptied that out yet. It's still there, my powder and lipstick and rouge, my perfumes, in the drawer that's still in my old bedroom. Clarke sits on bended knee in front of it all the time, as if he's praying, and makes himself up to look like me. We already look so much alike it doesn't take much, but then he takes the Elmer's glue he uses for his movie ads and puts that all over his face on top of the makeup. He looks straight in the mirror and waits for it to dry, and as it does, bit by bit, it crinkles up and

makes wrinkles around his eyes and mouth, little etches creeping
into the skin. It makes him look like I did at the end. Old. Tired.
Worn out. At forty-four years old.

Then he waits to start crying—it always happens, he doesn't
have to do anything—and his tears begin washing away the glue,
leaving watery streaks down his cheeks.

How many times have I sat in front of that very same mirror,
looking exactly the same.

My ten-year-old son, the makeup artist. More beautiful than I
ever was.

If I can just get inside his head and tell him to go there again, tell
him to put some of my pancake makeup on his face to cover the
mark, it will be like I'm on his cheek anyway. The powder puff that
touched my face once upon a time will now touch his.

And he does. At least I still have that power, to get inside his head.
My two little terrified boys roll out from underneath Clarke's bed,
covered with dust bunnies, and then Clarke slowly, almost roboti-
cally, walks to my makeup drawer in the room I used to share with
his father. I keep imagining Clarke there—*seeing* him there—and
it happens. I'm shimmering with so much willpower and concentration I think surely a few feathers will molt off me from the sheer
intensity of my thought.

As if hypnotized, he starts putting on foundation and powder.
Just doing what has to be done. No emotion. No feeling. Just sur-
viving. Putting on my makeup to cover the burning red handprint
on his face.

He would watch me put it on when he was little, sitting on my
bed as I "put on my face" in the morning, and laughing because he
said, "You already *have* a face. You don't need another one."

Now he has a new face too, to cover the mark that his father left
on it.

The mark of L.E.

He and Corey walk to school together, Clarke self-consciously
rubbing at the makeup and smearing it, then smelling at the slight

sweet smell on his fingers. It's a habit he'll have for the rest of his life, rubbing those two fingers against his thumb and smelling them to see if anything is there.

Now that I know the boys are safely on their way to school, I fly back to the house. For what? The damage has already been done. L.E. has slapped my son and slept with that woman in my bed—again. It's all changing too fast; the end is coming, I can feel it. I want to smash the cardboard model he's been making of his Ponderosa dream house—would God grant me touch for that, if He didn't let me touch my boys? Cardboard instead of flesh?—but I'm afraid L.E. will think the boys did it and punish them even more.

It's a model of the ranch house he wants to build, patterned after the one the Cartwrights live in on *Bonanza*. Two feet tall at the highest peak of the roof, L.E. has been constructing it from cardboard packing he brings home from work, with dowel rods he's carefully measured out and cut down for porch columns. Nothing he's done for me in months has been lavished with as much love and attention as that damn model. A doll's house for a grown man, complete with a roof you could lift off.

He'd said that we needed a fresh start, and a farm would give us one. "A plan and a plot and a promise," he said, where we would have room to grow, even further out on the edge of McKinney. He'd grown up walking in forests of maple trees and firs; now he just had a fenced-in backyard with a septic tank problem and a peach tree that only produced rotten fruit the birds got to before we could. He couldn't take it. He needed land. *Please?*

I said we couldn't afford it.

He said we couldn't afford *not* to buy it, the land was going so cheap. It was all part of a fantasy he seemed to have about Texas as a land of limitless borders where he could play at being a cowboy. Nothing but open fields and land to build on, anywhere you threw a stick. It's as if he really was living *in Bonanza* of the 1870s with land grants and gold rushes, prairie towns and saloons, instead of the atomic modern of the 1960s, in a town already dotted with Dairy Queens and marching bands, bomb shelters and suburban sprawl. But at least when he was lost in his fantasy, he seemed happy. And occupied. Productive.

It was all going so well—and then I died. I *bought* the farm that I wouldn't let *him* buy.

Money. That's what he wanted. And I wouldn't give it to him. The savings bonds that my father had given the boys when they were first born, or their college money that we were already tucking away, week by week, or what we'd put away for our own rainy day, in our joint savings account . . .

Our money. The bank.

It hits me for the first time, and I go into free fall, remembering even more of that last Wednesday, the part that was so bad I couldn't remember it, until now.

It wasn't just Corey's pills I'd gone downtown to buy, or tickets for some silly last-minute movie at the Ritz; it was to get my escape money from the bank. The boys always loved going there with me because the tellers made such a fuss over them, adding to their little passbooks and getting them their Social Security numbers, and letting them know they were "real citizens" now. The bank had cookies and coffee in the lounge downstairs, apple cider in the fall.

That fateful day, the cookies were there, but my money wasn't. L.E. had already beat me to it; our bank account was empty, and he'd cashed out the boys' savings bonds without my permission. The poor bank teller thought I already knew.

Ha! I wanted to tell the poor dear. The wife's always the last to know.

That's why, in a daze, I bought our three tickets to see *The Pied Piper* at the Ritz, a dollar and twenty cents, nearly all the money I had left in the world besides some spare change at the bottom of my purse, barely enough for popcorn. A movie or a future? At that point, the movie won out. I just wanted to lose myself, to be in the dark somewhere so I could figure out what to do next. I could plot in the dark while the boys had fun. They could laugh, and I could cry.

Just two nights left alive on this earth and there we were, watching what turned out to be the scariest movie any of us had ever seen. A man in a patchwork cape comes to an old German village and says he can get rid of all their rats—they have a lot of them—by playing a song on his flute.

"Okay, go ahead, do it."

After he does, they won't pay him what they promised.

"Okay, I'll take away all your children. Then you'll have to pay to get them back."

I'm making it all sound sillier, simpler than it was. It was . . . unearthly.

He plays the same song on his flute that he played for the rats, and the children follow him into the woods, hypnotized by his song, laughing and singing and having the time of their short little lives. They come to a wall of rocks that's so thick it's like a mountain they can't pass, and they think all their fun has come to an end. But the Pied Piper plays his flute one last time, and the wall magically opens up. The children scamper through the narrow passageway to the wonderful, bright, shining life that's waiting for them on the other side.

Then the mountain closes, and the children all disappear.

Except for one.

That's the part that killed me: the little boy who gets left behind because he's crippled and on crutches and can't run as fast as the others. You see him all alone, banging his crutch against the rocks, trying to wedge them open and screaming, "Let me in, let me in, let me in."

That little boy was like my Corey, with his angel disease. Screaming to be normal.

Let me in let me in make me well make me well don't let me die . . .

Corey squeezed my hand as we watched the movie at the Ritz, maybe because he saw me crying, maybe because he felt the same thing about the boy with the crutches. He knew that he'd always have his own version of a crutch to drag around with him.

When we got home, the boys knew something was wrong. I took one of my pills from Dr. Hill to calm down and tried to turn it all into a game. I threw one of my old scrap-work quilts around my shoulders and took Clarke's flutophone, and I marched the boys up and down the hall, singing that we'd get rid of the rats, one way or another.

Then I marched us outside into the front yard.

Then I marched us down the street, onto Woodleigh Drive, doing a little jig as I tried to bring that flutophone to life.

Maybe I'd taken more than one pill.

Every neighbor came outside on their porches to look at us. The boys were embarrassed, but something had taken over me. I couldn't stop. The boys pulled at me and begged me to go back home—"Everybody's looking at us!"—but I wouldn't do it.

I started laughing and crying, "Let us in, let us in," then "I have your children and you're going to have to *pay* to get them back! Pay me the money you *took* from me!"

Clarke grabbed the quilt off me and ran back home with it, and I was there by myself. I had my clothes on underneath, but I might as well have been naked. Corey held my hand and walked me back home, saying, "I'll let you in," in the tenderest little voice I've ever heard.

L.E. was there by the time we got back.

"What the fuck are you doing, parading around like that? Have you lost your mind?"

"No, HAVE YOU—going around with that whore! If you want to talk about parading somebody through town . . ."

The boys were standing in the hallway, too afraid to know what to do. I didn't care.

Unlike what I had told that poor ticket woman, just trying to get by at the Ritz, I didn't care about anything anymore except telling L.E. off, one last time.

"Are you going to leave us? Is that the plan? Take our money? Go off with her? Well, just do it, because *we're* going too! I'm the Pied Piper in case you haven't noticed, and I'm going to play *my* magic song all the way to Plano. That big rock candy mountain is going to open up for us, and the only rat left in this town is going to be *you*! I'm taking the boys with me and you'll never see them again!"

I grabbed the flutophone that I used to hypnotize rats and children and started banging it against him, like I had with the skillet. The skillet was strong, tempered metal, made to last. A cheap plastic flutophone wasn't. It broke into shards, flying all over the hallway.

"Creola, calm down. You're scaring the boys."

"*YOU* CALM THE FUCK DOWN! *You're* the one who's scaring them! And now you've taken all their money . . . oh yes, I know about that too!"

"I will kill you if you don't start flying right! I have tried my best to help you, we all have, but I am not going to let you run around embarrassing your children like this!"

"They're *your* children too, or have you forgotten that?"

I grabbed one of the plastic shards and tried to gouge it into my wrist, to hack an escape for all the blood that was boiling inside there, but Clarke grabbed me and held me still before he also started attacking his father, his little boy fists flying into his father's strong shoulders. "Leave her alone! This is all your fault! She's sick . . . can't you see! And you're not helping. You're a drunk, and that's why she acts like this! We all wish you were dead! Just leave us alone!"

"Creola, I'm leaving you, I swear . . ."

"Okay, go ahead, do it." I snarled the same thing at him that the Germans had said to the Pied Piper.

And he did.

— L.E. —

That night, L.E. took a brand-new bottle of Jim Beam that he kept hidden under the car's driver's seat, pulled it out, and put it on the seat next to him. He clutched the screw-top cap on it so hard he broke the paper seal, but he didn't touch a drop. He drove out to the new part of town, where McKinney was expanding. It looked like the New World yet to come.

He needed a new world.

Ten acres of scrub brush and clusters of trees and a stream that snaked through it all, dividing the acreage in half. On one side, a pond. It already had some fish in it; he'd stock it with more. They'd be pioneers, living off the land. He'd make it pay for itself. Pay back the money he'd just taken out of their bank account to buy it with. He'd raise things; he'd build them a house they could retire to, if he could only patch things up with Creola. He'd teach the boys how to fish and hunt and protect what was theirs. He'd give them driving lessons in the old stick-shift truck that came with the farm. He'd teach them to shoot at tin cans. He had a rifle and a pistol, no use letting them go to waste except for the once-a-year deer-hunting trip he took.

He'd finally be the kind of father he'd always wanted to be—the father he hadn't had; he didn't even know who his father was—as he showed Clarke and Corey how to bend the rifle in half and drop in ammunition, then snap it back into place and hold it straight out, propped up against their little shoulders. He'd tell them it would kick, and they would laugh because that's something they thought you could only do with a leg. It would be good, to teach them about the different meanings of words. He'd show them he was just as smart as Creola was. If Clarke loved words so much, L.E. would show him that he loved words too.

He didn't mind them having their heads in books and movies all the time; he wanted them to be smart. And he wanted them to have manners. He'd taught them to answer the phone by saying, "Perkins residence. Clarke speaking. Corey speaking." Even the boys made fun of that and balked every time he made them do it, but it was a sign of respect. A sign of pride for their house. He didn't even *have* a phone growing up; he barely had a house. But that didn't stop him. He wouldn't let Creola think he was some old hillbilly who didn't know how to act around decent people. Manners were fine, but the boys needed toughening up on top of them. They needed fresh air. He'd teach them how to get out of the car and open up the barbed-wire gate that fenced off the property, then close it back up so nobody else could get in. It was the barrier that said, "This Is Ours! Everybody Else Keep Out!" For L.E. and the boys, it would be like the private, backyard clubhouse the boys had with Mike Willis and Jim Poston across the street. Maybe they wouldn't even get a phone out here. They'd just stand on the land and shout out "Perkins Residence!" They wouldn't need to get in touch with other people, outsiders. They would just need each other.

All those things he could say in his head to Clarke and Corey, about all the things he wanted them to have and to do, but he couldn't say to them in person because he got so tongue-tied at the very enormity of having children. He wanted to give them things, buy things for them, so they'd love him. He didn't know if they could ever love him just for himself, not the way he'd been at least.

When he and Creola first got married, they didn't have anything and didn't need anything except each other. L.E. didn't even have a suit to wear at their ceremony, just his uniform from the army. They got married at the justice of the peace, and L.E. had promised Creola they'd redo it all, when they had money for a real wedding. Redo it, when they had "a plan and a plot and a promise."

They made love for the first time on their wedding night. Creola started crying, not because it hurt, she said, but because she was so happy. Through her tears, she started talking about babies and getting her teacher's license and their first little house. That night, she told L.E. about every dream she had for them, and he agreed with every single one of them. He prayed to God right before he slipped off to sleep—and he didn't often use God's name except as a curse—and asked Him for the strength to make all his wife's dreams come true.

Could this new farm be one of them, a dream come true, before it was too late?

The night his wife pretended to be the Pied Piper, he stayed out all that night on the farm that was already his, at least in his own mind. He drove through the gate, and in the glare of his car headlights he found the spot where he wanted to build his Ponderosa. He began marking it off with giant steps, dragging fallen-down tree branches and rocks from place to place, and outlining the footprint of his dream house with them.

And in the morning, to prove it *hadn't* all been a dream, he drove to the real estate office in town and put a down payment on their future, with the entire savings he'd taken out of his and Creola's bank account and the boys' savings bonds.

Only after he signed the property deed did he take a drink—the entire bottle, in fact—terrified at what he had just done.

That was then.

This was now, some six months later, and he was still drunk and terrified.

He couldn't raise two boys alone, without a mother. Without a wife.

He'd tried to, he really had. He'd tried to do all those things with them he'd first seen in his head: he'd taught them to shoot at old tin cans and calendars he nailed up to trees. They hated it. He'd told them his joke about how the rifle would "kick," but they hadn't laughed the way he'd imagined they would. They'd cried and said it hurt too much. Clarke dropped the rifle the first time it happened to him and almost killed them all when it fired accidentally.

L. E. had said—a last-ditch effort—that the fresh air would blow all the bad germs off Clarke, but Clarke had sassed back that there were more germs out in the country than in town. There were rabbit feces and deer feces and whatever snakes left behind, and you couldn't help but step in it.

L.E. was grateful Clarke had said even that much to him; his children barely talked to him anymore after he'd hit Clarke. He'd tried and tried to make up for it; he'd given them extra money for the concession stand at the Ritz and bought Clarke some of the Nancy Drew books he loved so much, but nothing helped. Even with three people living inside, the house stayed as silent as it had been when he'd found his dead wife in it.

How could he take care of two little children who wouldn't even speak to him? He couldn't afford Mrs. Angel for the rest of his life. Is that who he wanted raising his boys anyway, a babysitter? Somebody he drove home every night because she didn't have her own car? A drop-off mother, that's who she was. Could a new wife get his kids to start talking to him again, like they used to? Could they move away from Woodleigh Drive, with all its bad memories, and start out here fresh, in the country, on the Ponderosa?

It hadn't worked with his first wife. Would it work with a second one?

— RITA —

She'd told Perkins about every moment of Harold's death, mostly so Perkins could see what was waiting for him if he didn't quit drinking, but Perkins didn't take the hint. He just wouldn't talk about Creola, at least not about what killed her. He told Rita that they had fought a lot that last week, that he thought she was planning on leaving him. And then, she *had* left, but not in a way anyone expected. She just up and died. But what actually caused it? A heart attack? An accident? The coroner guessed a brain aneurysm, but that's all it really was, a guess. But even if it was an aneurysm, what caused it? Rita was no doctor, but if something in your head explodes, doesn't something have to cause it? They didn't know because Perkins wouldn't let them do an autopsy; he said he didn't want her body being desecrated like that. Wouldn't you want to know what killed your wife? L.E. said that was the past and it wouldn't bring her back alive, and he was all about the future now. In business, you might miss one sell, but you couldn't dwell on it. You had to get back on the horse and keep selling.

Rita snorted back at him, "Does that make me the horse then?"

"I'm not playing. I want you to marry me."

The night she'd spent over at his house had been a disaster, even though she'd left early in the morning before the boys got up. There would not be a repeat of that. Rita was more worried about upsetting Corey and Clarke by being there than she was about upsetting Perkins by *not* being there.

It would be day trips only from now on. One Sunday, Perkins

took all of them to a rodeo in Oklahoma where Clarke got bored and said he didn't like seeing animals used like that. Rita bought both boys mosaic-beaded belts and fake arrowheads in the souvenir shop there, but Clarke said Indians scared him. They might come back and scalp him since Texas was just over the border. For everything Rita offered up to him, he had a counteroffer.

That's why she was so surprised when Clarke asked her to help out with his Cub Scout skit at school. They were doing a medley of "Last Train to Clarksville" by the Monkees and "These Boots Are Made for Walking," and Clarke needed a go-go minidress in Day-Glo material so it would light up when they turned on the black light.

"Rita is not making you a shitass dress," Perkins said.

"She made me a nightgown from Mother's sheets!" Clarke snapped back in his defense.

"If he needs it for his little skit, Perkins, I'll make it." Rita was trapped between the two of them, the peacekeeper.

"He'll be a Monkee or he'll be nobody. He'll quit before I let him wear a goddamn dress."

"But my friends voted for me! It's the best part! They said I'd make a better Nancy Sinatra than I'd make a Michael Nesmith, which was the only boy part left. I'm the 'comic relief.' I get to wear a wig. And go-go boots!"

Perkins shook his head in disbelief. *"A dress? A wig?"*

"The Monkees have to wear wigs too. It's not a sissy thing."

"It *better* not be a sissy thing, little mister."

Rita ended up making Clarke the dress—in shiny canary yellow—but the night was a disaster anyway. Nobody wore the damn thing. The canary flew away.

Rita had been so excited; she was making inroads with Clarke, and it was yet another outside thing Perkins had taken her to: the big Cub Scout jamboree where all the troops in town gathered together to compete for best skit. Rita's giddiness wasn't just about them finally announcing they were a couple, no more sneaking around; it was about supporting Clarke. Doing everything she could to help him fit in, even if it meant helping him dress like Nancy Sinatra.

The den mothers were serving refreshments before it started, homemade cookies and lime-sherbet punch with ginger ale. Mrs. Gidney, whose daughter's go-go boots Clarke was wearing, had gone to ladle it out and found a fly—a single fly, wings spread, face-up—floating dead on an igloo of melting green sherbet in one of the cut-glass punch bowls. She started to just scoop it out and throw it away before anyone else saw, but another mother—from the nicer part of town—caught her and said "You can't serve that! You have to throw the whole thing away!"

Mrs. Gidney said nobody would notice, but she did it anyway. She was trying to fit in, the same as Rita.

Clarke, not yet in costume, and Rita were hovering near the cookies—they at least had a sweet tooth in common—when they both overheard another mother whisper to Mrs. Gidney, "Who's that woman?" Meaning Rita.

"Oh," said Mrs. Gidney, fresh from her humiliation with the punch, "that's Mr. Perkins new girlfriend. Humph . . ."

From bottom to top, with that single word, *humph*, the woman who'd just been denigrated for wanting to serve fly-spiked punch to thirsty children had found someone to replace her. To look down on, make fun of. Be better than.

Not knowing that Rita and the little boy she was so desperate to impress had heard every single word.

Clarke ran out of the two metal double doors in the auditorium, onto the playground, through the dark night, and all the way home. Someone else ended up wearing the dress that Rita had made for Clarke, a chubby Cub Scout who made the dress bunch up and squeeze in all the wrong places. The skit wasn't a complete disaster but only came in third place instead of first, which they surely would have if Clarke had gone on as planned.

He really had been funny dancing around in those go-go boots doing the Pony and the Swim like Nancy Sinatra. He'd shown his routine to Rita when she fit the dress on him. He'd laughed along with her in a way she'd never seen him laugh before. But she was the only one who got to see it.

Perkins wouldn't let her go after him. He said, "He's made his own bed, now he has to lie in it."

But Rita barely heard him because she was fixated on the song lyrics that were blasting out from a record player up on stage. "You been messin' where you shouldn'a been messin." When Nancy finally let loose with, "Ready Boots, start walking," Rita did. Out the door, to find Clarke. She knew none of this was about him or the stupid dress; it was about her. And she wasn't going to let that innocent little child carry her burden.

— CLARKE —

It's Halloween, the Day of the Dead, so it's a good day to try and hurt Daddy like Mother told me to. She actually told me to kill him, but I'm working up to it in stages so he won't suspect anything. I'm building up my nerve, which is different from being nervous. At night, I keep looking at myself in the medicine cabinet mirror, but instead of seeing myself, I see Mother. I see her everywhere I go now, blinking her eyes—except she doesn't have eyeballs—and pulling out her teeth, except she doesn't have teeth either. When I don't see Mother in the mirror, I see Daddy's handprint still on my face. It's turning purple and green, and even Mother's makeup can't cover it up anymore. It's sort of the color of Frankenstein's face, all put together in bits and pieces, so I guess I could go as him for Halloween.

The makeup wouldn't work anyway because it's not here anymore. Daddy cleaned out Mother's drawer and threw it all away. He took all my evidence I kept under my bed too, after I was dumb and told him about it. I came home from school one day, and everything was gone. The only thing left there were broom marks on the floor from where he'd swept everything up through the dust.

That night everything went missing, I saw a fire in the backyard and looked out my bedroom window. It was Daddy at the trash barrel behind the clothesline, tossing things in, one by one. As the flames flickered on his face, he turned around and saw me, but he kept doing it anyway. Mother's *Instructor* magazine. His own tie, the one he was wearing when he first introduced us to Rita. My *Psychopath* poster. The tape recorder that I stole from his store. *In Cold*

Blood and *The Boston Strangler*, which the library would never get back now. My Secret Sam Attaché spy kit, which you could smell burning, like tar and rubber, like that stuff they put on the streets to even them out.

After the fire died down and Daddy was gone, I went outside to the trash can, to see if I could save anything, but the plastic from my spy kit had dissolved over everything; the lids and covers and stuff on Mother's makeup were all melted shut. If I took anything with me, I'd carry the smell back into the house and give myself away.

Now I have to start fresh with evidence, so I'm doing it with the yellow go-go dress Rita made for me that I never got to use. I thought about wearing it for Halloween tonight and telling everybody I was going as Nancy Sinatra, but it has too many bad memories with it.

Bad memories = evidence.

So Daddy won't throw the dress away or burn it too (and I know polyester makes a mess when it burns), I wadded it up and put it inside my pillowcase, so I'll be sleeping on it every night. It will be something soft inside something soft, so he won't think about looking there. There's a little bit of the smell of Rita's White Shoulders on it from when she made it for me, but he's used to that so it won't stand out.

I got a better idea about how to hurt Daddy at our movie today, and I don't even need evidence for it. Not the movie that was supposed to be scary, the *Chamber of Horrors* one, but the double feature that went with it, *Cat on a Hot Tin Roof*, which shows how scary it is to be married. Elizabeth Taylor plays Maggie the Cat who goes around in her slip talking about "no-neck monsters," which I guess is why they showed it at Halloween. Paul Newman plays her husband, Brick, and goes around in his pajamas too. It's like they're always ready for bed, even in the middle of the day. Paul Newman drinks a lot and says he hears a "click" when the alcohol kicks in. The only "click" Daddy hears is when he locks the bathroom door behind him to drink in secret from the dirty clothes hamper.

When Elizabeth Taylor finally put on her dress, I took a bathroom break and went upstairs at the Ritz. Before you get there, you pass the projection booth, where Anita Welles's cousin Paul works. He's in tenth grade and runs the projector, and sometimes he lets me do it, since I'm a "regular." You have to be careful and watch for the "cue dot" that appears on-screen just six seconds before the first projector's film runs out, then you switch on the second machine. Then you've got twenty minutes to load up the first machine with the third reel of film. It's a little confusing with all the arithmetic you have to keep count of. The first few times I did it, I kept jumping the gun and starting the new reel before the old one was finished. Paul called it "anticipating" and said it's never a good thing. Now I don't "anticipate" anymore, and everything's fine.

While I was in the projection booth today, a rat ran across the floor. Paul says they have a "rodent problem" and to be careful because there's boxes of rat poison all over the place. "Kaboom! Little suckers don't know what hit 'em." He said "Ka-boom!" but I heard "Click!" and everything fell into place after I stole the rat poison.

Tonight, I mixed some in to Daddy's bottle, the one he hides in the dirty clothes hamper, so he wouldn't "anticipate" what was coming. I made a funnel out of the movie ad I cut out of the *Courier-Gazette*. Then I used that to make the poison powder slide into the whiskey bottle at the right angle. I tapped it to get it going, like Daddy does when he crinkles the cellophane on his BC powder into a glass of water. He nudges the powder in, and then it clumps up when it hits the water and starts bubbling.

That's what the rat poison did when it hit the whiskey, after I shook it up.

I sniffed it and my nose hurt, like it was burning. Daddy always goes "ahhh" and smacks his lips and sucks in extra air after he drinks, so he's used to the burning and won't notice anything's different until he's at the Kiwanis Club carnival where he's supposed to volunteer tonight.

By the time Daddy was ready to drive us there after trick-or-treating—we both wore our old hobo costumes, which at least re-minded me of Mother because she helped me sew the poor people patches on—he had been drinking a lot. (Click! Click! Ka-boom!) Our car shook like the bumpy car ride they'll have, and we almost hit another car. When we got to the Gibson's parking lot where the carnival is, he went off to help with the rides because he's a Kiwanis and that's what they do, and we went off by ourselves because that's what we do when he almost kills us with his drunk driving.

I was glad to get away from his whiskey and beer smells because there were better smells at the carnival: popcorn and coffee and ap-ple cider and corny dogs and cotton candy, which was sweet and burnt and had the best smell of all. I tried to win a prize by throwing rings on a bottle, but I didn't. I tried to make a man fall into a water tank, but I didn't do that either. Finally, I won a German chocolate cake when I stood on the right square at the cakewalk. That was Mother's favorite, so I think it was her way of telling me I'm doing the right thing.

When we found Daddy and told him we were ready to go home, he was throwing up behind the Tilt-A-Whirl. Another Kiwanis said he would drive us home, so the car wouldn't shake anymore. He didn't say that, but it's what he was thinking. It's what we were all thinking, even Daddy.

The last time somebody else drove us home was when Daddy came to school to tell us Mother was dead, so it was like things had come full circle, which means back to where you started.

Corey fell asleep as soon as we got home, but I stayed up look-ing out the window for dead people. They're supposed to split open their graves and roam the earth on All Hallow's Eve, so I wondered if Mother would be with them.

I turned out the lights so nobody could see inside the house, but that made it look like the wood knots on the paneling in the living room were moving. During the day it's fun to make up what the shapes look like, like a witch driving a spaceship or a bat flapping its wings, but at night it looks like they really are those things, coming alive and flying off the walls. And the water stains on the back of the curtains look like blood dripping down from the ceiling. And sirens were going off outside like there were crazy people or dead people on the loose and the police were trying to round them up.

Then something started scratching at the window. Maybe it was one of the branches from the yaupon tree in the front yard, but maybe . . .

Maybe it really *was* Mother trying to get inside to look at the scene of the crime one more time.

I got so scared I called Rita, because I didn't know who else to call. Mrs. Angel was gone, and Daddy was gone, and I didn't know where Mr. Ring was, and Mother was gone except for maybe being on the porch dressed up like a skeleton except it wasn't a costume, so Rita was the only living grown-up left that I knew how to find. She'd helped me out with my go-go dress, so maybe she'd help me out again.

"Can you come over? I'm scared. I think they're coming to get me."

"Clarke? What's . . . where's your father?" I could hear her licking her lips, like Daddy does when he tries to wake up and needs to make them wetter before he can talk.

"He's throwing up at the carnival. We're alone, and I hear sirens. Do you hear sirens? I think it's that air-raid siren they play to tell you the H-bomb is coming and to get ready."

"Clarke, what are you . . . your father left you boys *alone*?"

"This other man brought us here, but then he left and . . ."

"*What* other man? Are your doors locked?"

"Yeah, but . . . there's *noise* outside the house. I think dead people are trying to get in. They're already on the walls. And the curtains. The curtains are bleeding." I couldn't stop crying.

"Clarke, listen to me. You stay right where you are. *Don't move.* I'm going to get in a cab and come right over. Okay? Don't let anybody in your house. No *men* you don't know. Even if your Daddy gets there before I do and he's really drunk, just . . . just make him wait outside on the porch. I'll be there as fast as I can."

"I'm sorry I took the spy pictures of you and Daddy. I'm sorry I stole your grandson's picture." I needed to confess in case I was about to die.

I didn't hear anything, and I thought maybe the dead people had cut the phone line. But then Rita said, "Just stay inside. I'll be right there," and hung up.

I sat by the front door so I could hit anybody who tried to come in. But when Rita got here, I didn't hit her; I hugged her. And something else. I decided if she was going to keep *me* safe, then I needed to keep *her* safe. I had to tell her my secret, the one that would keep her alive.

"You shouldn't marry Daddy or he'll get tired of you and kill you the way he killed Mother, like he almost killed us tonight in the car, or the other day when he left part of his hand on my face. Don't marry him and you'll be fine."

It felt so good to let out all my secrets and feel safe again with a mother, even if she was just a pretend one, that I finally fell asleep in Rita's arms, like I used to do with my real mother.

— CREOLA —

Rita didn't listen. Instead, she had what you could call a Hollywood wedding, a movie sandwich, marrying the boys' father between *Dr. Goldfoot and the Girl Bombs* and *Fantastic Voyage. Dr. Goldfoot* was at the Ritz on the weekend, and *Fantastic Voyage* started on Thursday, and the boys' new parents got married after school on Tuesday at North Baptist Church. The minister, Brother Joe Bob, asked Rita and L.E. to say "I do," while he seemed to be shaking his head, *I don't. I don't believe this; I just buried your first wife six months ago.*

You tell 'em, Joe Bob.

It was the first time I'd been back in the church since Corey walked the aisle to become a Christian, and Brother Joe Bob performed my funeral. From a funeral to a wedding in six months. Time flies, when you're dead.

So do I.

I saw everything that day, flying from place to place like I was a wedding coordinator—something they'll have in the future—trying to make sure everything was in place and ready for liftoff:

L.E. getting dressed, standing with his hands on his hips and looking in the mirror, asking Clarke, "Does this go?" about the tie he had chosen for his new bride.

Clarke and Corey getting dressed, in their brand-new Nehru jackets and love beads, to be their father's best men.

And Rita at her house on Virginia Street, putting on her pillbox hat three different times before she got the angle just right. She wore pink, with shoes dyed to match.

The color I *should* have worn in my coffin.

I saw them go to the Townhouse Restaurant at Woods Motel afterward to celebrate. The very same place where, barely six months before, I had spent the night in a Shalimar-scented motel room with Maurice Ring.

I saw Maurice, on his waiter shift at the Townhouse, give a look of surprise when the four of them trooped in for their early-bird celebration dinner that Tuesday. (In the future, they'll call it, "Rolls eyes.") He hitched up his tuxedo pants and white socks and glued back on a button that was about to fall off of his gold poly-cotton blend waiter's jacket. No one else at the Townhouse would worry about such a thing, but Maurice would. No one else would say, "This way for the Perkins party," as he did when he escorted them to their banquette to try to make Clarke and Corey feel better about this new life, this new family of theirs.

L.E. plopped down on the plastic banquette seat, which made a sort of farting sound, and proclaimed, "You boys can order whatever you want for dinner tonight, a shrimp cocktail or a steak or even both, one right after the other," he said. "We want to celebrate having a new Mumma."

Then he raised his red plastic drinking glass, which Maurice had just filled with ice water and a special slice of lemon. Not a wedge, but a slice, which he was trying to convince management to switch over to because it was more chic. He'd heard the better restaurants in Dallas were giving it a try.

"I'd like to make a toast to the start of the rest of our lives," L.E. said. My old husband, now becoming a *new* husband.

Rita raised her glass so Corey and Clarke did too. They clinked them together, but the glasses thudded instead of clinked, plastic instead of crystal.

L.E. kept talking. "I'd like to officially welcome Rita into our family and thank her for being so good to us already."

Rita smiled, but it was the nervous kind, like she had just given Brother Joe Bob at church.

"Clarkie, you and Corey . . . you're my best men, my best boys, my best sons, so do you want to make a toast too?"

That part I could do without. It was one of the rules for being dead: you didn't have to stay and hear the toasts your children were forced to say to their new mother.

I should have stayed. The next time I saw my son, he'd be drowning in a swimming pool.

— CLARKE —

"Clarkie, you and Corey . . . you're my best men, my best boys, my best sons, so do you want to make a toast too?"

Corey asked, "With jelly or jam?" and everybody laughed. Except me. Corey started talking about much he loved the moccasins that Rita had given us while I tried to think how I could work Abraham Lincoln and John F. Kennedy into my toast. At the Townhouse, they have these little cards next to the cash register, right next to the bowl of free mints, with their restaurant ad on one side and a story about the dead presidents on the other. It's about how President Kennedy's secretary was named Mrs. Lincoln and she told him not to go to Dallas because something bad was going to happen, and also how President Lincoln's secretary was named Mrs. Kennedy and she told him the same thing, except about Ford's Theatre.

For my toast, I thought I could talk about how the president cards were next to the cash "register," which is the same as the book at Mother's viewing, which is where I found out about Rita, who was wearing a pink pillbox hat like the one Jackie Kennedy wore when her husband got shot. And then I remembered the bad luck thing that nobody had thought about in advance, which was that this *was* the anniversary of President Kennedy getting shot, November 22nd, three years ago. What a stupid day to get married. One thought kept leading to the next, and they were all connected by equal signs, like the one when I blinked to remember "Elvis = pills."

Which is what started everything.

Rita got up like she was reading my mind and put a quarter in the jukebox to play Elvis Presley's "Love Me Tender," which she said could be our song, but I didn't know if she meant hers and mine or hers and Daddy's. Then he ordered chicken, which is what Mother's body looked like in the funeral home under the hot orange spotlights. I saw the revolving case where all the desserts were spinning like the equal signs in my head, and I wondered if they had wedding cake in there. It was a "carousel" like the one they had at Daddy's Kiwanis Club Halloween carnival, and I couldn't stop counting all the different kinds of dessert inside. Black Forest cake and carrot cake and cheesecake with blueberries and cheesecake with strawberries and coconut cream pie and pecan pie and apple pie and chocolate cake...

The thought of so much sugar was making me sick, even though I love sugar, and that's when I did my toast.

"I'm happy Rita's here because she saved us on Halloween, and she can save us again. But I'm scared she's gonna have to switch to her black pillbox hat instead of her pink one like Jacqueline Kennedy did and wear that to her own funeral if something happens to her, like I told her it would."

Before Daddy could say anything, I looked straight at Rita. "You know what I'm talking about. I told you. I *warned* you. You can't say I didn't."

"I am going to KILL you, little mister!" Daddy reached across the table to grab the collar of my Nehru jacket, but he just broke my love beads instead. They went scattering all over the floor, and that's when I ran outside. In the dessert case behind me, I could see the reflection of him getting up and Rita grabbing him—"Perkins, Perkins," she said, and her mouth looked like the magnified fish lips in the tanks at Woolworths—but he kept spinning around, like my head.

I ran to the swimming pool behind the restaurant. It had a closed-off fence around it, but I climbed over the chain-link and got cut where one of the twists of metal poked into my knee. I was feeling so many other things by then I didn't feel it, even though it did start bleeding. Inside, the water was covered over by a big blue tarp since the pool was closed for the season, but I didn't have anywhere else to run, and Daddy was running toward me, and . . .

I stepped off the concrete ledge and onto the tarp. I heard the crunchy crinkly sounds it made when it started caving in, but then I didn't hear anything because the water was pouring over the top and into my ears.

The cold water put out the spinning in my head, it put out the equal signs, it put out me.

It was pouring into my clothes and making me sink faster. Then it was pouring into my mouth and making me die faster. But at least the water baptized me, without having to walk up the aisle first.

Right before I closed my eyes forever, I saw Daddy's face in the water. He was reaching out his arms, but the water made them so wavy I couldn't tell if he was trying to pull me out or push me back in.

— MAURICE —

Maurice Ring was the one who brought Clarke back to life; Maurice Ring, the last man Creola had kissed on this good earth, besides her boys, was now the one giving the kiss of life to her unconscious son after L.E. pulled him out of the Townhouse pool. L.E. didn't know what to do besides pull Clarke out so roughly his arms banged into the side of the pool and the left one, still tangled up in the tarp that was supposed to keep little children safe from drowning, got broken.

Just before it happened, Maurice had been bringing them a lazy Susan carrier filled with different salad dressings: Russian and Roquefort and French and Italian. He called it the "United Nations of salad dressing." That's when the fight broke out. L.E. grabbed at Clarke, who ran away; love beads flew everywhere; Mr. Ring slipped on them, and four different kinds of salad dressings went flying all over the waiter jacket he'd just gotten back from the dry cleaner's.

Clarke went running out of the restaurant first, then L.E., then Rita, then Corey. Maurice raced out too and saw them all making a beeline for the motel's swimming pool, closed for the season behind a fence. By the time Maurice had run to the manager's office and gotten the key to open the gate, L.E. and Rita were pulling Clarke out of the pool, his hair matted down, his brand-new gold Nehru jacket clinging to his spindly little chest.

Maurice pushed through them all and put his interlaced hands on Clarke's chest, with his perfectly buffed and polished fingernails (despite cleaning grade-school bathrooms and hauling around plastic tubs of dirty dishes), and pumped the first gulp of water out of him. He kept pushing until it all spewed out, and after that he started breathing fresh air into Clarke's mouth.

An ambulance with lights flashing and siren wailing took Clarke away, as the Perkins family hopped in their car and raced behind.

No one thought to bring along Maurice Ring, the hero of the evening. He just stood there alone, left behind, in shock, water dripping down his face like the Creature from the Black Lagoon. You couldn't tell where water from the pool left off and his tears began. The same way Creola had looked when they were at Woods Motel together three days before she died, when he saw her writing down a bunch of words on a sheet of motel stationery, tears running down her face, and then hiding it before he could see what she wrote.

— CREOLA —

By the time Clarke got out of the hospital, Rita got in: to her *new* house, my old one.

From high in my treehouse perch across the street, I watched new furniture get carted in by moving men, just as I had seen my dead body get carted out. Out with the old, in with the new! Isn't that what they say? With a new mother in place, there wasn't any need for Mrs. Angel, but she did leave her sugar cookie recipe behind as a wedding present. As Mrs. Angel was packing up her things, I heard her tell Rita, "You've got to get those boys to love something besides the movies. They can't keep you warm at night."

Tell me about it.

They replaced all the furniture that I had destroyed with new store-bought bedroom suites, using L.E.'s discount from the store. They replaced all the water-stained drapes, the ones that had scared Clarke so much on Halloween night. They put down wavy green carpet over the wooden floors; they turned the old den into a new bedroom for the boys, so they'd have a regular place to sleep—the *same* place every night, instead of wandering all over the house.

Suzanne McLarty, my student teacher, came by to bring Clarke the homework he'd missed while he was in the hospital. His broken left arm was in a cast; when he had Suzanne sign it, as so many visitors had already done, he told her, "Now I have a register on my arm too, only I don't have to be dead for it." I could see in her face that she didn't have a clue what Clarke was talking about.

There was so much I still had to teach her, but so much I *needed* to know from her too. She'd seen me close-up those last few days at school; there was some wisp of memory I keep having . . . what? I was down on the ground, looking up. She was looking down at me. Almost like *she* was the one who was floating above. But I couldn't make any sense of it yet. As soon as I tried to remember too hard, the memory evaporated like a cloud pushed away by a strong gust of wind.

Altha came by the house too, along with Beverly and Carolyn. It was a week or two before Christmas, and they came under the guise of bringing presents: a Batmobile for Clarke, a *Lost in Space* robot for Corey, a set of dish towels for Rita. Nothing for L.E. But my sister didn't fool me for a minute; she was really there to check out my competition: Rita. Altha could barely look at her. She walked around the newly decorated house, toeing the new carpet with her shoe tip. "I would have gone with a shag. Creola would have too."

Actually no, I wouldn't have—too hard to vacuum—but nobody was asking me. Rita had done a nice job with the house, I had to give her that. If I had been there, I might have told her that using shelf paper with a stained glass design on the accent window in the living room wasn't the best idea—you actually wanted to let the light shine *in* through the stained glass, not cover up the window completely with something that was solid and not see-through—but to each her own. She'd made a nice new room for the boys. Some of the things I'd always wanted to do but had never had the money for. That's what happens when you try to save money instead of spend it. Instead of *take* it, from a joint checking account.

Showing that house off to Suzanne and Altha and her girls, Rita was as nervous as I had been when I was a new bride. God bless her, because I couldn't.

And then the shocker, after Altha left, which almost brought me crashing back down to earth.

Rita brought in the oil portrait of me that L.E. had had done so many years ago, and asked the boys if they wanted to keep it in their

204   KIM POWERS

new bedroom. L.E. had done his best to make it disappear after the
funeral when he'd put it up on an easel behind my coffin. He buried
it facedown in the linen closet in the hallway.

At least they'd buried *me* faceup.

It was an old-fashioned kind of painting where what you see is
what you get, nothing "arty" about it. But it was a good likeness, an
apt likeness, which meant a sad likeness: I looked young and old at
the same time, even in the first years of my marriage. There weren't
any obvious age lines drawn on my face, but there was a sort of . . .
resignation, I guess you'd call it, which had nothing to do with
wrinkles painted on canvas. The painter tried to put a mirthful
crinkle in my eyes, but he couldn't lie and he wasn't good enough
to paint what wasn't there to begin with. There was a slight worry
to my brow; I was trying to smile, but the corners of my mouth just
wouldn't make it all the way up. Even so, it was nice to see myself
again, back from the days when my life seemed so full of promise.

Rita said, "It wasn't right to let a good piece of art go to waste."

Corey said, "Wouldn't that be weird to hang her up, with you
here and everything?"

I wanted to yell out for all of them to hear, "I've already been
hung out to dry, so don't start worrying about me now."

"I'm not here to take her away from you boys. I want you to know
that. She did a fine job raising you, and I hope to keep up her good
work."

Of course, Rita had started taking me away from them the first
time she slept with their father, the first time she even had lunch
with him at Shaw's Café, but saying that wouldn't do anybody any
good. Not now.

This was about to get interesting.

Corey kept talking, more than he had since he'd gone on and on
about getting baptized. "I don't want her eyes following me around.
You can put her over Clarke's bed, but not mine. I don't want her
there. I think about her enough as it is."

That was nice to know.

Rita propped up the painting on Clarke's new bed, on top of the black-and-white checked bedspread he'd picked out for himself. Then she stepped away to look at it. She moved this way and that, and I could tell what she was thinking: *Her eyes do look like they are following you around.*

I think she would have scared me too, and she *was* me.

"It was at the funeral home," Clarke said, forgetting for a minute that Rita had seen it there too. "Did you know her? Is that why you registered to see her?"

This was about to get *really* interesting.

Instead of answering him, Rita just kept looking at the painting, trying to get a safe distance from it. "Her eyes don't really move. It's just an optical illusion," she said, as if she were trying to convince herself as much as Corey. "That means it's not real."

Clarke looked at the painting too, but what he said next was aimed directly at Rita.

"I think he did it."

"Did what? Who?"

"Daddy. I think he killed her. He had her painted, like Goldfinger, then he killed her."

I caught my breath—well, my *something* since I guess I wasn't breathing anymore. It felt like a sucker punch, hearing it straight out like that.

Rita caught her breath too, then said, "Let me ask you this. Do you think anybody's ever loved me enough to make a painting for me? *Of* me? Why would he hurt somebody he loved so much?"

"Because he fell in love with . . ."

Somebody else. Clarke stopped short, suddenly realizing the "somebody else" was standing in the room, right in front of him.

Too bad they didn't know that I was *floating* in the room, in front of both of them, from my hiding place of ether in the air.

The air finally escaped from Rita's lungs. "Oh, Clarke. Let sleeping dogs lie. You know what that means? It means they'll bite you if you wake them up. It means nothing will bring your mother back, no matter how much we both wish it could. No matter how much I wish I hadn't ..."

"I like it," Clarke said, snapping Rita out of her reverie. "You can keep her here. Mother. Over my bed. She'll remind me of what I have to do." Then with his stiff fingers that were peeking out over the lip of the plaster cast on his arm, he held up my portrait so Rita could see where to hammer a nail in the wood-paneled wall to hang it on.

Bull's-eye.

The last nail in my coffin, so to speak, the one that had already been nailed shut.

– CLARKE –

SATURDAY, DECEMBER 24, 1966

It's been a while since I've written, so I have a lot to catch up on. And I didn't write because I thought things had gotten better. For a while at school, I was the most popular boy in my class because I almost drowned, and they had to pump out my lungs. I took a jar of water and told them that's what came out, even though it wasn't. At recess, the Beatles would pin me down on the ground and play like they were doing it again, until they pressed at my lungs so much I ran out of breath or slobber came out of my mouth. Because of my cast, they call me the One-Armed Man from *The Fugitive*, but I think they're doing it in fun, or because Miss McLarty told them to be nice to me. Now, I've started liking it when they hold me down.

My cast is dirty from being on the ground so much and from where everybody signed it. My Beatles club signed it with their Beatles names instead of their real ones, so Gary Keith is Paul and Ronnie Dunn is Ringo and Mickey Martin is John. Kathie Green is our mascot, so she signed it Cynthia, who is John's girlfriend. The skin inside the cast itches all the time now; I have to straighten out a wire coat hanger to stick down inside to scratch with.

Right after I went back to school, there was a picture of me in the *Courier-Gazette*, even though they had to make it seem like it was more about Thanksgiving instead of me drowning, so they wouldn't show favoritism. Cindy Riddle and Curtis Dickey were in the picture too, but I was the one in the middle with the best costume, an Indian bonnet and Indian vest that Rita got for me at Stuckey's to reward me for not being dead. The head of Curtis's horse covers my left arm so you can't see my cast, which is maybe a good thing. When the newspaper lady told us to smile because of what we were thankful for, I smiled because I was thankful Daddy didn't drown me.

But now it's almost happened again, just a month after the last time. I guess something always happens on a big holiday.

Since it's Christmas, Daddy gave me and Corey money to buy a present for Rita, so we bought her fake eyelashes. That's what she wanted, to go with her wiglet. Every lash cost a quarter, so Daddy gave us extra quarters for extra lashes.

After that, we went to see *The Fortune Cookie* with Walter Matthau and Jack Lemmon. It's supposed to be a comedy, but it wasn't very funny. I don't think it's as easy to laugh in black and white as it is in color. Walter makes Jack pretend he got hurt at a football game and wear a cast around his neck to get more insurance money. But that part reminded me too much of the cast I have to wear around my arm, except Jack's was pretend and mine wasn't.

When we were telling Rita about the movie after supper, before Daddy got home, she said, "Let's pretend we're *all* opening fortune cookies, to see what the future holds!" She went first and played like she was breaking a fortune cookie in half, then pretended to unfold the little piece of paper inside and read it. "Everything is going to get better," she said, still looking nervous like she did when she married Daddy and we made our toasts.

Then I "opened" *my* fortune cookie and it "said" the same thing: "Everything is going to get better!" I was trying to be nice and normal for Christmas.

Corey took so long time "opening" his I thought he wasn't going to be able to make anything up, but then he said, "You will be forgiven." He didn't laugh or smile, and he wadded up his "paper" before we could look at it.

Then we played Christmas carols on the hi-fi that Rita brought with her from her falling-down house, and she taught us how to dance to the fast songs that were about Santa Claus and presents.

When the slow songs about Jesus and the manger came on, we plopped down on the couch and looked at the silver aluminum Christmas tree we had just put up. It had a color wheel aimed at it that went from red to green to blue, and it was so pretty changing colors I thought maybe things *were* going to change and get better.

But then Daddy got home from work and he'd been drinking. "Christmas cheer," he called it, and he wanted to share it with us. He made us all get in the car in the pouring rain and go to our farm in the country where he wants to build his Ponderosa. Now he wanted to show us his idea to "make us rich!" But his words didn't sound rich, they sounded poor. They sounded drunk. I've heard him use words like that before. They mean we're supposed to stay quiet and let Daddy do all the talking. Even Rita knew that, and she's just been here a month.

He parked inside the gate and opened up the trunk of the car and said, "Here's our Christmas present, just in time!" All I saw was a long metal box, sort of bolted into the trunk. Daddy said I wasn't using my imagination—"the one you're so goddamn good with"—because it was supposed to keep your car from sliding on ice. "I'm gonna sell these all over town. You bolt it in your trunk, the gyroscopes go to work, and the money starts pouring in. You. Get. Rich. Quick." Only he slurred and said "jar-scopes" and "purring" and "get-ich-ick."

He said he'd prove it worked by driving us across the pond on the farm because that should be frozen like an icy road would be. Daddy gunned the car across the pasture where no road was, kicking up mud and rain, and the headlights bounced every time we hit a patch of weeds.

"Perkins, quit it." Rita tried to grab the steering wheel, even though she can't drive. "You're drunk. You're scaring the boys."

Daddy said, "The 'boys' have to grow up. I've babied 'em long enough."

The car was slipping and sliding so much I knew the thing in the trunk wasn't going to make us rich, it was going to make us dead. He kept racing toward the pond, looking for ice. If the pond had ever been frozen it was melted now because of the rain. All you could see was brown gunk. Finally, we got to the pond and he drove the car straight in, yelling, "I'll show you!" The car flew up and we bounced and hit our heads on the roof and came back down and hit our butts on the seats, and then we just sat there, conked out. Us *and* the car.

"Lloyd," that's what Rita calls him when she's really mad; his first name, which nobody ever uses or even knows. "Lloyd." She couldn't think of anything else to say.

He started trying to back the car out of the water and mud, but the wheels just kept whirring and not going anywhere. Wheels, rain, mud. Wheels, rain, mud. Finally he put some cardboard from the trunk under the wheels—the same cardboard his get-rich-quick scheme must have come wrapped in—and that got us out.

"Shitass." That's all Daddy said, perfectly clear, when the car hit a fence on the way back home.

Nobody else said anything until Rita ran to the bedroom and fell on her knees, crying. "Oh Jesus oh sweet Jesus thankyouthankyou-thankyouohmymercifulfather." It was like our other mother used to say, when she talked to the Great Apostle Paul. It happens to all the women in our family, sooner or later.

P. S. It's Christmas Eve, and we're in our new beds in our new room, me and Corey and Rita, looking up at the new TV Daddy got us for Christmas. It's the latest fashion, hanging up on a pole in our bed-room so we have to look up at it, like we do at the Ritz. The TV was in the back seat of the car and the screen on it cracked when Daddy hit the fence on the way home, but we're watching it anyway. *White Christmas* with Bing Crosby and Danny Kaye, and that's the only frozen ice we'll ever see this winter. Rita's putting glue on her fake eyelashes in Corey's bed and crying like Mother used to. I'm writ-ing in my scrapbook and pasting in my movie ad. Corey's in bed with me, eating glue and coloring on my cast with the new crayons I got him. Daddy's sitting up in the living room by himself, crushing his beer cans, then lining them up on the new TV trays that Corey and I saved up green stamps to buy for the whole family. We can hear the crunching of metal all the way back in our bedroom.

— CLARKE —

One time, I rode my bicycle to sleep on top of my mother's coffin.

Yesterday, I rode my bicycle to beg our new mother to come back to us, which is funnyweird since I didn't want her here in the first place.

When Corey and I woke up yesterday, the day after Christmas, the day after Daddy tried to drive us onto a frozen pond that wasn't, we found a note from Rita telling us that she had left and was going to live with her sister in town but that she loved us and our fake eyelashes and would always think of us when she wore them.

I put on my black Batman sweatshirt that I always wear when I go to find a mother who's gone, and I told Corey I was bringing Rita back. I tried to get him to come with me, to ride on the back of my banana seat and hold on, but he wouldn't. I even said we could stay with Rita and her sister and never come back, but he said he was too afraid of what Daddy would do if he came home for lunch and we weren't there. I told Corey he didn't want to find out, but he still wouldn't come with me. I think it's the worst thing I've ever done, leaving Corey alone, even worse than riding alone with Bobby Raines on his go-cart.

I rode my bike all the way to the east side of town where Rita's sister lives. For part of the time I tried steering with just my right hand and holding my broken left arm in my sling against my stomach, but it gets tough when you go over bumps or holes. But whenever I leaned over and rested the cast on the handlebars, I was afraid the vibration would break my arm all over again. And it was a long way—through downtown and past the big brick house of the man who's in Congress. I wondered if bad things ever happened behind brick walls, instead of just the new aluminum siding like we have, that Daddy put on the house to make it look better when Rita moved in. I kept on riding until I got to the part of town where they don't have brick or aluminum siding, just old rotting wood. That's where Rita's sister lives, where the streets are narrow and chalky, with ditches and black people. By the time I got there, I looked black too because the dye from my sweatshirt had sweated all over my body and I'd rubbed it on my face. That's how Rita's sister saw me when she opened her door.

She said, "You poor baby," and let me in to see Rita. She was wearing her new eyelashes, and they were black and runny too, just like me. We watched a movie on TV that night when she wasn't talking on the phone to Daddy. All through the night, her face stayed black and runny around her new eyelashes.

I don't know what they said during the commercials, but the next day Daddy came to pick us up. Rita said we had to go, that he'd promised to act better. I've heard that one before. I didn't want to get back in the car with him, but before I could get on my bike to ride away Daddy grabbed it and jammed it in the trunk where his machine to make us rich was still lying on its side, not doing anything. Right before Rita got in the front seat with Daddy, she whispered to me she wasn't doing it for him, she was doing it for us. Corey whispered that Daddy was so mad when he came home that he forgot to give Corey his pills, but Corey said he's growing up because he remembered to take them by himself anyway.

Blink. I cannot leave my brother alone without his pills, even if he is growing up.

Blink. I cannot ride my bicycle to find a lost mother again.

Blink. I cannot look at Rita with her runny black eyelashes and beg her to do something I know will hurt her.

Blink. I cannot think of Mother, knowing what Daddy did to her, and let him get away with it anymore.

— CREOLA —

Strange as it may seem, that's one thing that actually made me feel sorry for Rita, the woman who destroyed my marriage: watching her as she packed her little Samsonite suitcase and called a cab to take her to her sister's house. I know a lot about desperate, disappointed housewives who pack suitcases in the early morning, the minute their husbands leave for work. *Been there, done that,* as they will say. I know about riding in the back of a cab with tears running down your face and the cab driver looking at you from in the rearview mirror and wondering if he should ask if you're okay or just stay quiet and keep his eyes on the road.

I know about falling on your knees and thanking God that you're still alive after you've been in a car with a drunk behind the wheel.

Oh, yes, *girlfriend.* Rita and I had a lot more in common than most people could ever imagine.

And now we both have Clarke, who's braver than either of us. Rita and I just tried to pack up and leave. Clarke actually tried to fix the root problem; I saw him do it as I floated around and wished I could have given him a hand now that I can't get any deader than I already am.

While L.E. was gone away on his yearly hunting trip with the other drunks in town—oh, how I both dreaded and loved those trips, knowing the shape he'd be in when he came back, but so glad to be able to be alone for a while—Clarke sniffed out all of L.E.'s hiding places for his bottles: the dirty clothes hamper in the bathroom, the water tank at the back of the commode, the linen closet in the hall (the same one where L.E. had tried to keep my portrait buried away under some quilts), the tiny cabinet up above the ice-box in the kitchen, and the green metal locker out in the garage where L.E. keeps his tools.

And there's a new one since I died.

Rita brought a big ceramic milk jug with her, the antique kind that has a wooden pole that pioneers used to churn butter. It's a new "decorating touch" for the house. Rita originally had giant crepe paper flowers in Mexican fiesta colors in it, but L.E. had the bright idea to fill it to the brim with all the wheat pennies he collects. They stopped making them in the late '50s, when Clarke was born; the pennies have Lincoln on one side and two sheaths of wheat on the other. L.E. thinks he can cash them in as a coin collector, and they'll make him rich. (Where have I heard *that* one before?) He also thinks they'll be great cover for another bottle of whiskey, which he hides at the very bottom of the jug. It's like playing "Go Fish" when he pulls it out. He sticks his hand straight down and feels around, and all those copper pennies go sliding off when he pulls his amber liquid treasure out, his fingers smelling of metal.

Clarke lines up all six bottles next to the sink in the kitchen. My little soldier boy, with his left arm in a plaster cast and a gray cloth sling to hold it upright. Thank God it's not his right hand—the one he writes with, the hand and fingers that are strongest—because that's what he uses now to unscrew all six bottle tops.

But that's as far as Clarke gets. He looks at them for a long time, the four big bottles that are half-full, the little one L.E. hadn't broken the seal on yet (before Clarke did), and the square one from the water tank of the commode. But he can't empty them. He knows there will be hell to pay if he does.

He looks at Rita, now standing behind him in her new kitchen, but she can't do it either, and she's barely been married to L.E. a month. She knows it's her job as the boys' new mother, and she also knows it's her first failing to them that she can't.

I could have told her: that's no way to start a marriage.

Then Clarke just sighs; he sighs a lot these days. His cast sinks into his stomach as the air goes out, and he recaps all six bottles and takes them back to their original hiding places. When he gets to the commode in the bathroom and struggles to lift up the heavy porcelain lid with just one good hand and the elbow from the other, he turns to Rita and says, with complete resignation but no accusation, "If the H-bomb comes, the civil defense pamphlets say this is the water we're supposed to drink to survive. It looks kind of yucky, but I guess you do what you have to do. Daddy can drink this." He holds up the bottle one last time, then places it gently inside so it won't break. "Maybe we can all have a swig, to calm us down. We'll need it. Or use as an antiseptic if we get wounded in the fallout."

That's my boy, thinking ahead.

When L.E. gets back from his deer hunting trip, he has a new bottle to hide: a half-empty bottle of Wild Turkey, which he sneaked into the house via his duffel bag, which also held his rifle, a box of shells, and the bloodied orange jumpsuit that he wore in the woods so he wouldn't be mistaken for a deer and get shot himself.

Later that same night, after the boys and Rita are asleep, L.E. stays up at the dining room table Rita brought with her and works on the model of his Ponderosa dream house. I roost on top of the stereo hi-fi console that Rita also brought, just feet away from L.E.'s head, and watch him. His plumage of hair, sticking straight up, the same way he had worn it ever since we first met. I thought it was sexy then. When he's busy like that, he looks just like Clarke toiling away, writing in his movie scrapbook. Both of them hunched over their projects, their obsessions, biting their lips in concentration, the rest of the world disappearing around them.

On this night, L.E. takes some foil from the kitchen to lay down as a base around the cardboard model, then crinkles up Saran Wrap and glues that on top of the foil to become a lake. Not just any lake, but a frozen pond, silvery and tempting on bottom, clouded over by mushy ice on top. He then takes one of Corey's little toy cars, cuts it in half, and attaches it at an angle, headfirst into the "water." At least he remembers what he did to his family on Christmas Eve.

He lifts off the detachable roof of the house and fills the inside of the model with secrets only he can understand, like the secrets Clarke used to keep under his bed. Reminders. Evidence. I see L.E. put the Smirnoff bottle from his hunting trip in it, then my death certificate that lists my cause of death as "undetermined." He puts the empty bottle of Stelazine in there, which he had found in the medicine cabinet. And just before he puts the top back on . . .

. . . and maybe it's just my imagination—you tend to imagine a lot when you're dead—but I swear he senses my presence and turns around to look at me, eye to eye . . .

. . . he adds in the letter that I had been writing to him in the last few days of my life.

That's when I finally see what I had written on the outside of the envelope, maybe the very last thing I had ever written, in my signature red ink: TO BE READ AFTER I'M GONE.

— CLARKE —

It was a New Year, but it began the same old way, with Daddy drinking and hunting and shooting and killing. But this time, even after he unpacked, he still tried to keep doing it.

It was dinner, and he was trying to make us eat venison, which is a fancy word for reindeer. He brought it back from his hunting trip, which he takes every January. I didn't want to eat it because I couldn't stop thinking about the deer antlers he brought back too, still attached to a furry piece of skull. Rita said I could eat my venison with A1 steak sauce, but it didn't make any difference.

"C'mon," Daddy said to me, his eyes already glassy from all the Pabst Blue Ribbon beer he was drinking. "Just try it. It's like steak. You know how much you like steak."

"Steak's from a cow. You're supposed to eat cow. And chicken too. And sometimes fish. But not a reindeer. That's like eating Bambi."

"We saw *Bambi* at the Ritz. 'Man is in the forest.' I don't want to eat Bambi either," Corey said.

Rita said it tasted "gamey," which was not the same as Monopoly, but more like the woods and dirt, like what was around Mother's coffin. I didn't want to eat something that had been around a coffin.

"Perkins, it's not worth fighting about," Rita said. "I'll make the boys a hot dog."

"Yeah, what about that? That's from a pig. Porky Pig. Isn't that one of your little cartoons? You left that off your list," Daddy said, crumpling up his beer can with one hand.

"Perkins, leave it alone," Rita kept on, picking up our plates to take them off the table. "Just let them eat what they want. I've got mac and cheese, and I'll make hot dogs."

"*Bambi* is a shitass fairy tale," Daddy said and burped.

I looked at Rita. I knew we should have emptied his bottles because now he'd pretty much done it all on his own. Into his mouth.

"Eat the goddamn deer or you're not getting *anything* to eat. I go out and hunt for us and provide for us, and you'd rather have popcorn at your goddamn movies. You can't live unless you have *meat*. *Real* meat." Daddy picked up the platter in the middle of the table and slammed it down so hard it broke. Now ceramic and plaster and glass was all over the meat.

"Great. Now nobody can eat it. Let me clean this up," Rita said, her voice shaking. "Boys, go to your room." She wasn't saying it to be mean; she was saying it to protect us. But Daddy grabbed me before I could move.

"You're not going anywhere, little mister. In Vermont we were lucky to get *anything* to eat. I'll show you boys to count your blessings." He stood up at the opposite end of the table from Rita, like he was facing her down. "Get ready. We're going hunting. Daddy's gone-a-huntin,'" he said, wobbling and trying to get his balance.

"Perkins, you just got *back* from hunting. You're drunk. Leave the boys alone."

"I made a promise to their Mumma . . . a plan and a plot and a promise. Where we can get food . . . get Bambi."

From her end of the table, Rita put her hands down on our hands, mine and Corey's. Clamping them down so we couldn't move, and Daddy couldn't take us. "Lloyd"—she was really mad; that's the only time she ever called him by his first name—"you're not taking them anywhere. It's too dark. You're too drunk."

Daddy put out his arms on either side and grabbed us harder, on our collarbones. For an old drunk, he was very strong. "Oh yes I am. Yes, I am indeed. I am dark and drunk. Get used to it."

The words sounded like a slap, so Rita slapped him back. Then he slapped her for real and yanked me and Corey up from the table. He didn't let go and pulled us all the way outside and into the car.

Rita ran out to the porch. Looking at her from the back seat of the car, I remembered Mother standing there one of the last times I saw her, grabbing on to the post that held up the roof and looking like she didn't know where she was. Now Rita was holding on to that same post, watching us being taken away. Mother had just stood there, but Rita ran to the car and banged at the window. The fat on her upper arm jingled as she tried to yank at the door, but Daddy was already pulling out of the driveway and tearing down the street.

I was afraid he was going to drive us out on the lake at the farm again without even pretending it was frozen, but this time he drove the car straight to a bare patch of land. He slammed on the brakes and hopped out, then began taking giant steps and marking out a square with them. "This is where I'm gonna build it, my Ponderosa, OUR Ponderosa, and THIS is how we're gonna protect it. You've gotta learn to protect. Protect an' conquer. Protect an' destroy."

He opened the car trunk, and I thought he was going to show us that metal slidey thing that didn't work. It was still there, but he pulled out his rifle instead.

"We're coming for you, Bambi," he yelled, and his voice made an echo. So did the sound of the rifle, when he opened the long barrel and slid in bullets that looked like faded red penny wrappers. He snapped the two parts back into place.

Click. Click.

"I was providing for my family when I was just seven, so you're never too young to start. Corey too. A righteous kill. That's what we're goin' for. Hunt for our own food. If you ever wanna eat again . . ."

"You're a drunk." It was the first time I'd ever said it to his face. "And a killer."

This time it wasn't an open palm that came flying toward my

face. It was Daddy's balled-up fist. But making the effort threw him off balance and he wobbled, for just a moment.

That's when I yelled "Run" and yanked Corey away with me. It was cold, and the grass was crunchy with frost. I could see our breath when we ran, coming out of our mouths and noses like white smoke. Like we were on frozen fire.

We kept falling because it was dark and slippery. Daddy fell because he was drunk. "Come back. We've gotta practice. Gotta protect. That's our new motto. Gotta eat," he said, and started laughing. That made an echo too.

The leaves were mostly gone, so there was no good place to hide, but I pulled Corey behind a bunch of thick tree trunks. We were near the creek that ran through the farm, where we'd seen water moccasins once, but it was too deep to wade across and the bridge to the other side was too far away to get to. Corey was crying. I put my hand over his mouth and said we had to be quieter than we'd ever been in our lives, quieter than we were even when we heard that Mother was dead.

Daddy was thrashing through the trees close to us. Now he was crying too, instead of laughing. "She tried to take you from me. But she can't, she can't have you . . . if I can't have you, nobody can."

I started shaking harder than Corey ever has with one of his seizures, but it was weird; it was all inside, like the Ice Age had slid over me and weighted me down with a million pounds of ice. I was so cold and shaky I thought ice cubes were going to start flying off me and give away where we were.

"Get out from your hiding place. We're looking for shitass Bambi."

Daddy shot his rifle, and the blast tore through the trees. It made a clumpy sound, like a little H-bomb. A bunch of birds flew away. Dead leaves lifted up off the ground. I heard the rifle click open, one shell pop out, another one go in, and then the rifle close.

Click click.

Daddy fired again.

We weren't wearing orange like you're supposed to when you go hunting. We weren't even wearing our coats because Daddy pulled us out of the house so fast. We weren't wearing anything that could keep us warm or stop a bullet.

Corey stood up, and one hit him.

My mountain of ice melted and the avalanche started. My mouth came unfrozen and I yelled. "Nooooooo..."

There was an echo, but it wasn't me, it was Daddy. He ran through the trees faster than his bullet did. "Oh my God oh my God oh my God..." It's like he heard the bullet stop in Corey's arm. It's like he heard the world stop when he shot his own son.

Corey was the only one not screaming. He was just looking at the blood pouring out of his upper arm where the bullet had zipped across his flesh. But his shirt sleeve was ripped through and all the threads hanging off it were turning dark red and purple as they soaked up more blood.

"Am I dying? Am I dying?" was all he kept saying as he fell down.

"Don't look. Don't look," was all I kept saying. "I'll save you. I'll save you."

"I didn't see. I didn't see," was all Daddy kept crying now that he was on top of us, ripping off Corey's shirt and wrapping it around Corey's arm to stop the bleeding.

And then, something else was on top of us, a siren sound and lights and Rita, running toward us, her fat skinny arms swinging, trying to take flight to get to us faster.

"GODDAMN YOU, WHAT DID YOU DO TO HIM?"

It's what Daddy yelled at me when I split Corey's head open. Now it was Rita yelling it at Daddy, for splitting his arm open.

"It was an accident. Oh Jesus oh Jesus Christ oh my God..."

Rita pulled Daddy off Corey and grabbed his arm to stop the blood, and one of the police pulled Rita off Corey and raced him back to the police car, yelling back to us, "It's a flesh wound. He'll be okay. He'll be okay."

"He's got epilepsy! He's an angel!" That was me, yelling to everybody.

"What did you DO to him?" Rita was screaming, beating at Daddy's chest, slapping his face. He put his bloody hands up to protect himself, and drops of blood flew everywhere. "I called the police as soon as you took off but . . . OH MY GOD!"

Another policeman pulled her off Daddy, again, and put Daddy in jail overnight, for "drunk and disorderly."

P.S. Corey's arm has a big bandage and stitches now, like he used to have in his head, but at least he's home. At least he's alive. He says it doesn't matter because he would have "gone to heaven anyway. It's what I deserve, after what I did."

And he crawled in his homemade cardboard box coffin under the bed and wouldn't come out of it, no matter how much Rita and I begged him to.

— L.E. —

The first time he and Creola ever slept together, the first night
they were married, she wasn't repulsed by the scar on his right leg.
She looked at it, almost transfixed. She'd never seen a scar that
big—eight, nine, ten inches; a shiny indentation on his thigh the
color of undercooked pork—and wondered aloud how it had kept
growing with him, stretching out his skin even more as he grew
into adulthood. Creola asked him if it hurt when the weather was
damp. She even did that thing the boys would come to do later:
pressing in at it to see if she could feel the metal plate underneath
that held the shattered bone in place. She came to hate so much else
about him, but she always said she felt sorry for him because of that
scar, and the childhood that went with it.

Now, through his pants in the jail cell, L.E. tried to gouge at it
himself so his leg would start bleeding all over again. So he could
feel that same searing pain that he had felt when he was a little boy
run over by a truck. The same pain Corey must have felt when that
hot flash of metal went glancing off his arm. Now they'd both been
wounded at seven years old, marking them for life. Father and son,
blood brothers.

L.E. wanted his own hot blood to mix with his son's, which had
already dried on L.E.'s pants. He hadn't been allowed to change
when the police hauled him in; they told him they wanted him to
"stew in his own juices" and remember what he'd done, although
there was no chance he would ever forget.

Clarke's scream, then Corey's whimper.

Of all the sounds that day, that's the one he'd never forget. The quietest one.

None of the ones that came later could hold a candle to that: not Rita screaming at him, not the thud of her fists hitting his face and chest, not the sound of the police siren or the door of the jail cell as it clanged shut.

He knew that he had almost killed his son. He knew that he'd almost killed all of them that night he drove into the frozen pond out on that farm. Maybe he'd been sleepwalking; maybe that "other Perkins" is the one who had packed up his family on Christmas Eve and bundled them into a car and driven them into a lake. Maybe he was trying to prove he was Superman. Maybe he was trying to prove he was Jesus of Vermont who could drive on top of water, not just walk on it. Maybe he was hoping the car would sink, and the cold water would finally wake him up.

Now it was the sound of the drunk in the cell next to L.E. that would keep him awake. All night long, he'd been wailing, "Just as I am, without one plea, but that Thy blood, was shed for me." L.E. thought of his own family's blood that had been shed that day, and that he had no pleas left. Maybe not even a family.

But finally, he did have success: fresh blood started seeping into his pants as he kept digging his fingers into his scar, digging deep and hard enough, pressing the fingernails he hadn't trimmed in weeks through the fabric. Enough to make things really hurt. Enough to make things really bleed. Enough to feel the pain he knew he deserved. If he only had one of his bottles with him, he'd pour the scorching alcohol on top of the wound, to make it hurt even more.

— CLARKE —

Everything has been quiet all week except for the sound of Rita changing Corey's bandage and running water to wash his wound, giving him his antibiotics and pain medicine while we wait for his stitches to come out. When they do, I'm going to ask Dr. Hill if I can keep them for evidence. Although the police have all the evidence they need now, from when they locked Daddy up.

At home, nothing's going on; nobody's saying anything, except for Daddy crying and adding little plastic toy figures, for me and Corey, to his Ponderosa model. He's made a bunch of bare trees without leaves out of brown pipe cleaners, and the two little boys are hiding in them. One of them has blood dripping down his arm, which Daddy made from Rita's red fingernail polish.

She's not talking to him, so he just took it.

Nobody's talking but Daddy, who just keeps saying, "I'm sorry. I'm begging you. Forgive me. It was the drink talking."

Daddy said he wanted us to protect things, so now I'm going to protect *us*. Me and Corey. And even Rita. For now, we're safe from his rifle because the police took it away, but I've found something new to keep us even safer.

I got the idea at our movie today, which was *Who's Afraid of Virginia Woolf?* We almost didn't get to see it because they almost wouldn't let us in. That's never happened before. The ticket lady said it was "some sex thing" and kids wouldn't understand.

I made her look at the movie poster, which said, "You are Cordially Invited to George and Martha's for an Evening of Fun and Games."

"It says so right there!" I told her. "We're *invited*! Cordially! That means really!"

The ticket lady finally gave in and let us have tickets when I promised I'd keep us both hidden in the back corner where it's the darkest and nobody can see unless they shine a flashlight in your eyes.

But there wasn't any sex in the movie, at least not that I could figure out, and I still didn't understand it. They kept their clothes on all the time, although Elizabeth Taylor's clothes were very tight. She dyed her hair gray and says, "What a dump," and bugs her husband, George, who's played by Richard Burton, who's her husband in real life too. He wears glasses and a sweater and drinks a lot, like Paul Newman did in *Cat on a Hot Tin Roof*, which Elizabeth Taylor was also in. I guess you just want to drink a lot when you're around her.

They invite their friends Nick and Honey over. Sandy Dennis plays Honey. She gets scared and wants to go home because Richard Burton and Elizabeth Taylor keep yelling at each other, and then Elizabeth does a dance and Richard gets mad and points a gun at her. Honey screams, but when he pulls the trigger an umbrella shoots out instead of a bullet. They keep talking about their son who's supposed to come home from college, but he has a car wreck and doesn't make it. They stay up all night long, and then Sandy Dennis throws up and goes home, but Richard Burton and Elizabeth Taylor are stuck with each other and don't have anywhere else to go. She says, "George and Martha, sad sad sad," and I agreed.

After the movie, I walked around home running my finger over the dusty furniture and saying "What a dump." I ran my finger over the chest of drawers Daddy keeps his underwear and socks and tee shirts in, and that's when I remembered what else was in there, that I saw when I stole Mother's funeral register.

Because the movie had "fun and games" in it, I made up a game to play before I let myself actually open the drawer.

I thought of every time Daddy has scared me so much I think I'm going to die. Like when we had to hide under my bed after he said he'd cut out my vocal cords, and at Halloween when he left us alone, and at his wedding when he tried to keep me underwater, and at Christmas when he drove us into the pond. I thought of him making Rita go to her sister's and making Corey go to the hospital after he shot him at the farm.

For every one of those thoughts, I let myself move one step closer to the drawer.

Vocal cords.

One step.

Halloween.

Another step.

Swimming pool.

Another.

Christmas pond.

Another.

Dead mother.

A big giant step.

Almost dead little brother.

Bingo. I reached the handles, opened the top drawer, and took out the pistol that Daddy kept in there. With my left arm in a cast, it would be a lot easier to shoot than his rifle.

— CREOLA —

One son dragged out of a swimming pool, half dead, his arm mangled, brought back to life.

Another son shot down, his arm mangled too, on the farm that was supposed to be my plan and my plot and my promise.

Some promise.

I don't know what you're planning, Clarke, but I'm afraid. I see you going out in the backyard by yourself late at night for target practice. Putting on your black sweatshirt and shooting your father's pistol into that old rusted-out trash barrel where we burned the garbage. The smell of rot and wet newspaper and moldy trash and old food at the bottom of it, which the fire never burned away. Where I made you both throw your pacifiers into the flame when you wouldn't quit using them. Where I held you over the lip of the barrel, one in each arm, and made you watch your childhoods melt.

What kind of mother does that—and screams, "Rubber's not a substitute for the real thing"—even if it's for your own good?

I'm scared of so much. The ultimate thing has happened to me—"*You're dead, snap out of it!*"; it can't get any worse—but I'm still terrified, as scared as I was when I was on the verge of leaving L.E. and starting over by ourselves in Plano. A woman on her own, in 1966, with two little boys. That's scary. As scary as the idea of burning my bra and becoming "liberated"; *that's* never going to happen. I wasn't that kind of woman. I wasn't the kind of woman who got divorced either, but I was going to have to put that into action as soon as I got settled.

As scared as you were, Clarke, hiding in the woods with your brother while a madman with a rifle hunted you down. As scared as you were looking at all of those liquor bottles and knowing you were too afraid to empty them all out, just as I had always been.

Can a ghost be scared? Most people would think the only real thing to be scared of was being dead, or the pain you might feel in dying, but since I'm already dead, what's left to scare me so much? Fear that I'm going to feel that pain all over again?

But *was* there pain? Did it hurt? I still don't know. I can't remember.

My thoughts are coming faster now. I can feel it. I'm getting closer to seeing my end, and I'm not sure I want to know anymore. I used to think that was the only thing I wanted to see—how I died. Now I think it's the one last thing I *don't* want to see. Even if it means I'm cursed to wander here, in limbo, for the rest of my life. What does that even mean—"the rest of my life"—if I'm already dead? Would that be so bad, getting to see Clarke and Corey all the time, seeing them grow up, even if I couldn't touch them or let them know I was there?

Before I drove to school that last Thursday morning, I drove to the downtown square. I can remember that much. A big courthouse in the middle, four squares of commerce around it. The next day I would be driving us to Plano first thing, after L.E. went to work, so I knew this was the last chance I'd ever get to see it like this. People going to work, before the day has them beaten down. The women's dresses are still fresh; the men look dapper. They have steaming cups of coffee; they tip their heads at each other, say hello. By noon, all of that is gone.

I want to see it one last time before I'm gone too, to Plano. I don't ever want to come back to this town. I just want to take my memories and make a clean break.

Outside the courthouse, on the west side of the square, is where Santa's little North Pole log cabin goes up every Christmas, next to the steps that lead down to the basement fallout shelter with its black-and-yellow air raid sign. Once, Clarke brought a list of what he wanted for Christmas; he'd been working on it the whole night before. An elf outside the log cabin let him reach inside a little basket and pull out a cellophane-covered candy cane, and Clarke started chewing on it, because he said, "I want to have clean breath for Santa."

As Clarke waited for his turn, I saw him look at the fallout shelter sign. He couldn't quit staring at it. By the time he finally got plopped on Santa's lap, I saw him wad up his list and say this: "All I really want for Christmas is to be safe from The Bomb."

What kind of a child says something like that, let alone thinks it? The child of someone like me, who dragged him to see dead bodies in their coffins, who made him walk through storms to get ice cream, who made him chase me down the street while I wore a patchwork quilt for a magic cape.

From then on, every Saturday afternoon when I dropped the boys off at the Ritz, Clarke would point out the air raid shelter across the street and tell me he felt better just knowing it was there. Then he'd look up to a window at the top of the courthouse, four or so stories above, and say, "Lee Harvey Oswald hid out at a place like that. It's a good place to hide a rifle. I think he acted alone."

My son, the expert on the Warren Commission.

Many years from now, Clarke will appear as an extra in a TV movie filmed in that courthouse. It's about what would have happened if Lee Harvey Oswald *hadn't* been shot just days after the Kennedy assassination but had gone on trial instead. Clarke won't allow them to cut his long brown hair into a period haircut, so he'll be stuck in the back of the courtroom, wearing a hat. That's the closest he'll ever come to fame as an actor. He'll sit in the courtroom with the heavy, hot film lights all around him, and wonder, *What if?*

Like mother, like son; we both thought that a lot.

I just want to stop now, to breathe in all these memories, to let them fill my body like blood. Is that all there is of this life I've led? All these silly little stories adding up to . . . what? We live, stuff happens, we die. Is that enough? Now that I have nothing to do, an eternity stretched out in front of me for nothing but reflection, I look back and think, *Did I do enough?* Who will really remember me? The boys, L.E., Altha, Mr. Ring. A pretty small circle of friends. And someday, they'll all be dead, and then I'll be well and truly forgotten. You can always look at the first line of someone's obituary, and that tells you everything you need to know about them. One-stop shopping. "Elementary schoolteacher Creola Perkins." That's me in a nutshell. I guess some of those kiddoes will miss me. Maybe I've taught them a few things. Maybe I've inspired some of the girls to be teachers themselves when they grow up. Maybe I've read a book to them that they'll read to their own children when they're as old as I am. Was. But nobody will be building a statue to me, like the one in the courthouse square. He's there in cement, but I couldn't tell you his name, or what he did, unless I go up close to look at the burnished plaque that's embedded with him. I just know he did something once, but now . . .

He's covered with pigeon doo.

Is that all there is? In a few years, Peggy Lee will have a song called that, a tinkly, sad little thing, and I think, *Thank God somebody finally had the nerve to say it out loud.*

It will become one of Clarke's favorite songs.

I'm getting nostalgic about leaving, and I'm not even gone yet.

Oh well, I still have time to make my mark. Or that's what I thought, that Thursday morning, my last fully conscious morning on this earth. I drove away from the square and all those memories and went to school. It was Suzanne's third day, and she was already there. I thought, "She's off to a great start. She's going to be a very good teacher."

I can remember everything until recess that afternoon: someone throws up in the hall, and Mr. Ring has to mop it up. He looks up at me from the vomit and mouths the words, "I'm sorry," and I mouth back to him, "Me too." I'm glad we got that out of the way; I felt bad for the way I'd been ignoring him after he told me he loved me in Woods Motel. I went there with him; he didn't toss me over his shoulder and force me to go. I just wasn't the kind of woman who was used to declarations of love. L.E. was the only man who'd ever said that to me. And then Mr. Ring. That was some dance card to carry dangling around my wrist into the hereafter.

Then Mr. Walker came into my classroom and asked the boys which one of them had written "Eat Me" on one of the bathroom stalls. Judy Goodman started crying because she said she didn't want to get eaten. None of the boys confessed.

It was about two o'clock—a beautiful spring day, the kind they write about in children's books and poems—and we went outside for recess. I was still a little dizzy and distracted from the day before: dressing up like the Pied Piper and trying to cut your wrist with a plastic flutophone can do that to you.

Other than that, it was a normal day. The day before the day I died.

— MAURICE —

Sometimes when he's finishing up work at North Ward—right after the final bell rings at 3:30 and the teachers stampede out of the place as fast as the students, before he has to switch over for his dinner shift at the Townhouse—Maurice thinks he hears someone trying to get his attention. A "pssst" in the hallway, near the glass display case in the middle of the hall. He clicks off the switch on his floor polisher and cocks his head this way and that, to hear where the sound is coming from. But no one's ever there, at least that he can see.

Just yards and yards of wooden floors and polished wood, his frayed extension cord whipping like a snake as he pulls it along behind him. His life is made up of extension cords: this one for the floor polisher, the one he uses to plug in the record player on top of the audiovisual cart that he drags along with him, the one on the *other* audiovisual cart that carries the school's lone television, brought into the classrooms on special occasions. Maurice likes to have hot-and-cold running sound all around him to keep him distracted whenever he's alone. He blasts the hallways with his movie soundtracks and original cast recordings: *West Side Story, Camelot, Sweet Charity,* even *Baker Street,* a musical about Sherlock Holmes that he got super cheap from the sales bin at Woolworth's. When he's tired of those, he'll switch over to the television and turn on *Sump'n Else,* the live after-school dance party that comes on from the Dallas station, and practice the latest dances as he's pushing his polisher along.

Sometimes he thinks that polisher is the only dance partner he'll ever have.

Nothing helps him forget Creola, as busy as he tries to keep himself. He's tried to turn Miss McLarty into his movie date, but it's just not the same. She doesn't cry at the sad parts or laugh at the silly parts the way Creola did. She doesn't gossip about the other teachers the way Creola did. She's not lonely the way Creola was. She's engaged to "Brad," and that's all she wants to talk about: shopping for her dress and planning her wedding and pink engraving or silver on the invitations? He's helping her out, nixing various color schemes and fabrics she comes up with for her bridesmaid dresses, clipping recipes for her reception from the *Good Housekeeping* magazines that his mother gets at home. He's even promised to teach her and Brad their first dance, to "Lara's Theme" or "Somewhere, My Love" from *Dr. Zhivago.*

But then he thinks how he and Creola could have been the *second* couple to hop up on the dance floor at the wedding and how he would have taught them an even *better* version of the dance to show-up the married couple, and everything comes falling back to earth again.

Just like Creola did that last day she was at school; the day no one knew would be her last. Even when Maurice drove her home to make sure she got there alright, he didn't know it would be the last time he would ever see her alive. She steadied herself against the car door when she got out at 815 Woodleigh Drive but waved him away when he offered to help her into the house.

So very much like Creola: *I can do this on my own. I have to do this on my own.*

At least she blew him a kiss when she went inside the house; that was Creola too. Something a character in a movie might do. He put out his palm to catch it—probably the first thing he's ever caught in his entire life without fumbling or getting hit in the face and his glasses falling off.

At least he has that one kiss to remember Creola by, even if it's a pretend one, carried to him on nothing but thin air.

— CLARKE —

WEDNESDAY, FEBRUARY 1, 1967

My cast is finally off my arm, split in two and added to the start of my new evidence collection. Now I'm keeping it between the mattress and box springs instead of under the bed. I took the two halves home with me because I didn't want to leave all those names that people had signed on my cast behind on the "cutting room floor." That's where Dr. Hill cut the cast off but also what they call "the parts they didn't use" in Hollywood. Dr. Hill used a buzz saw, and the plaster started melting and burning like your teeth do at the dentist. Like cotton candy that's cooked too long. Dust blew all over my face and made me look worn-out, like Daddy does now. He doesn't have any words left over to say to us at the end of the day when he gets home from work. I have more words than I know what to do with.

Now they're about a movie I'm actually going to be in, instead of just watching up on a screen. Well, I'll do that too. It's called *The McKinney Story*, and Rita's the one who found the article about it in the *Courier-Gazette*. It said a real, live movie director is coming to McKinney to make it because he wants to discover "fresh new talent" here. That's where I come in. I just tried out for it at the Ritz. Being there felt like something Mother would want me to do.

It was the first time I'd ever been inside during the middle of the week and the middle of the day with the lights on. It's definitely better in the dark. With all the lights on, you can see how the red velvet curtains have holes in them and how the wallpaper has big brown water stains and some of the ceiling tiles are missing. The stuffing's coming out of the seats and the springs are poking up; the backs of the seats are carved up with names of girls and boys who love each other or hate each other or do other things to each other. Everything smells moldy and syrupy. You can't see and smell all that when the lights are off.

The director, Mr. Barker, sat behind a big microphone at a table down front. His face was all wrinkly, and his nose was covered with broken blood vessels, like Daddy's. For your audition, all you had to do was walk up to his microphone and say your name out loud, plus pay him five dollars, which Rita gave me. Seeing you walk up to him lets Mr. Barker judge your stage presence; saying your name out loud lets him judge your speaking ability. I put my hand around the base of the microphone and really looked at everybody in the "house," then said my name: "Clarke Perkins." I made sure my K's were strong and clear and the S at the end of my name really popped off, which made it sound like *zzzzz*, which was not what I intended. I just got carried away.

I said my name so loud, and the sound from the microphone boomeranged so much, that it seemed to be coming from the walls and the ceiling, from the back of the theater and up in the balcony and everywhere. I closed my eyes when I heard it, partly to block out the kids who laughed, but mostly to pretend I was already in the movie and my voice was coming from up on-screen. People were paying their money to watch me instead of the other way around.

I kept my eyes closed even after my name stopped ringing, just to keep hearing it in my head. Then everybody quit laughing, maybe because they thought something was wrong with me. I know it myself. I know something's wrong. I know it's not normal to think about Mother all the time or boys or killers like I do. I know that the other kids make fun of me and want to leave me by myself, like the kid on crutches in *The Pied Piper* that we saw with Mother the very last time we were ever here in the Ritz with her. She started crying then, when the little boy tried to stick his crutches through the hole in the rocks. I know because I looked at her then, out of the sides of my eyes.

But what I should have told her was not to be sad; he was the only one who was safe, because his crutches kept him back. He was the only one who didn't get kidnapped by the Pied Piper. He could still be around for everybody. I wish I had told her then. I wish I had let her know that *I* was like the boy with crutches, not Corey, because I was still going to be around after everybody else was gone. After I did my plan.

— RITA —

She was going to buy the boys new outfits for their big events: a suit for Corey for his baptism and a new "mod" getup for Clarke, for making his movie. She'd never met two little boys from the same family who were more different: Corey had never cared about clothes at all, but now he wanted a blue suit with a matching clip-on tie. He kept saying he wanted to look "good for Jesus." And Clarke, who would change clothes every three hours if he could to keep germs off his skin, wanted hip-huggers and one of those stretchy "poor boy" ribbed-knit shirts with a zipper down the front. He was already so skinny Rita didn't think it was a good look for him; the poor little thing had no hips to hug! But she'd made such good strides with him she didn't want to break his heart over a pair of pants and a silly shirt. It had been so long since he'd been able to wear shirts he really liked because of the cast on his arm that she wanted to celebrate him getting back to normal clothes.

She wanted to celebrate everything getting back to normal.

Perkins was on his best behavior these days; he hadn't had a drop to drink since the accident. He hadn't emptied his bottles or thrown them out, but he hadn't touched them either, as far as Rita could tell. Instead, he'd switched to eating ice cream and chocolate-covered cherries all the time, to replace all that sugar in his system. She'd rather have a fat husband than a drunk one on the loose with a rifle, so she didn't say a word. She was an old pro at punching extra holes in leather belts at the shoe shop for men who were packing on a few extra pounds, and she could do it for her new husband.

But she'd do it at home, with a hammer and nail; she wanted to forget about how she'd met Perkins there, at the shoe shop, and start fresh. Occasionally Mr. Leif, the man she sold the shop to, would call her with a question, but as far as she was concerned, that was the past. Mr. Leif would share his print-out diets from Weight Watchers with her, even though it was against the rules for people who hadn't paid their dues—oh, Rita Cobb Perkins had paid her dues alright—but other than that, she didn't want to step foot in her old shoe shop or eat at Shaw's Café next door ever again.

Any business she had from now on, she'd take to the new Westgate Mall out by the high school. There was even talk they were going to build a new movie theater out there, but she'd believe it when she saw it. She didn't think she'd ever get Clarke to go anywhere but the Ritz to see a movie; he was tied to that place like a homing pigeon, but one thing at a time. She never thought they'd actually come around to liking her, but that was happening too. Maybe this *is* how things were supposed to be.

There'd been an odd moment when they were shopping at Bealls, out at Westgate. Rita had wanted something bright and springy, to celebrate everything that was good and new in their lives, but Clarke thought she should get a dark blue suit. He told her it was more "versatile" and she could get more use out of it. "Whatever happens," he'd said, in his little boy soprano. "You need to be prepared."

Shaken—between flashbacks to that disastrous wedding dinner at the Townhouse and her own hot flashes, she didn't know if she was going or coming most days—Rita honed in on a *light* blue dress. Turquoise, to match her wiglet case. She was going to celebrate. No child, not even her own, was going to tell her how to dress.

But when the day came for Corey's baptism at North Baptist Church, she was careful not to wear her pillbox hat. The last time she'd been there and worn that hat, one of her new sons had ended up floating, nearly dead, in a swimming pool. Now, her other little boy was going under in a different pool, getting baptized. When

Brother Joe Bob got ready to dunk Corey, covered in a white choir robe, Corey made the funniest look on his face, squeezing it tight and smashing shut his eyes to brace for the cold water. When he came back up, he flicked it all off, like a dog after a bath. He dried off and came to sit by them in one of the pews, now dressed up in his brand-new suit. Rita said, "See, that wasn't so bad, was it?" Corey even let his father squeeze his upper arm, until he realized it was the same one he'd shot, and shook him off.

At home after church, Perkins was making his special okra gumbo with salt pork, which he'd learned how to make as a cook in the army and also made for them on special occasions. Rita was in the bedroom getting out of her new dress, and in the distance, she heard Corey say "the okra looks like it has boogers." His father said back to him, "Well, since you like eating boogers so much, we know you'll like this." When they both laughed, Rita knew that father and son were, maybe, going to be okay.

Maybe *everything* was going to be okay.

Smiling to herself, she pulled out the top drawer of Perkins's dresser, where he kept the little velvet box that contained his only pair of cuff links, which she'd given him for a wedding present. Cuff links on a man like Perkins; she knew it was as silly as having a pill-box hat. But still, she wanted him to have a pair. Black onyx, with an L in gold on the right one, and an E on the left.

It was only then that she noticed that the pistol he always kept there—the one he'd left the army with, the one she'd warned him shouldn't be in a house with children—was gone.

— CLARKE —

Before I got to the movie set, I was deciding if I should wear my glasses or not, to see my cue cards if I got too nervous to remember my lines. Miss McLarty says the eyes are the windows of the soul, so I didn't want my glasses to get in its way.

But when I got to Finch Park, where we shot the movie, I found out I didn't have any lines. I just had a word: "Run!" And I didn't even get to say it by myself; I said it with a bunch of other kids. And the movie's not really a movie, just a "short." The director, Mr. Barker, doesn't even have a script, he just has words in his head. He's gone around the southern part of the country making the same movie so many times, since the 1940s, that he just closes his eyes, puts his thumb and forefinger on either side of his big spidery nose, then comes up with the lines. Line. Word.

"Run."

The very same thing I'd said to Corey when Daddy took us out to the farm and started loading his rifle.

In the movie, we all say it—actually, we yell it—after two crooks kidnap Bette Davis when she's just a little girl, and all the children in town find out where she is and "run!" to save her. Mr. Barker just has one big camera, so he can only shoot one thing at a time. But it always ends up pointing at the same thing. Trees. The parking lot. The concrete picnic tables. There aren't even any scenes like in real movies, just the kids who paid up, standing in a straight row, looking directly at the camera. And saying the same stuff over and over.

"Bette's been kidnapped! What do we do!"

"Let's go find her!"

First the big boys say it, then the little boys, then the girls. "Bette Davis! I'd hate to be in her place! Wonder what they'll do to her?" But the weird thing is nobody talks to each other, like you'd do in real life. You just say your line straight to the camera, which isn't a close-up, but very far away. And some of the kids laugh or smile or pick their noses while they do their lines or show off their clothes. They don't seem sad that Bette's gone.

Then we hear that Bette's parents have offered a thousand-dollar reward, so everybody talks about what they'd do with the money. Originally that's where I had my big line: "A thousand dollars! Gee whiz, that's a lotta dough," but Mr. Barker didn't like the way I said it, so he gave it to somebody else.

It's a stupid idea for a movie because Bette Davis isn't a little girl anymore; she's at least sixty years old. But I thought maybe if I told Mr. Barker how many of her movies I'd seen, he'd be impressed with me and give me a new line. A better line. More than just "Run!" So when we were on a break, while everybody else was just playing on the seesaws, I went up to him. I told him how much I liked *Hush . . . Hush, Sweet Charlotte* and *What Ever Happened to Baby Jane?* and how *The Nanny* was at the drive-in a while back but I missed it, and even how Rita sort of looks like the young Bette Davis.

I said all that, then stopped to catch my breath. He kept scratching his big drunk nose and finally said, "What the hell are you talking about, kid?"

"Bette Davis. The actress. How you made her the little girl who gets kidnapped. That's a great idea because it'll bring in the movie fans."

"Bette Davis? BETTY Davis. B-e-t-t-Y. I've been using that name for years, no reason to change now. It's all-American. *Bette* Davis? You mean you thought I meant the *actress*? Jesus. Hey, Patton, get the hell over here." He called the big guy who ran the camera. "Kid, tell him what you just . . ."

But I was gone. For the rest of the day, I hid as much as I could instead of wanting a new line or trying to stand out on camera. Mr. Barker had told us just to wear jeans and a tee shirt—"like normal kids"—but I had ignored him and worn my new hip-huggers and poor boy zip-down shirt. Now I regret it because it makes me stand out too much.

At least I took off my glasses so I couldn't see if Mr. Barker was still laughing at me.

— CREOLA —

There's a makeshift baseball diamond at Finch Park: a bunch of sand and grass and gravel, some old bags for bases, and a rickety old backstop behind it all made of rain-soaked wood with chicken wire stapled to it. A straight section in the middle, maybe ten, twelve feet high, seven or eight feet across, with two panels that angle out on either side of it. That's what is supposed to keep children and spectators safe from baseballs.

But what keeps them safe from old drunk directors who can't recognize a lonely child? *My* child?

I was in my familiar stooped position on top of that dilapidated baseball backstop—feet clenched on the top board for stability, my growing wings feathering out from my back for balance, shielding me. Not that anyone could have seen me anyway. But I could see Clarke. And I could see and hear Melton Barker saying, "What the hell are you talking about?"

At that moment, I wished I were a real bird, not just this half-creature that I've become. I wanted to have a beak and talons so I could attack him.

I see my kids more now that I'm dead than when I was alive.

Sometimes I think I'm a better mother now, dead instead of alive.

I want to protect them more, hide them in my sheltering wings.

But I can't. That's the biggest rule of all for being dead: whatever you want to do, you can't. Especially when your children are involved.

I want to see *The McKinney Story* live on-screen. Live in the *audience*, despite having had my own version of *The McKinney Story*.

(That's the title Clarke will always call it by, although it has a more official name, *The Local Gang in the Kidnapper's Foil*. In the future, it will even be listed on something called a website, along with dozens of other "itinerant" films that the director, Melton Barker, went barnstorming around the South to make from the '40s through the late '60s. I wish I could have been there to tell Clarke's new friend Paul, in the projection booth, to save the film; that it would one day be wanted for the National Film Directory at the Library of Congress.)

I was there at the Ritz the night they put up the marquee letters for *The McKinney Story*, along with the real movie they'll show after it to give the audience its money's worth. *The Brass Bottle* with Burl Ives and Tony Randall. They must own their own copy; they play it every time there's a special event, like the toy drive around Christmas.

Maurice was there that night too, watching *Alfie*, when they changed the marquee. Maurice still goes to the Ritz a lot, sitting up in the balcony along with teenage couples who are making out. He's that one lonely man up there, killing as much time as he can before he has to go home to his mother's house. Sometimes he falls asleep and starts snoring, and they have to wake him up when the last movie of the night is over, around 10:00 p.m. He'll still be rubbing his eyes, stretching, and yawning as they begin putting the theater to bed for another night. Money counted, floor swept, popcorn bagged; sometimes, they give Maurice the leftover popcorn at the end of the night.

I'm not making fun. I'm usually there too, just invisible, outside on the marquee, watching one of the high school boys on a ladder change the big red plastic letters to the next day's feature. I wish I could give them a hand; actually be useful for something besides just spying on people, envious that they're still alive, that they have jobs to do, places to go.

Maurice walked outside the theater as the RITZ sign made its final sputter of the night, a death rattle of neon. He crossed to his car, parked at an angle right off the courthouse. That late there are usually just a few cars left around the square. He'll be there the next night too for Clarke's movie. The boys like him, and I'm proud of that. I'm proud they say "hey" to him in the halls of J. L. Greer, when no one else does, just because he's the janitor. Or because he's the . . . other thing he is. I'm proud they don't judge; at least I taught them that before I . . .

I *what?*

Whatever happened, it involved Maurice. I remember that much; something happened at school, something bad. Suzanne had to read *A Wrinkle in Time* to the kids to calm them down afterward. I'm having my own wrinkle in time; I can't put everything together.

I remember seeing Maurice drop me off at home after school, pulling his car up next to the stenciled numbers on the concrete curb of our house: 8-1-5, in Day-Glo silver. The boys had spray-painted them last summer, so anyone could find their way home in the dark.

Maurice parked in a hurry; the car wasn't straight. I stumbled out of it, and Mr. Ring hopped out too to help me, but I waved him away.

That was the last time I saw him until my funeral.

I should have called him back, but it was too late. I should have let him come live with us in Plano, at the apartment for "young singles" he wanted so much, but it was too late for that too.

By the time I got home from school that day, it was too late for everything.

— CLARKE —

Most people would say *Alfie* was too grown-up for me and Corey to see, so I won't tell Miss McLarty on Monday that we saw it because she'll be upset. She'll say we shouldn't see "adult only" movies, even though I could make her feel better by telling her I didn't understand the "adult only" parts where Michael Caine looks straight out at the audience from the screen and talks about how he dates all these different women. He calls them "birds," which is what they call women in London, and Michael Caine dates a lot of them—old ones, young ones, married ones, even Shelley Winters. But then she starts dating somebody else, somebody younger, and he gets upset and winds up walking all alone on a bridge. Cher sings "Alfie" at the end of the movie, and I sang along because I know it from when I almost sang it for my *Peter Pan* audition, before I decided to go with "Edelweiss."

We probably won't even be at school on Monday if everything goes according to plan tonight at the premiere of *The McKinney Story*. Although I guess it's not really a premiere if there's just one showing of it. It's sort of like a premiere and a closing all at once.

With so many people watching, I knew it would be hard to sneak in Daddy's pistol, so I snuck it up to the balcony today during *Alfie*, like Lee Harvey Oswald snuck his rifle into the Texas School Depository before he shot Kennedy. The floor up there is so sticky nobody would be feeling around under the seats and find the gun by accident. Going up the stairs, I ran into Paul, the high school boy who runs the projector. "Hey, kid, haven't seen you in a while. Give up on the movies?"

I liked seeing him. He sort of looks like a McKinney version of Michael Caine but with pimples. "No, just . . . I've been busy making one."

Did I sound like I was bragging?

"The one tonight. The McKinney Story. I'm in it." I didn't tell him I just had one line. One word. In unison. "If you're working tonight, you'll get to see it."

"Wouldn't miss a chance to see *you*, little bud."

He put his hand on my neck and squeezed it. I got goose bumps, but I tried to act grown-up. He winked at me before he went back into his projection booth. "See ya 'round, Hollywood."

I blinked to remember Paul winking at me and thought I'd never been happier in my life, even with what I was about to do.

— CREOLA —

What's it all about, Alfie, indeed?

I think that was on my mind a lot my last twenty-four hours on earth. What's it all about, L.E.? What's it all about, Creola? Well, don't look at me for answers. If I had them, I wouldn't be asking the question. Life belongs only to the strong, and only fools are kind. Well, no more. I'm not going to let anything get in the way of leaving L.E. and taking the boys to Plano with me. Even if I have to call Altha to come pick us up and hear her say "I told you so" for the entire drive back.

That day, the day something happened at school, the day Maurice drove me home to make sure I got there okay, I unsteadily walked up the three concrete steps to the front porch. The house needed so much work: fresh paint, a new door to replace the one that never hung straight, new rolls of sod to replace the crabgrass that had taken over the yard, but that could all be L.E.'s problem. The boys and I had a brand-new apartment in Plano waiting for us; they had their own room to share, and I had a nice big bedroom all to myself. The back of the complex dipped down toward a creek, so the boys would have their crawdads to hunt down right outside the back door.

Eager to get a move on, even as sick as I felt, I went inside the house—and another woman was there, staring right back at me.

L.E. had already let Rita in, and I wasn't even cold in my coffin yet.

I wasn't even *dead* yet.

No . . . wait . . . it was just *me*, hanging on the wall. That oil painting of me, or at least the person I used to be. I knew she looked familiar. After our fight, maybe L.E. had put it up to say, "Remember
this? Remember her? Let's try again."

Hope springs eternal, doesn't it?

Have I said that before? Time's turning in on itself.

But I didn't want her to see what I was about to do, so I turned
her around, facing the wall.

Wait. Did I just think *what I'm about to do*?

What *was* I about to do?

I was about to take some aspirin, take a nap, then take the boys to
the drive-in that night to see a movie, our last night in McKinney.

That's all I was about to do.

— CLARKE —

They've put a red carpet outside the Ritz, just like at a real Holly-wood premiere, and they have spotlights aimed upward to criss-cross the sky. All the actors get to pose with the director, Mr. Barker, and you can buy your picture with him at the end of the movie for an extra $2.50. I hear Daddy introduce himself and thank Mr. Barker for giving me such a "life-changing opportunity. We can all use one of those."

When Daddy says that, he winks at me, but it just makes me think about all the blinking I have to do to remember things. Like what he did to Mother. What he did to Corey. What he did to Rita. What he did to me. I have to remember enough for four people, to remember what I have to do tonight.

"Oh, he's got a promising future alright." The last time Mr. Barker saw me he was laughing at me, but it's nice to hear anyway. I'm glad one of the last things Daddy will ever hear about me is something good, even if it's a lie.

Daddy has Corey and Rita go on into the Ritz and makes me stay behind. "Listen, son, I know I've scared you to death. I've scared myself. I'll make it up to you, I promise."

"You promise that all the time. You promise you'll get better. You promise you'll change." I couldn't believe I was talking back to him like that.

"I know, I know, but this time I really mean it. You have to be-lieve me. We'll go through the house together. We'll empty out all my bottles ..."

Then he runs out of words and starts blinking too. He puts his lips on top of my head to say something else. I think it's "Your Mumma would be so proud of you," but it's all mushed in with my hair and I can't tell. Then he goes inside to find Corey and Rita. I stay behind to go up to the balcony by myself.

I'm scared. I wonder if Lee Harvey Oswald felt the same way.

I go by the concession stand and pass Mr. Ring and Miss McLarty, who tell me "Congratulations," and Mrs. Angel, who gives me a sugar cookie even though you're not supposed to bring in food from the outside. So many people from this past year are here, people who've tried to help me since Mother died.

It's just two weeks until April Fools' Day, when she did it, so it's like she's been leading me to this night all along. All the times I saw her in the medicine cabinet mirror and the rearview mirror in the car, all the times I've seen her in my dreams, it's all been leading me to tonight. I walk up the stairs to the balcony, and it's like I'm walking toward her, tiptoeing past posters hanging on the walls of the old movies she liked so much.

I hear the hum and whir of the projection machine as it starts up, so I keep moving in its direction. I want to say hi to Paul, who's inside his booth, but I'm afraid he'll distract me from what I have to do, and I've got to pay attention for the end of the movie. I won't have a second chance. I keep on walking to the very top of the balcony. It's a little bit like I'm walking through fog, because you can smoke in the balcony so there are a lot of cigarettes going on. I don't like getting the smell of it on my opening-night outfit, but I don't have any choice. What I have to do, I can only do from up here.

The credits start, and all of the kids from Finch Park, where we shot the movie, come up on-screen in black and white, singing "London Bridge Is Falling Down" and playing like we're at a birthday party. A title comes on that says THE MCKINNEY STORY, and everybody starts screaming just to see themselves and the name of our town. You can look at yourself in a mirror all you want, but it's not the same thing.

I get sidetracked for a minute and can't look away, even though I feel around with my feet under the seat to make sure I'm in the right one that's hiding Daddy's pistol. I give it an extra kick, just to get it unstuck from all the gooey stuff on the floor.

On-screen, "BETTY Davis" is with her parents and friends, having a birthday party at Finch Park with hats and balloons and a cake on one of the concrete picnic tables. Just when the mother's knife starts to slice the cake, I stand up and move in front of the projector light. It's shooting out in a triangle shape from a cut-out square in the wall right above my head.

Suddenly it looks like the knife goes sticking into this big black shape like the Blob. Like *The McKinney Story* has suddenly turned into a horror movie. The Blob takes over Betty's party on-screen, and everybody in the audience boos. I see the Blob too, but I don't realize it's me. I keep looking at it until I move, then it moves, then I move again, and it moves, and then I know what it is. Me. I'm the Blob until I duck down to get out of the projector light and pick up Daddy's pistol from under my seat.

The light from the projector shows all the cigarette smoke and dust particles in the air, dust we breathe in all the time without knowing it, and I think it's not just dust in the light that I'm now seeing, it's me. That's what's carrying the movie from the projector to the screen, that beam of light. I'm floating in there with all the dust, back in time, to when we made the movie at Finch Park weeks ago. It's a movie machine, a time machine, a magic machine. But even something as magic as the movies can't take me back as far as I'd like to go, back to before Mother was dead or even further back than that, to whenever Daddy met Rita and started making his plan.

I have my own plan now, even if Daddy did say he was sorry.

It's not enough.

How many would be enough? Well, Charles Whitman killed sixteen people from the tower at the University of Texas in Austin, Richard Speck killed eight nurses in Chicago, and the two guys from *In Cold Blood* killed four people, an entire family. There's a name for that in arithmetic, where every number keeps doubling up: two becomes four becomes eight becomes sixteen.

In Daddy's pistol, I have six bullets but just one target.

I didn't know how I was going to use the gun until I saw Alfred Hitchcock's *The Man Who Knew Too Much* on *The Late Late Show* on Channel 11. In the movie, Doris Day and Jimmy Stewart have a little boy who gets kidnapped, but that's really just a "subplot" to the villains killing a foreign leader during a symphony concert. Doris Day is listening to it at the back of an auditorium, crying and thinking about her little boy and singing *Que Será Será* to him when the cymbals in the orchestra come crashing together. She figures out that's when the gun will go off, but nobody will hear it and the killer will get away with murder.

I'll just have to take my chances during *The McKinney Story* and hope there's something loud at the end, like music or applause.

CREOLA

My last night on this good earth, and the boys are making such a racket that I can't sleep. That's all I want, to just close my eyes, but my head is killing me. Pounding. Hot. I take some aspirin and think *Why not take an extra one or two to help my headache go away faster?*

I'm so scared and nervous about leaving tomorrow.

I can hear my heart beat, my head is so . . . what? Not congested, just . . . something's building up in it. My ears are red-hot, probably glowing. I feel like if I touched them, they'd start bleeding, the blood feels so close to the paper-thin surface.

I want to close my eyes, but when I do, I see all the veins inside my eyelids. They're throbbing, and that makes my stomach start churning and I want to throw up. But when I bend my head over the commode, nothing comes out. My whole body is turning inside out and exiting my throat, but nothing's there.

I have to pull it together, though, and get us to the drive-in, no matter how crummy I feel. I've promised the boys, and you can't break a promise to such impressionable, sensitive young children. They don't know we're going to Plano tomorrow, so I'll need everything good I can throw at them to make up for taking them away from their little friends. Maybe the drive-in will make me feel better. The dark outside will be good for my eyes. Nothing bright. The fresh night air, the spring air from a dark, cloudless sky with our car window down for the speaker.

Fresh air. I want to gulp it down, drink it by the gallon to keep from throwing up.

I load the boys up in the car. Clarke sits between my legs to help me drive since my head is still spinning. He watches his father drive; he's a quick learner, and thank God he gets us there in one piece.

Before the boys were born, there had been a terrible accident out by the drive-in, in all that flat emptiness. The road goes on for miles and miles out there, and nobody's around to get in your way. No cars, no people, no husbands. Nobody was around to get in the way of that carful of drunk high school boys, who took the corner too fast. They'd been racing through town, faster and faster, egged on by the promise and wonder of the night, past the point of stopping. Their car flew out of control and smashed into a telephone pole. One of them, the youngest, was thrown across the field; the police determined the quickness of his death by the look of surprise on his face. The other boys stayed in the hospital for the summer, their bodies slowing knitting back together. Of course, I had taught them all, so I took them flowers and read to them. *Stuart Little. Charlotte's Web. Danny Dunn and the Homework Machine.* Children's stories for boys who had almost died, who'd had to grow up much too fast. Who would never be children again.

The town council voted to hang traffic lights at the very spot they crashed so nobody would ever crash there again. On our way to the drive-in for our very last time, we stopped to watch those lights, blinking on and off, rocking on their cables in the wind, and I thought, *Lights won't do the trick, not by themselves.*

But what *will* do the trick?

Tammy and the Bachelor. That's what. How perfect. I couldn't have planned it any better myself. It was the movie I'd seen on my first date with L.E., and now things have come full circle. Things are finished.

We get there and find a good spot; we practically have the place to ourselves. It's early in the season—it doesn't get dark until quite late—and there isn't much of a crowd. For a minute, I think maybe I should use the telephone in the concession stand—that little stucco building that smells of fried things, corny dogs and onion

rings and French fries—and call Mr. Ring to join us, to make up
for the week, but then I think those smells would make me sicker. I
should have let him take me to the doctor like he'd wanted to. I've
never felt worse in my life. But it's right that I'm alone with the boys
for my last night.

My last night in McKinney, I mean.

The nauseating smell of fried food, the only thing standing between me and salvation.

We hear the *Tammy* song through the metal speaker that hooks
onto our rolled-down window, and I begin to feel a little better.
This night air is doing the trick, or maybe it's just the movie. Debbie Reynolds and Leslie Nielsen. (Years later, the boys will think he
only came into being with those silly *Airplane* movies. They won't
remember that the first time they saw him was with me, a million
years ago, the night I left them.)

I smile watching the movie and wish the boys had been awake to
see that. It's been a long time since they've seen me smile. I remember smiling—beaming really, a smile that was so ecstatic it was
about to fly off to the moon—when I watched the movie that first
time with their future father. I thought I was as lucky as Tammy
walking through those elegant French doors into a house that was
new to her. I thought no moment could ever be so bright.

I thought I could change him.

Now I know I can't, as I sit there at the drive-in, watching the final credits up on the screen.

Finally, we get home. Clarke wakes up grouchy and helps me
carry Corey in. Corey looks at me more strangely than he's ever
looked at me before. I put the boys to bed, and he keeps looking at
me like that, not saying a word.

I stay up late, finishing the goodbye note that I will leave for L.E.
in the morning after he's gone for work. I've been carrying it around
with me for days, writing a bit here and a bit there whenever I had
a spare minute, to tell him the story of our lives together. The "that
was then, this is now." Some written on a page torn out of my grade

book with my red pen writing across all those tiny little squares in green meant for numbers and letters and check marks instead of goodbyes. Some on a sheet of stationery from Woods Motel, from the night I was there with Maurice. Plain, cheap white stationery with their logo of a girl in a modest 1950s bathing suit, diving into a pool.

Now, I decide to write about our final movie in McKinney, on what is, to me, the most precious paper of all: the stationery the boys bought me last Christmas. It's a soft pink with a border of red roses and green thorns at the top. The note L.E. will find when he comes home for lunch tomorrow, telling him that I'm starting a new life without him, that I have the boys with me and he can never get them back. I've never been more excited, or more scared, to put pen to paper, and I don't stop until I've written everything down.

By the time I'm finished, my fingers are burning from holding the pen so tightly, but that is that. It is finished. I don't need to sign my name; the only thing I want to sign are divorce papers.

L.E. will know who it's from, and he'll know why.

— CLARKE —

At the Ritz now, I play like I'm the character in *The Man Who Knew Too Much*, the man who's going to kill somebody while everybody else is just watching what's up on stage.

Except I'm "The *Boy* Who Knew Too Much."

On-screen, Betty's parents bring out a giant box that she unwraps, and there's a pretty pink bicycle inside. She decorates the white basket on its handlebars with flowers left over from her party. Then they kiss her goodbye so she can go ride her new bike. I sneak out of the back row as Betty goes pedaling through Finch Park. The sun's streaming through the trees and hitting her, but then something else does too—the kidnapper. He sneaks out from behind one of the trees and grabs her, and the camera cuts to the wheels of her new bicycle just spinning and spinning on the ground, even though no one's riding it anymore.

You hear Betty scream in the woods, and then nothing, and then she disappears.

I disappear too as I slip into place behind the red velvet curtains that separate the balcony from the little hallway that goes to the projection booth. I hide in them like I did when we were in *Peter Pan* and I'd peek out from behind the curtains to look at the audience.

On-screen, the children of McKinney hear that Betty has been kidnapped, and her parents beg us to find her, saying they'll give us a thousand dollars if we do. The older kids start looking for her first, beginning with where they find her bicycle tossed over by the side of the trail. Its wheels are still spinning.

So am I. I'm getting dizzy inside the curtains.

I open them just a crack to get some fresh air and start thinking about how much I want to be an actor; how much I like dressing up in costumes and playing like I'm somebody else. Like I was Michael in *Peter Pan* and got to wear a nightgown and footy pajamas. Like how I was almost a go-go girl in our Beatles skit at school until something bad happened and I was gone-gone instead. I thought of Miss McLarty letting me be Joseph in the Christmas pageant at school and how I came up with my own line when I see the baby Jesus in the manger: "Allah be praised." I thought of Dr. Hill giving me my cast on my arm so I could be the One-Armed Man. I even thought of Aunt Altha giving me mother's dress so I could put it on and pretend to be her.

I'm distracting myself. I've got to focus.

Back in Finch Park, the older kids find a trail where a body has been dragged through pine needles, and they follow that to an old shack in the woods, which in real life is the log cabin home of Collin McKinney, who founded our town. They peek through the window and see Betty tied up there, and the kidnapper writing a ransom note.

In the audience, everybody starts clapping and yelling, "Get him, get him!" They mean the kidnapper, but their chant takes over the "dialogue" on-screen and I start thinking they mean Daddy, because it's the only thing I can hear anymore.

"Get him. Get him."

The older kids tell the rest of us that they've found Betty, and it's time for all of us to rescue her from the shack. They give the command and we "Run"; my one word that blends in with all the other kids, so loud it's the loudest noise in the movie so far. There's no music, but it sounds like music anyway. It sounds like cymbals crashing as we start chasing the kidnapper through Finch Park.

It's time.

I peep out from the curtains and know there's only one victim. There's only ever been one victim, no matter how mad or upset everybody else has made me along the way. There's only one person Mother wants me to get even with. There has to be "just cause" for doing something like this, and I have it.

I have Daddy.

I have an eye for an eye and a tooth for a tooth, except my eyes are crying and my teeth are grinding and biting the inside of my cheeks.

And now, I have the back of Daddy's head in my sights, downstairs and near the front of the theater.

— CREOLA —

I finish up my letter to L.E. and put down the pen on my bedside table, which is still splashed with white paint. The upper part of my forefinger is stinging where that red ink pen has been resting for hours, rubbing a blister. It feels like the skin has opened up and let the ink into my bloodstream, it burns so much. I want to go to the bathroom to hold it under cold water, but I don't think I have the strength left to run the faucet. This letter has taken everything out of me.

I feel so hot. Burning hot. I just want cold.

Corey comes into my bedroom, shuffling his feet so slowly from the kitchen and down the hall. Walking so carefully so he doesn't step on the splinters of wood that are still on the floor, from where I took an ax to the bedroom furniture. Stepping over those pieces of wood as if it were the most natural thing in the world. When we're at our new apartment in Plano, he won't have to step over anything. He's holding out a glass of chocolate milk to me with both hands and not spilling a drop.

"Here Momma, drink this. It will make you feel better. I don't want you to be so sad all the time."

"It will all be over soon, I promise."

"I don't want you to be so sick. I'm sorry we make so much noise and upset you. I promise we'll be better from now on, so you can get better too."

"What a good little boy you are. Momma's littlest angel."

He kisses me goodnight and pads back to bed.

I want to go with him and scoop up both boys and drive us to

Plano right now, but I'd be a menace on the road, the way I feel. The way my hands are shaking. The way my whole body is shaking. If it comes down to it, I can get Maurice to drive us there tomorrow, in my car, which is still sitting in the school parking lot.

It's so quiet in my bedroom except for the tick of the alarm clock that will wake me up tomorrow morning. I turn it around so I can see the time and realize tomorrow is already here. Tomorrow is today. It's 2:00 a.m., and L.E. still isn't home. He's probably with Rita, doing "inventory." I just have five hours until I have to get up for school . . . and then I remember I'm not going back to North Ward tomorrow. Today. Whenever. I'm taking the boys to Plano.

We're starting our new lives.

I look up from the bed—just barely, any movement sets off one of those Tilt-A-Whirls in my head, that L.E. promised me—and see my face in the big mirror that's over the bureau. Even in the dark, with just the moonlight coming in from the windows, my eyes look so huge, like one of those giant-eyed Keane paintings. With fear? From feeling so sick? From wearing my eyes out writing that letter in the near dark? Maybe all of the above.

I hear sounds from outside—night birds, trucks ambling along the highway that's on the other side of the Marshalls' yard behind us. The early morning world of McKinney, Texas, is already waking up; life goes on, and soon mine will too. Away from this place. That highway is the only thing between me and freedom.

If only I could get rid of this headache! There was a brief respite during *Tammy*, but now my eyestrain has made it worse than before. I don't think I've ever been in as much pain since I gave birth to the boys: like my head is going to split wide open and give birth to a third child ripping out of my skull if I don't do something.

So I take some more of the pills Dr. Hill has given me and close my eyes.

I think I hear L.E. tiptoe in at some point during the next few hours. He has so much practice at taking off his shoes by the front door and sneaking down the long hallway to our bedroom; he knows which spots to avoid to keep the floorboards from creaking. He knows exactly which spot in the hall to steady himself on, by the little cut-out phone caddy, so he can give the floor a chance to settle. He's practiced at sliding in and out of his clothes and sliding under the covers, so he barely makes a sound. But I seem to have developed bat ears now; most wives in my position do, at some point or another.

I can hear everything, even if I can't rouse myself to respond to it.

In the morning, I'm vaguely aware that he gets the boys dressed himself—Clarke wants to wear his "hobo" pants from an old Halloween costume. He says all the kids are dressing up since it's April Fools' Day, but L.E. won't let him. He says no son of his is going to school looking like a bum; he remembered all the days he'd gone to school in Vermont and he *did* look like a bum, but it had been no costume. It's all he had to wear. So no child of his was going to turn it into a joke and look like he didn't have decent clothes to wear or parents who didn't care enough to dress him properly.

Before they leave the house, Corey looks at me and says, "I thought you were going to get better. I'm sorry. I just wanted you to not be so sick all the time."

And somehow, I know those are the last words—while I'm on this earth, at least—that I will ever hear him say. And I also know I'm too sick to say anything back to him or Clarke, not even "I love you."

It's too much effort to talk; it's too much effort to open my eyes. L.E. asks me if he should have Dr. Hill come over, but I shake my head *no*. At least that's what it must look like to him; I think I'm just shaking and he interprets that as a *no*.

Maybe that would have made all the difference.

L.E. calls my principal, Mr. Walker, instead, to tell him that they'll need a substitute for me.

The next call L.E. makes on that same phone, four or so hours from now, will be for an ambulance, but by then, it will be too late.

– L.E. –

"Creola?"

He walked in the front door and immediately knew that his house had never been quieter, not even when no one was in it. And he knew Creola *had* to be in it; she'd been too sick that morning to leave.

"Creola?"

He didn't rush because he was thinking, *Has she really left me? After all her threats?* and he didn't know if he wanted that to happen or not.

He was suddenly afraid. For one of the first times in their marriage, he was afraid.

He walked down that hallway as slowly as when he had snuck back in the night before, careful not to wake anyone up.

He sensed something back there, a feeling of hot and cold coming out the door at the same time.

Before he saw Creola, he saw a wet puddle by the side of the bed, vomit or something.

He saw pills and empty pill bottles and their white plastic caps spread on the chenille bedspread.

He saw his wife, half hanging over the bed, face down, and he ran to her—three or four giant steps—and he knew she was dead even before he even touched her. He didn't feel any breath coming out of her, but he was barely breathing either so what did he know?

"Cre, oh my God, wake up, wake up . . ."

He pulled her body back onto the bed ever so gently, as gently as he had touched her the first time they made love; he held her body in one hand as he tried to dial the phone on the bedside nightstand with his other.

His hands shook so much he had to dial three times before he could get the call through. Never had his big, thick fingers—so perfect for thumping Corey or Clarke on the head—gotten in the way so much. But once he got the call through, he couldn't remember his address. His mind had gone blank, and he found himself rattling off numbers from the three or four other houses he'd lived in along the way—1611, 1332, even 719, Rita's address. The right number, 815, 815 Woodleigh Drive, just wouldn't come out. His own address flew out of his head and so many other wrong addresses flew in because he knew it was no use calling anybody, she was dead.

On the phone, the operator kept asking, "What happened? What happened?"

But he didn't know. He wasn't thinking about what happened.

He was thinking, *Oh sweet Jesus Lord, what am I gonna do? How am I gonna tell the boys that their Mumma is gone?*

He sat there, her face up against his, kissing and kissing her gray-streaked hair and trying to warm up her body and feel any last little whisper of air coming out, but there was nothing.

And then there was something.

An envelope. A letter, tossed onto the bed alongside all those empty pill bottles.

He picked it up and read; his thoughts switched to *How am I ever going to let the boys read this and hate me as much as their Mumma did in her final minutes?*

His fist tightened up and formed into a ball around those pages, but he couldn't throw it away. He couldn't destroy what amounted to his wife's last will and testament. He couldn't get rid of the letter, but he couldn't look at it again. Ever. But he couldn't leave it for the boys to find. And then find out about him.

So he smoothed out the pages, folded them and stuck them back

inside the envelope. Where to put it? The boys were always sneaking around in their parents' bedroom, digging in drawers and clos-
ets, trying to find secrets; they could find anything.

And then he spied the perfect hiding place: his Ponderosa dream
house. L.E. lifted the roof off and put the envelope inside along with
all his other secrets.

Let the boys think whatever they wanted about him; what a
bad father he was, a bad husband. He could take it. But they would
never be allowed to know that their Mumma killed herself. As long
as L.E. was alive, they would never know that. The letter didn't say
that, not exactly; it just said she was leaving him, but how else could
he interpret all those empty pill bottles all over the bed cover, all
the hate in those pages?

Such a goodbye, such a Fuck You. How could she do that to her
very own children?

Let them hate him but never know enough to hate her because
of what she had done her last day on earth. Which he had caused.

— CLARKE —

From up in the balcony, behind an opening in the curtains, I'm pointing the pistol at the back of Daddy's head down below.

I don't hear anything except the noise on-screen. And in the Ritz. Everybody's cheering because the older kids have found Betty inside the log cabin. They're untying her and rubbing her wrists and ankles to bring her back into circulation. They're putting her on their shoulders to bring her back to her parents. Mr. Barker's camera is circling around and making Betty look like she's spinning around in slow motion, and it's the most beautiful thing I've ever seen.

Betty's finally free.

And now I can be too.

I aim the pistol and hold it firm and steady with both hands against the kick I know will be coming.

That's when I see myself up on-screen, in a close-up. It's like my smile is something they did in editing, it's such a surprise. I forget I don't like my teeth and the big gap between the two front ones, and I smile back at the version of me that's smiling on the screen.

And then someone comes running at my knees and knocks me down inside the curtains. The curtains come down with me as I'm tussling with something I can't make out that's beating on me from the outside of the red velvet while I'm trying to dig out from inside.

It's Corey, hissing at me, trying to find the opening in the curtains. "Don't do it! Don't do it!"

"What are you doing? Get away! You're gonna get hurt," I whisper at him, still trying to be quiet, still trying to carry out my plan.

"No," he snaps back. "I read your scrapbook. You've got it all wrong."

The heavy curtains are soaking up all the noise we make, and the clapping and cheering in the theater are covering up the rest as Corey and I fight for the pistol. "Get out of the way! Daddy killed her! Mother! He almost killed you. Now he's just getting what he deserves."

"NO! I'm telling you . . ."

"I'm telling *you*. He gave her pills, so he could be with Rita! He's got blood on his hands!"

"No he doesn't. I do. I'm the one who gave her pills. *I'm* the one who killed her."

The final credits from *The McKinney Story* are rolling up on-screen, and our names are there, but I'm missing all of it because I'm trying to untangle myself from the curtains. Trying to get Corey off me. Trying to understand this outrageous thing that Corey just said that makes no sense, just like me thinking I could shoot Daddy and make the pain go away. And that would make Mother go away. I don't know which thing I'm crying about more.

Corey's crying too, like everything he's held in for a year is finally pouring out. "I killed her. After *Mary Poppins*. I wanted to make her better, but I killed her. It's all my fault."

"Corey, you've gone nuts. Daddy killed her. You're all mixed up. Everything's gone crazy."

Downstairs, they're playing a Looney Toons cartoon before they start showing *The Brass Bottle*. There's so much noise with people leaving and laughing and the cartoon playing that nobody can hear us. Only a few people are still left in the balcony anyway.

"You don't know everything like you always think you do! You don't know what I did, that last night. After Tammy. After *Mary Poppins*."

"What does Mary Poppins have to do with it?"

"She gave me the idea. A spoonful of sugar helps the medicine go down."

I'm getting scared again. I don't want to hear anything else. Daddy did it. I know it. Mother told me, in my dream. She wouldn't lie to me.

"Mary Poppins is a movie. She's not real. She's not a person."

On-screen now, *The Brass Bottle* is starting, and I know Daddy and Rita will be looking for us, but I'm thinking back to when Mother took us to see *Mary Poppins* in Dallas. Julie Andrews and Dick Van Dyke sang and danced with penguins, and men with sooty faces climbed up chimneys, and a poor old lady fed the birds.

And Corey had a seizure. A bad one.

"Mary Poppins said a spoonful of sugar helps the medicine go down, that's how Mother gave me my medicine, in a glass of Bosco with sugar stirred up in it, so that's how I'd give *her* some medicine. She was so sad and sick all the time, I thought if my medicine helped me, wouldn't it help both of us?"

"Corey, *what did you do?*" I've finally got the curtains off us, and I'm trying to pull him back into a seat so I can make sense of this. But all I can see in my head is us at *Mary Poppins* when Corey had a seizure and threw up his popcorn and Coke on everybody.

I want to throw up too; everything's getting mixed up. Mother and Mary Poppins and Tammy and Rita and a new lady coming in to take care of us, when the other lady dies. They're all the same person.

"Sorry sorry sorry," Mother had said at *Mary Poppins*, to the people around us.

"Sorry sorry sorry," Corey had said to me and Mother, and kept saying it, crying too, when we walked out of the Majestic Theater in Dallas. It was a foggy night outside—I looked for the bird lady, to give her her tuppence—and I could tell something was different. Something was broken.

I was embarrassed by Corey, even though I hated myself for it.

I hated myself for everything. For this whole past year. For what I thought. For what I did. For what Corey's saying *he* did. "I'm sorry, I'm so sorry. I just wanted to make her feel better. I didn't want to make her die."

"Corey, *what did you give her?* Is that why she was so sick the next day and didn't go to school?"

"I don't know. I think so. We got home from *Tammy*, and that's when . . . that's when I did it. I crushed up some of the blue pills she took and some of the pink pills I took. I mixed 'em together in some Bosco. Seven pills, for as old as I was. One pill for every year. That's how many years I'm gonna have to spend in hell, to be punished."

Corey's never said that many words in his whole life. He's never cried that much in his whole life.

Just then, Paul, from the projection booth, comes into the balcony. He's smoking a cigarette in one hand and blowing smoke rings, and in the other, he's twirling a big flashlight like a baton. Doing tricks with it, aiming its beam right in my eyes. "Hey, Hollywood, good job, but they're looking for you downstairs. I'm the search party. S-O-S. S-O-S."

With every letter, he flicks the light on and off: first aiming it up from under his face like a candle inside a jack-o'-lantern, then shining it in our faces. On-off, on-off. Like that traffic light swinging on its cable out by the drive-in. There's too much going on at once. Too much to think about. Too much to remember. Too many places to be.

Paul's blinking flashlight makes Corey start shaking, like his nerves are suddenly going on and off like the light.

Another seizure. Just like at *Mary Poppins*.

"Stop it. I'm getting sick," Corey is trying to say to Paul, but his voice is whispery and so up-and-down and back-and-forth, like he's trying to keep from throwing up, that nobody can hear him but me.

I grab his body, to keep his shakes from exploding. Now I don't care who hears us. I yell at Paul, "Go get somebody! Help!" Paul stamps out his cigarette on the carpet, then runs down the stairs. I hold Corey even tighter. "Shhhh, shhh, it'll pass . . ." I think that's what Mother used to say to him; I can't remember anything I'm supposed to do.

"It's all my fault. I didn't mean to . . . I swear I didn't . . ."

"You're just a kid. You didn't know." Am I really saying that to the person who killed my mother? I can't believe it, not after all this. After everything I've gone through and thought this year. After I've brought a gun into the Ritz and almost . . .

Above us, through the cutout in the wall for the projector, I can hear the film strip start flapping around because Paul isn't there to switch over to the next reel. A plastic thwacking sound every time it makes a complete turn. There's nothing but pure white light pouring onto the screen now, and everybody downstairs starts yelling.

"Hey, wake up! Fix the movie, asshole! We want our money back!"

Daddy and Rita run into the balcony now, and I think they're going to start yelling at us too, just like the kids downstairs. Mr. Ring and Miss McLarty and even Mr. Barker, the movie director, come running in with them. I hear Paul in his booth above us, trying to get the movie back on track. It's playing on the screen again, but now he's pushed the wrong button or something and it's running backwards. Burl Ives is getting sucked back into his brass bottle, and a cloud of smoke is pulling back in after him.

"What the hell happened?" Daddy's yelling, as he squeezes into our aisle. "This shitass place should be condemned. Making children sick." He grabs Corey and holds him, then sticks the edge of his hand into Corey's mouth so he can't bite his tongue. Corey's knees are jerking up and down against the concrete floor, and his whole body is vibrating.

"I'm here now, I'm here, we're all here," Daddy whispers to Corey. "It's your angel disease. Just let it pass." Now Daddy's crying too, except his tears are going onto Corey's head and his big scar, from where I flung him against the edge of the couch.

Daddy reaches toward me and I think he's going to slap me for causing Corey's seizure, but he just squeezes his hand on my shoulder and pulls me into a group hug with Rita. The four of us are so heavy piled up around Corey that he doesn't have any more room to shake. He finally stops, then looks at us like he can't quite remember what just happened.

"Give him room, give him room to catch his breath. There's my boy. There's my good little angel," Daddy says.

Rita wipes the snot and tears off of Corey's face with the lapel of the new dress she bought.

Nobody knows what to say now except for Mr. Barker, but I think he's just saying it to make us all laugh. Cuss words around children do that. "Betty Fucking Davis. Gotta hand it to ya, kid. You're one of a kind. You see the close-up I gave ya at the end? Next time I make this crappy movie, I'm gonna change her name, in honor of you."

I guess it's a compliment, but it makes me . . . I don't know. Sad? The movie's over, Corey's still sick, Mother's still dead, Daddy's *not* dead, and nothing's like it was supposed to be. Nothing in the past twelve months is like it was supposed to be.

Mr. Ring slides into the row in front of us. "Corey, we can't have you getting hurt too, like Clarke did at the pool. Like your mother did, out at the playground. I can't take much more!"

Now Miss McLarty chimes in too, talking to all of us, like at a parent-teacher conference. "Oh, that was the scariest thing I've ever seen. Makes me think maybe I've chosen the wrong career. To see a fellow teacher laid out like that . . ."

Daddy looks up from Corey. "What the hell are you talking about?"

Miss McLarty looks confused; even in the dark, I can see it. She looks at Mr. Ring like *Did I say something wrong?*

But she keeps talking, and everything she says turns into a movie. Something that can't be real. Something I'm watching from some other balcony. "Well, the accident . . . out on the playground? I still feel so guilty about it. If I hadn't been yacking away . . . if she hadn't been turned around and looking at me instead of where she was going . . . then she wouldn't have run into that tether ball."

Now Daddy's getting mad again. "What accident? What tether ball?"

"Well, the one that knocked her out," Miss McLarty says. They're laughing downstairs at the movie, but nobody's laughing up here. "I thought you knew. Didn't she tell you what happened?" She looks at Mr. Ring, "I thought you told him."

He looks back at her and all of us. "I thought *you* told him."

"*Nobody* told you?" Miss McLarty looks like she's about to get as sick as Corey just was. "We were out on the playground and she got hit, and I guess her brain started bleeding so bad . . . wait . . . is it bad, or badly?"

Badly, I would have said, if I could talk just then. But I couldn't. Nobody could.

— CREOLA —

I feel like I'm getting knocked in the head all over again.

Nobody told *me*, either.

Creola on the playground with a tether ball, like in some demented, real-life version of *Clue*? It knocked me out and I didn't remember? A silly playground accident and . . . I didn't kill myself? How could that be? I wrote a letter. A goodbye letter. I took pills. Too many pills. How could I . . . But maybe I took them to make the headache go away and *I* just went away instead. Maybe the tether ball just did the work for me, that I was too cowardly—too afraid—to do myself. Maybe . . .

I don't know.

It was the perfect storm—something they'll have in the future— of being a teacher and being an unhappy wife and being a not-perfect mother and wanting to leave everything behind, not be *tethered* to so much sadness anymore, even if it meant leaving the boys.

But what kind of mother would do that?

A very sick and sad one, like I had become.

Maybe that damn tether ball hit the exact part of my brain where memories reside. Maybe I didn't tell anyone about the accident because there wasn't anyone to tell at the very end. I never told L.E. because he wasn't home that night. I didn't tell the boys because I didn't want them to worry. Maybe I didn't *want* to remember myself and know that it was all going to be over so very soon. I knew my hours were already trickling down, just like the blood in my brain.

Just like the memory comes back to me—not a trickle, but a deluge.

It's a beautiful spring day. Blue sky. Green leaves. Solid brown earth. That first sweet-and-sour smell of sweat on children, when they can get out and really play in the sun after months of being cooped up.

I'm out on the playground with Suzanne, admiring her rust-colored poor-boy top and thinking maybe I should buy one too, after I get to Plano. Throw out all those boring teacher dresses I have, those prim-and-proper outfits, and really make myself over. Get a new hairdo. Do something different to celebrate my freedom. I'm thinking how lucky Suzanne is to still be free. To be just starting out. I was like her once.

My students call me over to the tether ball pole; they want me to referee!

I'm barely taller than they are, ten-year-olds; I feel as if I've shrunk so much this last year, all the trouble with L.E. eating me up alive. My clothes just hang off me now. Maybe I'll start filling out again once I get free of all this. Altha would love nothing more than to fatten me up.

I get close enough to the tether ball pole to see that the silver paint is flaking off and layers of rust from underneath are peeping through. I'm close enough to see that the rope the ball is attached to is gray. It's left out there on the playground year-round, through every kind of weather. Rain, sleet, snow; tornadoes of love. That rope is always there, fraying bit by bit.

I'm about to tell the kids to be careful; my mouth is open.

Just then Suzanne asks me something. I think it's, "But if there's *just one thing* that makes a great teacher, what is it?"

She's got a steno pad out, eager to record my every precious word. Looking for lessons, even out on the playground. I turn toward her, teaching until the very end, and that's when it happens.

I get hit in the back of the head by a tether ball.

Black-and-white leather, gridded off in triangles like that air raid sign Clarke is so obsessed with. All that pressurized air inside, smacking into my skull harder than I've ever been hit before. The back of my head, the side of my head, that flat plane of skull and skin right next to my right eye socket—it feels like the ball hits me everywhere at once. In all the anger L.E. will have when he finds out I've left him, he couldn't have hit me that hard.

I feel it for just a second—I think I even hear something crack— and then I don't feel anything at all. I don't feel myself hitting the ground; I don't feel all those hands lifting me up—Mr. Walker, the principal; Maurice, finally getting his hands on me just like he wanted to at Woods Motel; some of the bigger boys who will drop out before they even finish high school (size and brute strength all they have going for them, and all they ever will).

I don't wake up until I'm back in my classroom and my leg starts hurting. My eyes flicker open; I look down and see a big run in my stockings, a new pair I had put on fresh just that morning. A cascade of blood has already ruined them from where my left knee must have hit a rock or something; the dried blood has practically glued the stocking to my leg. Maurice is spraying Bactine right into the wound, right through my stockings, and it's burning. And smelling. That's what brings me back to consciousness.

I slowly take in more and more, starting small and working my way up: my bloody stockings, Maurice kneeling at my feet as if he's proposing, my battle-scarred desk with the little apple from Suzanne already drying up on the corner. And everyone, my students included, staring back at me.

I gather from their faces that something bad has happened, but I tell them I'm fine; I just need a drink of water from the fountain out in the hall. But when I try to stand up, I wobble. I guess something bad really has happened.

Somebody asks—I couldn't tell you who, I can't make out individual voices—if I want an ambulance or a doctor.

How ridiculous. I teach fifth graders. I'm not made of glass. "Just let me rest for a few more minutes, and I'll be fine."

All the students are looking at me, clustered around my desk. Judy Goodman is crying. Judy Goodman cries at the drop of a hat, usually while trying to explain that she has a thyroid condition and that's why she hasn't done her homework.

They shouldn't see their teacher like this, so I put on a brave face for them. "Miss McLarty, why don't you read to them while I just rest my eyes for a few more minutes?"

I hear her read the opening words from *A Wrinkle in Time*, not knowing that it will be the last book I ever hear. (Well, I'll hear some words from the Bible at my funeral, but I won't really *hear* them. They'll just be white noise.)

Suzanne clears her throat and starts, "It was a dark and stormy night."

And I think—then *and* now—so *that's* how it starts, this children's book Clarke will come to love so much and reread once a year, even into adulthood. I thought that was a joke, that opening sentence. I didn't remember the book really started that way. Just look it up if you don't believe me. "It was a dark and stormy night." I promise.

My "few minutes" must have stretched because by the time I open my eyes again, the three weird sisters, Mrs. Whatsit, Mrs. Who, and Mrs. Which, are well along on their journey, and so am I. The children in the book, Meg and Charles Wallace, so much like my little Clarke, are looking for their father on some other distant planet, and I'm looking for . . . what? The three o'clock bell has rung. But for once, the children aren't racing away. They linger behind to make sure I'm okay.

Of course, I tell them, although I'm not really so sure myself.

My head has never hurt so much in my life.

Maurice volunteers to drive me home; his hands are as shaky as mine would have been, putting the keys in the ignition. If only he had stayed to make sure I was as okay as I said I was. But I'm not blaming him; I can point to my own litany of "what ifs" and "if on-lys" as well.

That night, I take the boys to the drive-in and then I write a letter; I cry some, and then I try to sleep.

I *think* I remember the boys kissing me goodbye that next morning, but it's more a memory I *think* I should have, an important one, maybe the *most* important one.

Could I have known that then? Yes. Somehow, I did. Somehow, I knew that is the last time that I will ever see them, at least while I'm still breathing, even if it is through eyelashes that are almost glued shut with tears and sleep. I hear their footsteps go down the hall one last time and the door open, and then close.

I sleep some more; I wake up some more, covered in sweat, the pillow wet underneath me. I take the aspirin we buy over the counter and Dr. Hill's pills and some of L.E.'s BC powders; pretty much anything and everything I can get my hands on, squeezed tight to try to ward off the pain. Redirect it. The only time my fingers come unclenched is to pry off the medicine caps. Somewhere along the way, I lose track of how many pills I've taken; I just reach for anything, and I feel empty pill bottles all over the bed covers. Finally, there are no more pills to take, and my headache has gone away.

I use that last moment of pain-free clarity to scribble a final TO BE READ AFTER I'M GONE on the front of the envelope. Gone to Plano, I think I mean—I *must* mean—but it doesn't turn out that way. I use the last little bit of saliva in my mouth to lick the gummed seal on the back of it and close it shut.

Just like my eyes. My lungs.

I hear my own heart stop pounding, and the red-hot echo in my ears finally quits.

The air goes out of my body, and it's even quieter.

I think, *I guess I should tell somebody,* but I never get the chance. There's nobody left to tell.

I thought . . . I don't know . . . I thought that when I finally saw it, the very end, my last breath, it would be worse, but . . . I'm just floating, and looking. I'm not feeling any great emotion, no sadness or terror; those haven't kicked in yet. It's a strange feeling, being in the house with nothing to do but watch what goes on without me. No dishes to wash, no food to prepare, no boys to separate from fighting or cheer up if they're pouting, no lesson plans to prepare, no . . . nothing.

By the time L.E. comes home for lunch to check on me, I've been dead for hours.

— CLARKE —

By the time we get home from the Ritz, nobody can sleep. Normally I'd go paste my movie ad in my scrapbook, but I don't even want to remember the movie anymore, after what we learned there. I don't even understand exactly what we *did* learn, or if it's good or bad or it means Corey still did it, or Daddy did it, or what. Nothing I thought is real anymore.

Daddy acts like he doesn't understand either, yelling that he's going to sue the school district. His eyes are as watery as when he was drunk, but this time the only thing he's had to drink was a syrupy Coke from the concession stand at the Ritz. He got them for all of us, to "calm us down," he said, but the Coke's not working. We're not calmed down at all.

"But she *killed* herself," Daddy let out, falling down into his Barcalounger. "Pills everywhere. A goddamn *tether* ball? Nobody said anything about a shitass tether ball. Somebody would have told me."

"What did Dr. Hill say?" Rita pipes up, as confused as the rest of us.

"He said a goddamn aneurysm. How the hell do I know what an aneurysm is? I thought it meant that's what the pills caused. A brain bleed. All those pills. I thought she planned it. She left a note. A letter. For me."

"*What* note? I thought *you* killed her," I say. It's out of my mouth before I can even think.

"Are you outta your mind? Your *Mumma*? You thought I killed your Mumma?"

"You tried to kill *all* of us," I snap back at him. "She was gonna leave you, so you killed her so she couldn't. You wouldn't let them cut her open to find out! At least that's what I thought until Corey . . ."

"Corey what?" Daddy almost whispers, like he doesn't want to add any more noise to the room. It's dark in the living room. A slant of light from the window goes across Daddy's eyes, and they look like they have big red spider webs in them.

"I killed her," Corey starts to cry again. "To make her feel better. I killed her. I gave her chocolate milk. That's why I had to get baptized."

"What the hell is going on? Corey? Clarke? What the hell are you . . . wait a minute. She *wrote* about that," he says, like he's suddenly remembering something. "The chocolate milk. She didn't . . ."

He pulls himself out of his chair and I think he's going to hit us, but he uses the forward motion to keep going down the hall. I'm waiting to hear a door slam, but instead one opens. The linen closet in the hall.

"Boys, maybe you better go to bed. Maybe . . . maybe you should . . . maybe we should just all stay together now," Rita says. She doesn't know what to do, so she grabs us both, like she tried to do the last time Daddy took us away.

We hear him coming back down the hall, into the living room.

"I always knew this day would come." Daddy shakes his head, carrying his Ponderosa model in both hands. I thought he'd quit working on it, but he's done even more. It actually looks like a home now, where people could live. He's added a cutout door that swings open and windows with toilet paper curtains. He's glued on Lincoln Logs for siding, and for smoke from the chimney, he's used the cotton balls that Rita wipes off her makeup with at night, pulled apart so they're see-through.

It scares me seeing the model, like he's going to start drinking again and take us back to the farm. Or shoot at us.

I think it scares Rita too. "Perkins, what are you doing? Haven't we all had enough of that thing?"

He puts the model down on the dining room table, then puts his left hand on the roof. I can tell that his fingers have gotten so thin lately, without drinking, that he's had to put a Band-Aid under his wedding ring—the one from Rita, not the one from Mother—to keep it from sliding off.

Daddy pulls up on the roof of the house, and it falls back on hinges, showing everything inside. A box of chocolate-covered cherries. A paperback of *Tai-Pan* by James Clavell. A whiskey bottle that's full. A bunch of papers. And an envelope that looks like it's been opened and closed a lot. Its edges aren't crisp and sharp anymore, but crumpled up and sort of dirty.

"I should have done this a long time ago." He hands the envelope to me and Corey. "This is yours. Your Mumma . . ."

My Mumma what? I don't want to know about "my Mumma" anymore. I thought I knew, and I was all wrong. I feel like I'm back at the Ritz, about to hear a story I don't want to hear. I'm seeing things I don't want to see. How thin Daddy's fingers are. How yellow they are from all his cigarettes. The envelope he gives us is creamy pink, but Daddy's fingers are so yellow and callused against it, they look like Cheetos. Five Cheetos, instead of fingers, on each hand.

He puts his Cheetos on our heads, rubbing our hair. "I've made so many shitass mistakes. I wanted to protect you boys. I couldn't let you see . . . I thought she hurt herself. Everybody did. Well, a lot of people did. But it was that damn playground, not that it makes any of this any better. What she said. I deserve it . . ."

He starts to give the envelope to me, but now he's having a hard time letting go of it. He makes a big swallowing sound and starts squeezing the envelope down the middle, so it looks like a bow tie with a knot in the middle. Then he shakes his head and lets the envelope fall on the table, like it was burning him.

I'm the first one to pick it up. On the front of the envelope there's writing in red ink, like the pen Mother used to write with when she put letters and numbers in her grade book, getting ink on her fingers. It's like she's alive again now, in the room with us. Not just with me, but all of us. I open the envelope, and Corey looks over my shoulder. I recognize Mother's handwriting, her Jungle Gardenia smell still on the paper.

It feels like she's here with us, even though it's our other mother, our new mother, Rita, who takes the letter from me and starts reading it out loud.

My husband,

Remember the movie we went to see, your third or fourth leave in town? Tammy and the Bachelor? I took the boys to see it tonight and thought a better movie has never been made. Oh, maybe it wasn't just the movie, but the flood of memories it set off in me. I want to get them all down on paper while I can, before it's too late. I want you to remember too.

You laughed at the movie, but I cried. At the end, Debbie Reynolds and Leslie Neilsen held hands and walked into that beautiful old mansion that his family owned. He was going to give that poor country girl everything she deserved. I thought if I'd been Tammy, I'd have let him go in first, so I could stay outside, by myself, in the cool night air. I'd squeeze myself, not quite believing my luck. Just then you put your army jacket around my shoulders, like you'd read my mind, like you'd felt the chill that had just gone through my body. Nothing so romantic had ever happened to me.

You kidded me, with your kidding that was never mean, not then; with your love that was never mean either, not then. When I told you I was pregnant with our first son, you cried with happiness. I said, "He'll be smart, and he'll see things, he'll know things. We'll name him Jack for Jack and the Beanstalk, because our dreams for him will reach all the way to the sky."

You laughed at me and my fairy tales, and got me to laugh too, at how silly I was. What a beautiful laugh you had when you

*weren't drinking. When you weren't hiding things from me. That
laugh took away everything bad. So did the words we both knew
weren't true, that you said anyway, after I told you we were going
to have a son. "Creola, you are so goddamn beautiful."*

*I wasn't beautiful, I was afraid. What if I wasn't a good
mother? What if I wasn't a good wife? What if I wasn't a good
teacher? Your lies always made my fear disappear. "You are so
damn beautiful, Creola, you just don't know it. You just needed
someone to tell you. And that's me. Our son will be just as
beautiful."*

*You told me you wanted pearls and roses to lay at my feet,
but all you had was Juicy Fruit. That became our joke. When
Clarke came into the world, there I was at the hospital, looking
like something the cat dragged home, and you came in and laid a
bouquet of Juicy Fruit on my breast. Juicy Fruit instead of flowers, because that's all we could afford, but I still felt like a queen
who had just given birth to a prince. It was our joke, our future.
We said that gum would hold us together, forever.*

When Corey was born, you said it again.

I thought no moment could ever be so bright.

*Now I think no moment could ever be so dark. You've found
another woman, not the first, but the first time I don't know what
to do except leave.*

Rita gives the letter to Daddy then; she can't keep reading it.
She's crying, and her eyes can't see. "Perkins, I can't . . ."

Daddy says, "It wasn't your fault. It was mine. And now we've got
to finish what I started." He puts on his bifocals. "It doesn't get any
easier the more you read it. I've tried. A dozen times at least since
I found it. Boys, you can hate me all you want. I deserve it. But you
have to promise . . . never hate your Mumma. And don't hate Rita.
It was all my fault."

Now he takes over, pulling me to sit on one of his legs and Corey
to sit on the other. Six legs are on the floor now, and his big arms

are reaching around us to hold the letter in the middle. I don't remember him ever reading us bedtime stories when we were little, Mother always did, so it's weird to hear him reading like this. I don't want to listen, but I have to. We all do.

For a while, I thought about really leaving and taking the boys with me, on the ultimate journey. Coming home from the drive-in tonight, the streets deserted, it would have been so easy for me to just press my foot down on the gas pedal. I'd turn it into a game and we'd all laugh and laugh, fast and faster and fastest until we hit something. But I couldn't be certain it would take us all, and the boys have done nothing to deserve that. I've had my life, but they haven't. Let that be my final gift to you: that I didn't take your sons. I got them home safely. I got them home, where you weren't to be found. They deserve better than that.

Corey fell asleep at the drive-in, so Clarke helped me carry him in. I was right about Clarke. He sees things. He knows things. He tucked Corey into bed tonight, better than I ever could have. Corey, my sleeping angel. He is beautiful when he is still and asleep, but just as beautiful when he shakes with his angel disease.

I kissed him one last time, and that woke him up. He felt my tears on his precious little face, and he tried to make me feel better. He brought me a glass of chocolate milk, to help me sleep, then toddled away, back to bed. But I couldn't drink it. Holding that glass to my lips would have made me think of how much love you and I used to share, when the boys first came into our lives and I thought things could get better; I should give you a second chance. A third chance. A fourth. But now, I've given you all the chances you deserve.

So I emptied the glass onto the floor without taking a sip, and it disappeared into the rug. A glass of spilt chocolate milk is letting you off too easy. You and your girlfriend can clean up the mess it leaves, just like I'm leaving you.

"You mean . . . she didn't drink it? I didn't kill her? She spilled it?" Corey stops Daddy cold.

"Corey Banorey, if I had thought . . . if I had known, in a million years, that you were thinking that . . ."

"But I did it. I mashed up the pills."

"*She* mashed up the pills. She took those, but not the ones you gave her. She spilled all that. You have nothing to feel bad about. It all makes sense now. That goddamn tether ball. Goddamn *me*. Not smart enough to take her to the doctor. Out so goddamn late . . ." Daddy is crying so hard the paper's getting wet, and her red handwriting is getting all smeary.

I grab the pages from Daddy. "That night at the drive-in? She came back and wrote all this?" Before Daddy or Rita can stop me, I start reading what's left aloud.

> *My Clarke, my Corey, the two names I will shout aloud at my Final Judgment, which is fast approaching. At least you gave me them. That's the one thing—the two things—I can't hate you for. For the rest of their lives, and mine, I will surround them with the carousels and Tilt-A-Whirls and tornadoes of love, which you once promised me.*

That was the end. There wasn't anything else, not even her name.

"Your Mumma . . ." Daddy says, the thing he always says when he can't think of what else to say. "She wasn't in her right mind when she wrote that. She was . . . confused. The tether ball, the pills made her all confused . . ."

He doesn't know what else to say, and neither does anybody else. So nobody says anything. And nobody stops me when I take the letter for myself and walk back to our bedroom to put it under my pillow, as evidence of love.

— CLARKE —

It is April Fools' Day, exactly one year since Mother died. We didn't go to school today; we went to her grave instead. It's the first time I've been here since that night I rode my bike to the cemetery and tried to dig her up. It looks different in the day, not nearly as scary. You can see the stained-glass windows on the church better, and they make things very colorful. They're tall, and they give the graves something to look up to.

Aunt Altha brought us. She's a teacher too, so she said it was alright to play hooky for something as important as this. She was doing okay until she read Mother's tombstone. "Wife, Mother, Teacher." Aunt Altha said, "*Sister*, we should have put *sister* there too, because that's what we were, just like you and Corey are brothers." She started pointing at her palms again, "stigmata" no one could see but her. That's one of my new words.

The cemetery is completely empty except for us. Daddy didn't want to come, and Rita said she didn't want to be an "intrusion," even though she bought us flowers to put on the grave. Yellow roses, since they were Mother's favorite. If somebody was getting buried here today, it would be a "Funeral in McKinney," not a *Funeral in Berlin* with Michael Caine, which is on at the Ritz tonight. But I think we're going to skip it because I don't want to think about funerals anymore and besides, I want to save our money for next weekend and *One Million Years B.C.*

We all helped troweling off some weeds and dirt on top of Mother's grave and stuck the foil-covered flower pot in so it wouldn't tip over. Then Aunt Altha said she had a surprise for us. "I was going to wait until your birthdays, but since we're all here loved up to-gether, well . . . there's no time like the present. You never know what's around the corner. Just ask Creola."

That made her start crying, even though she's the one who said it, and she had to use the handkerchief she always carries with her to blow her nose.

"Here goes. I've bought these two graves right here, next to your Momma, for you guys to be buried in, so you'll always be near her. What do you think of that?" She stopped crying and started smil-ing then, so you could see the lipstick smeared on her teeth, just like Mother used to have.

I didn't want to tell her I'd rather have a new dictionary or my own subscription to *Tiger Beat*. Being outside in the fresh air, feel-ing the sun, and looking at Mother's flowers and her name on her tombstone, I feel happy. I know it's stupid and won't last, but right now, I don't think I'll ever need a grave. I don't think I'll ever die. I think if I really try hard enough, I can be the first person in the world to live forever.

Before we left, I took one of Mother's yellow roses and stuck it in my pocket. I don't think it's stealing anymore, just remember-ing. Since nobody else is here to do it, that's my job now. But I don't need a flower to remember her by. I have her last letter. I have her last words, and I said them out loud for the whole cemetery to hear.

"My Clarke, my Corey . . . for the rest of your lives, I will surround you with carousels and Tilt-A-Whirls and tornadoes of love."

— CREOLA —

"That's all she wrote," they'll say years from now, and they'll be right.

The last words I ever wrote, but hearing Clarke say his version of them, they're almost not enough. When you know what I know now, you want them to be so much more. You want them to be *everything*, a worthy summation. At the very end, you want to have screamed from the mountaintops; you want to skywrite that you're fighting with everything you have to stay alive, just one more second, one more breath, one more look, just so you can be in the world with them that much longer. But how can a few hundred words on a few sheets of stationery ever do that? A thousand sheets of stationery couldn't do it.

One minute you're alive, writing a "Dear L.E." letter, and the next, you're sitting in the crook of two limbs in a tree across the street as an ambulance races down your street to take away your dead body away. ("I *hate* when that happens." The kids will say that in the future, turning anything and everything into a joke. A joke to keep from crying? A joke to keep from feeling anything real, *sharing* anything real with people? I hate when *what* happens? A kids' ball on a playground hits my head and, what, *kills* me?)

I *hate* when that happens.

I really do.

Did I try to kill myself?

Did a tether ball kill me?

Does it matter? (It will, to the boys. I wish it did more to me.)

The boys can have their answer—and do; they *need* an answer—

thinking it was the tether ball. Not murder. Not suicide. Nothing but a horrible playground accident. But I have to face facts, even in the afterlife. I just don't know. Was I trying to kill myself, and if the tether ball hadn't come along, just in the nick of time . . .

I want to be honest. I want to find "my truth"—as they will say in the future—and face it. And is part of the truth that I was in so much pain I wanted it gone, whatever it took? The thing that should be impossible for any mother, and yet I wanted to just make everything disappear, without thinking far enough ahead to know that meant leaving the boys to face life alone.

It is a possibility, one I can barely admit to myself.

After all this, I just don't know. It doesn't change anything. At the end of the day, at the end of all eternity, I'm still dead.

Do all mysteries finally need to be solved, or is that all that keeps us going, the looking for answers? For the alive and the dead.

It shook me, finally hearing that letter all put together. It's not the kind of bedtime story I would have planned to leave the boys with. *Carousels and Tilt-A-Whirls and tornadoes of love.* It sounds so ferocious, so terrifying. And the boys are terrified of enough already; now they'll be afraid of the weather. And carnivals. And maybe even love. But at least they will know, will forever know, the depth of *my* love. At least I left them with that. Maybe that's all I ever wanted: not to know *how* I died, but to know that *they* would know how I died—loving them. Ferociously.

That's really all the answer I need.

I think I've finally been set free, and I'm not sure I want to be. I didn't think it would come so soon. I've gotten used to how things are: seeing the boys and floating around them. I can't really help them, but at least like this, I can see them grow up from afar. Like Barbara Stanwyck looking in the window at her daughter's wedding, at the end of *Stella Dallas*. Forgotten, washed-up, dead; it doesn't matter. At least I'd get to see what happens to them if I'm still here.

But something's definitely different. Something's changing, since that night they came home from the Ritz. I'm lighter. (What woman *doesn't* want to feel that way? LOL.) God is getting me ready for something; the feathers on my back are twitching. I think that means He's forgiving me.

"Magic time" has never felt more real, more alive.

I've never felt more alive since I actually was.

I can fly faster, higher. I'm moving further away from the day-to-day. Already, things are harder to see down on earth, like my head is strapped into one of those optometry machines and they keep moving different glass filters in front of my eyes to see if it improves my vision. "Can you see better with this one? This one? Read that fourth row of letters." Blurry, then clear. Things are just a speck down on earth now, I'm flying so far away from it. I'm scared, but excited. I think I'm smiling; I can feel my cheek muscles moving in an all-new way. I feel flesh there too; something 3-D, because I can feel tears on it as I'm allowed to see these last few things:

Clarke's final weekly movie at the Ritz, a week after the triumph and disaster of *The McKinney Story*, will be *One Million Years B.C.* Raquel Welch, a fur bikini, and a bunch of cavemen. All she does is grunt. For the first and only time in its history—well, besides *The McKinney Story* and John Huston's *The Bible*, which every church group in town will descend on like a plague of locusts—the Ritz will be packed. But Clarke isn't much interested in Raquel; he's more interested in the loin-clothed cavemen chasing her. (As is my dear Maurice Ring. He'll be there too, without Suzanne McLarty but with the new line cook from the Townhouse. They'll hold hands underneath the largest tub of popcorn that they can buy. I'm happy for him.)

That Saturday matinee, Clarke will walk up the carpeted stairs to the balcony, to the projection room where his friend Paul works. Paul will once again show Clarke how to thread the machine, how to fool the audience into thinking it's all one continuous flow, not six big canisters of still pictures embedded on celluloid until light and artistry bring them to life.

Well, he doesn't use those exact words, but I'm sure that's what
he means.

Who needs words when you have Raquel Welch?

For once, Clarke won't be paying attention to his beloved words,
but flesh and blood. Paul will put his nimble fingers on Clarke's hand
as he shows him what to do, then move his nimble lips to Clarke's
cheek. Clarke will put his own fingers around the back of Paul's
head, and hold them there. And that will be that. His first kiss, a
May–December romance, however inappropriate. It happened at
the movies. Doesn't it always? A new beginning, after the misery
I've put him through this past year. Clarke won't need the movies
anymore—he'll enjoy them, but he won't *need* them—when he has
bigger fish to fry.

Clarke won't always make the wisest choices in men, much like
his mother. For better or worse, that's one of the things I've passed
on to him, and I just have to live with it. Or . . . you know, be dead
with it. At a certain point, you just have to accept *it is what it is*. I've
learned that rule better than most.

Raquel Welch. Cavemen. Maurice Ring and my Clarke will both
owe them a debt of gratitude while Corey will start a new obsession
with dinosaurs.

That night, Clarke will dutifully cut out the movie ad, but he'll
just leave it a loose clipping in the back of his scrapbook. Too distracted, still thinking about Paul the Projectionist and the "funnyweird" feeling he got from him. That night, lounging on top of
his black-and-white checked bedspread, like Ann-Margret in *Bye
Bye Birdie*, wishing he had a telephone cord to twirl around he's so
happy, Clarke won't glue down his movie ad with the paste he always teases Corey about, saying it comes from the dead horses they
kill at Derryberry's Animal Clinic.

My son, the comedian.

My son, the overachiever, with a first kiss at just ten years old.

My son, the only boy in McKinney, Texas, circa 1967, who kept a
scrapbook full of movie ads and secrets from that fateful year when

one mother left his life and another came to take her place. He'll keep the scrapbook under his twin bed along with all the other telltale pieces of "evidence" from that year, the ones that survived L.E.'s purge. Every sweep of Clarke's hand under those sagging box springs will bring out another bit of history: the flattened-out cardboard box that Corey played "buried alive" in; Clarke's disintegrating cast from a broken arm, buzz-sawed down the middle and crumbling into chunks of plaster and cheesecloth. Later, in their high school years, a *Penthouse* magazine Corey bought, a *Playgirl* calendar Clarke stole from the 7-Eleven on the outskirts of town.

He'll look at it every year on the anniversary of the day I died—the scrapbook, not the *Playgirl*—for as long into the future as I can see. (God will continue to grant me those little one-day passes.) He'll get sad on that day—Clarke, not God—and sometimes skip work. Those who know his story, and he will tell many people his story, will know why.

April Fool's Day. It's a hard date to forget.

Corey and Clarke will always call each other on that day, wherever they are in the world, to say hello and wish each other "tornadoes of love."

Clarke will carry that falling-apart scrapbook with him for the rest of his life. From apartment to apartment, house to house, city to city, job to job, year to year, everywhere he goes. He'll use the fleshy edge of his hand to wipe the dust from its fake green leather cover, embossed with gold. He won't bother with a cloth, the same way he'll clean house as an adult. He'll tenderly turn the pages, which grow more brittle with each passing year; he'll see the old movie ads and that pressed yellow rose from my grave as he continues to cram in the newspaper clippings that Rita sends him from McKinney every few months.

About the Ritz becoming something called a "fern bar."

About Altha's death, the one person I thought would outlast everyone. She'd had her hair done just the day before, shellacked with enough hairspray to last for all eternity, so she didn't need anything extra.

About L.E. fading away, never waking up, three days after a stroke. The boys will have his beloved Ponderosa model buried with him.

Finally, the clippings will stop when Rita herself dies, and there's no one left to clip out anything. (If there's anyone who had to raise my boys instead of me, I'm glad it was her. She did a good job, even though I don't like how she *got* the job.) Not many people will come to her funeral. Not because she wasn't loved, but because she just didn't get out much, at the end. Her funeral will be as quiet as the life she led.

On their way to the funeral home from the airport in Dallas, Clarke and Corey will make the exact same trip they made together so many times in high school, mindlessly cruising around the downtown square, then taking a long detour out by the Westgate Mall, to the Dairy Queen. Through the drive-in window, they'll both order the largest, sweetest iced teas that are available. (Corey, who lives on iced tea and coffee, will even get a second one for the short trip to the funeral home they're about to take. No matter how much he tries in New York, he's never been able to reproduce the recipe of that sweet, syrupy, brewed iced tea.)

My boys will sit there together at Rita's funeral, the handsome, polite, slightly nutty young men they've become, and they will laugh through their tears, remembering stories of their childhood.

Clarke will be good at that, laughing through his tears, after losing so many of his friends and boyfriends, and not knowing why he hasn't been killed himself by the Great Plague. Corey will be good at it too; both of them will have tried to kill themselves over their secrets and their pain, with neither one ever quite going through with it. Neither one really wanting to be dead, when all was said and done.

I could have told them that.

Every time one of his friends passes, Clarke will say, under his breath, "Flights of angels, sing thee to thy rest."

And when it's finally time for my sons to join me—and that is truly God's grace, that He will not allow me to see that in advance— I will be here waiting. To sing the very same thing to them, to make them less afraid on their journey home.